Power Chord

Power Chord

Ted Staunton

orca currents

ORCA BOOK PUBLISHERS

Library and Archives Canada Cataloguing in Publication

Staunton, Ted, 1956-
Power chord / Ted Staunton.
(Orca currents)

Issued also in electronic format.
ISBN 978-1-55469-904-9 (bound).--ISBN 978-1-55469-903-2 (pbk.)

I. Title. II. Series: Orca currents
PS8587.T334P69 2011   JC813'.54   C2011-903427-1

First published in the United States, 2011
Library of Congress Control Number: 2011929395

Summary: Fourteen-year-old Ace starts a band and learns a tough
lesson about plagiarism.

*Orca Book Publishers is dedicated to preserving the environment and has printed this
book on paper certified by the Forest Stewardship Council®.*

Orca Book Publishers gratefully acknowledges the support for its
publishing programs provided by the following agencies: the Government
of Canada through the Canada Book Fund and the Canada Council for the Arts,
and the Province of British Columbia through the BC Arts Council
and the Book Publishing Tax Credit.

Cover photography by First Light

ORCA BOOK PUBLISHERS
PO Box 5626, Stn. B
Victoria, BC Canada
V8R 6S4

ORCA BOOK PUBLISHERS
PO Box 468
Custer, WA USA
98240-0468

www.orcabook.com
Printed and bound in Canada.

14 13 12 11 • 4 3 2 1

Thanks to Liz, Kim, Bernice, Tabitha,
Sue, Florence, Roma, Lindsay and Daniel,
for great suggestions, and to my son Will,
for great music.

Chapter One

Denny is yelling, but I can't hear his words. Onstage, Twisted Hazard has just ripped their last chord. It's still bouncing around the gym.

"What?" I yell back. I pull the tissue out of my ears. I always take tissue to Battle of the Bands.

"*I got a great idea*," Denny yells.

Denny gets lots of ideas. His last one called for coconuts, shaving cream and our math teacher's car. If this is a *great* idea, it'll be the first time he's ever had one.

"What is it?" I say.

Denny says, "We hafta start a band."

"What for?"

"What *for*?" Denny waves at the stage. The Hazard bass player is a hobbit in red plaid pajama pants. He's talking to two girls in amazingly tight jeans. The lead singer looks too young to stay out after the streetlights come on, plus he's in chess club. Three girls, one very hot, are chatting with him. The drummer has glasses and is wearing flood pants. He's handing his snare and a cymbal to two girls in grade *ten*. One of them is his sister, but still.

"Look at those guys," Denny says. "Imagine how we'd do."

I hate to admit it, but maybe Denny has a point. Those guys are in grade nine, and we're in grade nine. They are nerds, and yet those girls are all over them.

We're not nerds—even if Denny's ears do stick out—but we're invisible to girls. There are girls all around us, in cool shapes and sizes and smells. They don't help *us* with anything, except maybe give us something to stare at.

Maybe a band is the answer. I bet playing in a band is easier than playing basketball, especially for someone my size. There's a problem though.

"Uh, Den," I say, "don't you have to play music to be in a band?"

Up onstage, the next group is plugging in. It's No Money Down. The guitar players are in my English class.

"Well, *duh*," Denny says. He's patting his pockets. He pulls out his cell and flips it open. "No problem. You've got that stuff at your house."

There is a bass and a guitar at my place. I fool around on them a little.

Denny says, "And I play guitar and sing."

Denny did take some guitar lessons a couple of years back.

"Since when do you sing?" I ask. In between ideas, Denny has been known to lie.

"Me?" he says. "I sing great. I was in that choir, remember?"

I make a face and say, "So was I, Den. That was grade four."

Denny says, "Yeah, well, I sing all the time at home. While I'm playing guitar. I just don't do it around other people. Anyway, it's your band style that counts."

"Band style?" I say.

Denny says, "Yeah. You know, your look, your attitude. That stuff. Like, notice how cool bands never smile in pictures? Anyway, most of them don't even play, they fake along to their records."

"How do you know?" I ask.

Denny shrugs. "Everybody knows that."

"One problem, Den," I say, "we won't have any records to fake to."

Denny is too busy texting to answer.

How did we end up talking about starting a band? Really, we only came to see who was around. And to look at girls and make jokes about them we don't really mean. Soon we'll probably yell and fake wrestle with some other guys. Later we'll walk back to my place to watch downloads of *Python Pit 6* and *Facemelt* and laugh at them. I mean, you have to do *something* on a Friday night.

Up onstage, some goof from the student government introduces No Money Down. One of the guitar players hits a power chord behind him. Everybody is crowding the stage around them. Girls are crowding the stage around them.

I look at the two guys from English.
They look the same as they do in
English, only they don't. They have
sweet guitars that I don't know the
make of. Lights are shining on them,
and everybody is watching. They're
trying to look cool, but you can tell they
want to giggle like little kids.

Do I want that? Yes I do. I turn to
Denny and say, "Let's do it."

"Wait." He's still texting.

"Who are you texting anyway?"
I ask.

"I'm not texting." Denny looks up
and grins his big maniac grin. "I'm
tweeting."

"What?" I say. "Since when are you
on Twitter?"

"Since today. Look, I just told the
world." He holds up his phone as No
Money Down stomp off their first song.
On the screen it reads: **Hot new band**

startup 4 u. dr. d & ace will rule. watch for more later.

"Let's do it, Ace," Denny says.

"Props." We bump fists. I'm in.

Chapter Two

We decide the first thing we need to do is find a drummer. We start at three on Saturday afternoon. We're not what you call early risers.

"We'll get Pigpen," Denny says to me on the phone.

"I didn't know Pig played drums," I say.

"His older brother has drums. He was in that band, remember, when we were in grade eight."

I do remember. They were pretty good, even though at the time, I said they sucked.

"His brother plays drums, but that doesn't mean Pig does," I say.

"I heard Pig tapping pencils in study hall," Denny says. "He's great."

We meet at the bus stop. Pig lives a ways from us. When the bus arrives, Denny insists we sneak on the back doors as other people get off. Not many people get off on a Saturday.

Right away, the driver calls, "You in the green hoodie!"

Denny looks around as if he's not wearing a green hoodie. He's also grinning.

"And your buddy," calls the driver. "No free rides. Get up here. Pay your fares or get off."

Everyone stares at us, which I don't like. Denny grins bigger than ever. We shuffle up front, digging in our pockets for cash.

It's a seven-stop ride. When we get to Pigpen's house and ring the bell, his mom answers. Denny blathers all over her, the way he always does with adults. I wait. Actually she is pretty nice.

"Jared!" she calls down to the basement. Jared is Pigpen's real name. "Friends!" She sends us downstairs.

Pigpen is not exactly a friend of ours, but we knew him in grade three. Then his family moved. We met him again this year when we all started at the same high school. His nickname is kind of a joke, because he's a neat freak. He has a buzz cut and always tucks in his shirt. His jeans are pressed. Even his locker is organized. It's spooky.

When we get downstairs, Pigpen is polishing a pair of black combat boots.

I wonder if he's a closet punker. Sure enough, a drum kit is set up in the corner.

Denny makes his pitch. Pig listens, then nods. "Okay," he says.

Pig isn't a talker. He could have been in silent movies. Denny is a talker. In fact Denny is a motormouth. I can be a talker with my friends, but not around adults.

"Cool," says Denny.

There are more props all round. I notice Pig is wearing latex gloves to keep his hands clean as he polishes.

Denny says, "I'll bring over my Tely, and Ace has got a bass and amp and—"

"Can't," says Pig.

"Huh?" we say.

"Can't." Pig dabs more polish on a boot. Then he says, "Mom won't let us. Too loud. Said New Teeth made her grind her own." New Teeth had been the name of Pig's brother's band.

"But the drums are here," I say.

"Gotta move 'em," Pig says. He starts buffing the toe of a boot with a brush. "My brother won't care. He's away at school till Christmas. We can use his microphone too."

"There's no room at my place," says Denny. He's right. That leaves us with my place. They both look at me.

I sigh. "I'll have to ask my mom."

"So call her," Denny says.

"She said not to call unless there's a disaster. She's showing a house." Mom sells real estate. She says the market is slow.

"Then let's take everything over. How can she say no?"

"She can say no lots of ways, Den," I say. "I'll ask when she gets home."

Denny grabs the hi-hat anyway. The pedal clunks off on his foot. "Ow, Jee—" He cuts off. Pig's mom is upstairs.

"So let's go," I say.

Denny is limp-hopping around the room.

"Call me," Pig says.

"Aren't you coming?" Denny looks back at him, still limp-hopping.

Pig picks up an unpolished boot and nods at it.

"Later," I say.

"Later."

Chapter Three

We're out of cash, so Denny and I walk
the seven stops back to my house.

Denny says, "Pig didn't even want
to come with us." He shakes his head in
amazement.

"He was busy, Den," I say.

"Yeah, see those boots? What was
that about?"

I shrug. "Maybe he's a professional grape stomper."

Denny says, "Don't you wear hip waders for that?"

My mom isn't home when we get back to my place. We get snacks. Archie, our cat, pads in and stretches. I give him a snack too.

"Let's check out the stuff," says Denny, as if we haven't a million times before.

We haul everything out from under the basement stairs. There's a microphone stand, a Yorkville bass amp, two guitar cases and a cardboard box. All of it looks pretty battered. Inside the cases are a Squier electric bass and a Cort acoustic guitar with a pickup. I know there are straps, patch cords, a couple of picks, and an electronic tuner with no battery tucked in there too. When you open the cases they let out a whiff of wood polish and plastic, cigarette smoke and beer. The bass case also smells of cat pee. Arch once took a leak in there. It doesn't matter. I like it. It reminds me of Chuck.

Chuck is the owner of all this stuff. He was a boyfriend of Mom's when I was eleven or twelve. Chuck was a goof, but in a good way. I liked him. I think Mom did too, but she said he had "reliability issues."

When Chuck wasn't driving a truck, he played in a band called Razorburn. He said he was only driving truck until his music took off.

Mom said the truck would take off before the music did. She was right.

Inside the cardboard box is a pile of leftover copies of Razorburn's CD, *Mullet Over*. I haven't listened to it in a million years.

Denny is trying to tune the guitar. He gives up and strums. It's not music, but it gets your attention.

"Power chord," says Denny. "See what I'm doing?"

"Mangling the guitar," I say. We hear the door open upstairs.

"Hi," Mom calls.

"We're down here," I call back.

There are footsteps, and then Mom's feet and legs appear on the stairs. I spend a lot of time in the basement. I always like how people on stairs seem to sprout magically in front of you. Mom is wearing her house-showing pantsuit. Mom looks at all the gear spread out. She raises an eyebrow.

"Ask her," Den hisses. "Go on, ask her."

There are reasons I shouldn't ask her. I am supposed to be getting better marks. I am supposed to be looking for a part-time job. I am supposed to be more reliable. Thanks to Chuck, I don't think Mom thinks *reliable* and *music* go together.

On the other hand, Denny and Pig need this too. And getting out this stuff reminds me of how Chuck showed me chords and bits from songs. I liked that. Chuck said I was good too. Above all, there are girls everywhere who don't know I exist, but who soon will—if I ask. I ask.

"We want to start a band. Can we practice here?"

Denny takes a running step off the carpet. He slides toward my mom on his knees across the patch of lino. It's a good rock-and-roll move, actually. He stops in front of her and looks up, his hands together, begging, "Please Mrs. C, please?"

Mom looks from him to me. I am trying to look hardworking and reliable.

Her mouth twitches. She says, "This is going to cost you straight Bs, minimum, on your next report card."

Denny starts tweeting.

Chapter Four

Mom invites Denny to stay for supper, but he has to go. She asks me to make salad while she cooks spaghetti. I start by looking in the junk drawer. "Do we have any batteries?"

"What size?" Mom asks. She's running water to fill a saucepan.

"I don't know," I say, "The square ones."

"Nine-volt," Mom says. "I think there's one. What do you need it for?"

Man. Already she's piling on questions. I say, "The guitar tuner thingy."

"Look in the computer desk." She passes me the knife and cutting board. "After you make salad."

Instead, I look in the computer desk right away. I can't find it.

By now, Mom is browning ground beef in the fry pan. She has stacked the salad vegetables beside the cutting board. "Who else is going to be in the band?"

I say, "Pigpe...Jared."

Mom says, "Really? Jared from grade school?" She turns to look at me.

"Uh-huh."

"That's nice," she says. "I haven't seen Jared in ages. What does he play?"

"Drums." I tear off chunks of lettuce to wash. Will the questions never end?

"Anybody else?" she asks.

"No," I say.

Mom nods and says, "What are you going to call yourselves?"

I turn off the tap. "We haven't decided. Either Green Day or the Beatles."

"All right, smart guy," she says as she takes spaghetti down from the cupboard. "Just..."

"What?" I start chopping carrots, ready for the lecture.

"Never mind," Mom says. She tells me about the people interested in the house instead.

After supper I hit Facebook and try to line up the evening. It is Saturday night, after all. For way too long I write on walls and don't get anything back. Where is everybody?

Finally, Denny writes back and asks if I want to go to Rock 'N Bowl. I'm a bad bowler, but I like Rock 'N Bowl. You don't tell people you like

Rock 'N Bowl though. It sounds lame. I message back **better than death** and ask Mom if she'll drive us.

There's an hour to kill before we pick up Denny. I go down to the basement and open the guitar cases. I look at the instruments, nestled in plush. They are full of music I want to get at. I remember Chuck showing me chords and a bass pattern for playing blues. The guitar had felt big as an army tank. Now it feels light—and hard, for something so curvy-looking. I pluck the strings softly. I don't want Mom to hear. I also don't know what it's supposed to sound like.

I take the neck in my left hand and press down on the littlest string with a finger. It's tougher than it looks. In fact, it hurts a little. I pluck with the pick. *Cluk*. I press harder. Now I get a twang. I stop the sound with my hand. I remember a chord Chuck showed me, a G, I think.

Anyway, it's the one where you reach across with two fingers to the two thickest strings. It's tough tucking my little finger in behind. I try a quiet strum.

Yuck. I need that tuner.

I put the guitar down and pick up the bass. It's heavy, and the balance is different. After the guitar, the neck is like a tree. The strings feel thick as snakes. They push back under my fingers, vibrating through me when I pluck them. Cool.

I have to take the next step, even if I'm not in tune. I have to hear the sound, the real sound. It's time for power. I plug the patch cord into the amp and the bass. I flip the power switch. A red light pops on, and the amp starts to hum. I feel my whole body hum with it. I set the volume down low and try again. The strings slither under my fingers. The sound vibrates right into my gut, like it's the center of the Earth.

All at once I can see myself on a stage with Pig and Denny. I feel music swirling all around us, loud music. I see bright lights, and beyond the lights are faces and waving arms. *I want that.* I want it to be me you hear at Rock 'N Bowl, especially if you are a girl.

I start fake singing at the empty microphone stand. I blump at the bass like an idiot. Already my fingers hurt. I close my eyes and make a rock singer face. When I open them, Mom has sprouted on the stairs. I freeze in mid-*blump.*

"Sorry," she says. "I thought you might want this." She's holding a battery.

I say, "Oh. Yeah. Thanks." I can feel my face turn the color of spaghetti sauce. This is worse than being caught on certain websites. I take off the bass, then grab the tuner from the case. "Where was it?" I ask.

Mom smiles. "In the kitchen drawer."

"Oh. I'll just—" I'm fumbling so hard I can't get the tuner open.

"Let me try," Mom says. She takes the tuner. She opens the back and hooks in the battery. She presses the button. Bingo. "Remember how to use it?"

I nod.

"Good," she says. "Didn't Chuck write out some things to get you started?"

"Oh yeahhh…," I say. My face is cooling off. I look in the guitar case. There are pages with writing in pen. One says *How to Tune*. Another has chord charts. I remember practicing making the chords. Another sheet has bass patterns for songs marked on it. There's "Smoke on the Water" and "Sunshine of Your Love." I remember Chuck showing me those. They were cool.

Then I think of something. "Is it, like, okay to—"

"To use Chuck's things?" Mom smiles. "I think so," she says. "In fact, I think he'd like it. Besides, he'd have been back if anything had been important." Her voice changes, and her smile fades.

"Okay," I say. "I thought that since he used to show me stuff…"

She smiles again. "You're right, he did. He was good that way."

"Maybe he forgot it," I say.

Now she laughs. "I wouldn't be surprised. Forgetful was a way of life for Chuck. Remember the time he used two tins of Archie's food by mistake in the—"

Now I laugh and say, "Yeah, and we all had to go out for dinner."

Mom stops laughing. "And I paid. No, Chuck did pay. I shouldn't be so hard on him. He was a nice guy…" Mom sighs and looks at me now. "I'm glad you're giving this a try. Focus is good. But remember your promises, Davey."

David is my real name. Everybody calls me Ace because when I get asked about marks, I always sarcastically say, "A's." Everyone but Mom thinks it's funny. Now I nod my head. "I know," I say.

"Good. We should get going in ten minutes."

I turn off the amp. Mom starts back up the stairs. "Cat food." I hear her chuckle. She vanishes a step at a time.

Chapter Five

"How long till the next bus?" I ask.

Pigpen shrugs. Denny is busy tweeting: **nmbr1 rd. trip w/drums. need rdies nxt time 4 help. R U up 4 it girls?**

We're at the bus stop near Pig's house. It's Tuesday after school, and it's hot for late September. I'm sweating and thirsty because we're carrying the whole drum kit. Also, the fingertips of my left hand are sore.

I've tuned the instruments that are waiting at my house, and I've been practicing. I don't tell Pig and Denny. I want to surprise them with how good I am. Instead I say, "We could have waited till tomorrow. My mom could've given us a ride."

"Rock and roll doesn't wait, Ace." Denny snaps his cell shut. "And Pig's mom wanted the stuff out."

"It was only until tomorrow," I say.

"Who cares?" Denny says. "It's cool. Anyway, it's like free advertising for the band. People will remember us: *I used to see them carrying their drums down the street.*"

This could be true. We're hard to miss. The drums take up a lot of sidewalk. I've got the bass drum, pedal and a cymbal stand. Denny's got the toms, the snare and stand. Sticks are poking out of his back pocket. Pig, the biggest of us, has the cymbals, a stand, the hi-hat stand and another set of sticks. How did he end up carrying so little?

"What we really need," Denny goes on, "are band T-shirts. If we were wearing them, everybody would know who we are and remember when they hear us."

"The T-shirts would be blank, Den," I say. "We don't have a name."

"*Oh yeahhhhh*," Denny says. "Okay, I think we should be Corruption."

"Incoming," says Pig.

"What kind of name is that?" I ask.

Pig jerks his head. I see he means that the bus is coming.

As we pick up all of the drum parts, Denny says, "Remember, slip in the back door. Nobody will notice."

This time it's nearly rush hour. Getting on by the back doors is like swimming upstream to Niagara Falls.

With a drum set. Tired-looking adults glare at us, especially when Denny backs into someone with his drum sticks.

"Hey!" the guy says.

The driver's voice comes on over the intercom. "Boys with the drums, come to the front."

Have you ever tried squeezing down a bus aisle with a bass drum? It's hard to do. I feel like a human bowling ball, but this is not Rock 'N Bowl. I get stuck between a sweaty fat guy with grocery bags and a tall skinny lady who looks away. This is not what being up close and personal with your fans is supposed to mean.

The bus rumbles. I stare at the top of the drum. As we slow for the first stop, Denny squeezes back to me. "We gotta get off," he says. "She says we're creating a disturbance. Besides, I don't have money for a ticket."

I have to back out when the bus stops. I keep my eyes on the drum, but I feel the staring and hear the grumbles. At least we're going with the flow. I make it to the sidewalk before I have to put the drum down. My arms are killing me.

"I bet *they'll* remember us—even without T-shirts," Denny says.

"Incoming," says Pig.

"We just did that," I say. My back is killing me too.

"For a name," Pig says. He doesn't seem tired.

Den is busy tweeting. "I kind of like that," he says. "What about…" Then he forgets to say anything.

We have to walk the rest of the way to my house. At every rest stop, Denny tweets how far we've gone in case any girls want to rush on down to help us. Nobody does.

"Gee, Den," I say, "Maybe you gave the wrong directions."

"Aw, Ace. You watch," Denny says. "Give it one month, and we'll be chick magnets."

"That's how long it's going to take to get to my house," I say.

Denny changes the subject. "I think we should call ourselves The Spank. We could play in jock straps, like the Chili Peppers."

"Spitfires," says Pig.

Denny shakes his head. "That would be like a Kiss cover band. You know, spitting fire? This drum is heavy."

Now Pig shakes his head, but he doesn't say anything. We walk, talking names. Then we stagger, talking names. At least, Denny and I stagger. Pig doesn't even break a sweat.

Pig suggests Surface to Air and Wing Commander or something, and Chopper. I like Chopper. Denny doesn't. Then Pig goes back to Incoming.

I can't think of anything good that isn't taken. Every name I think of reminds me of some other name. By the time we turn down my street, we're back to The Spank or Incoming. Finally, I vote with Pig for Incoming.

"I was just kidding about the jock straps," Denny complains.

"I don't want to get spanked," I say. "I'm not a little kid."

"It's okay," Denny says. "Lots of rock stars are short."

"I'm not short, either," I say. I change the topic. "Incoming, for now."

"It can't be for *now*," Denny says. "We have to start a Myspace page, post pictures, list influences."

He's right. I hate it when Denny's right. I hate carrying a bass drum even more. Luckily, we're at my house.

"Incoming," I say again as I put the drum down on my front step. My fingers stay bent. Archie watches us from the porch.

"Too bad Archie can't take pictures," Denny says. "He could take our first group shot." He drops the snare on the grass. Our lawn isn't much bigger than the drum.

"Hey," says Pig.

"Sorry." Denny lays the other stuff down to tweet again. "Okay, influences?"

Maybe there's blood getting to my brain again. I say, "Nirvana."

"Billy Talent."

"Green Day."

"Chili Peppers."

"Doors."

"Alexisonfire."

"Led Zep."

"Slayer."

"Hendrix," says Denny. His thumbs fly, tweeting. More names come up. It's cool to sit here like real musicians and toss around names of bands we want to sound like.

I imagine our video. I get that image of playing onstage in my head again. I press my fingertips. It's cool that they're sore. Only musicians have sore fingers. And maybe martial-arts guys, from all that eye poking they do. But that would be different. When we stand up again, I'm all stiff. That's cool too. It feels like a sacrifice for my art. I'll blow off some homework and practice again tonight.

Chapter Six

We have our first practice the next afternoon. I discover seven important things about starting a band.

One: *You can't look cool if practice is at your house.*

Denny has spent the whole day carrying his gear around school. I've always made jokes about guys who carry guitars around, but I wish I needed to do it. I know it would make me look way cooler.

Two: *You need all your strings.*

When Denny unpacks his guitar, I say, "Hey, your guitar is missing the high string."

"Oh, yeah. It broke." Denny plugs in. He slips the strap over his shoulder. "Don't worry, I don't use that one much yet anyway. I'm all about the power chords."

He sets his fingers, then jabs at the strings. Out comes a sound like pigs in a blender.

"You got that tuner thingy?" Denny asks.

I hand it to him. I look closer at the head of his guitar. "I thought you said you had a Telecaster."

"I said it was a Tely."

"That says *Teleporter by Thunder* on the head. A Thunder Teleporter? A five-string Thunder Teleporter?"

"So I'll get another string. Anyway, it's a good amp."

The amp says Melodia. It looks like a kindergarten toy.

Three: *Bring earplugs.*

I figure I'm good with tissue, like at Battle of the Bands. Pig pulls on a monster set of noise-blocker head phones.

"What's with those?" I say to him and point.

He pulls a giant padded yellow cup off one ear. "Industrial strength," he says and puts it back on.

Denny finishes tuning his five strings, plugs in and turns up his amp. He tries his power chord again. The top of my head almost comes off. I yell something that not even I can hear. Archie streaks for the stairs.

"Told you it was a good amp," says Denny.

As I dig for more tissue, Pig yells, "Turn up your guitar. I can't hear it."

"What?" yells Denny. "My ears are ringing. I can't hear you."

"What?" Pig hollers as he lifts off a headphone.

"What we all need are earplugs," I say.

"What?" they both yell.

Four: *Don't kiss the microphone.*

Since they can't hear, I lean close to the microphone. Too close. The microphone is also plugged into Denny's amp. There is a shriek louder than the Thunder Teleporter. Upstairs, Archie howls. I pull back and try again.

"What do you want to play?" I ask.

Five: *Your own voice will surprise you.*

I don't hear their answers. Instead I'm thinking, Why does my voice sound whiny and crappy? Do I always sound like that? That can't be me. It must be a cheap mike.

Six: *It's harder than you thought.*

We all look at each other. This is it. We are going to play music. There's a lot of music in the world. Where are we going to start?

It's a no-brainer. We choose "Brain Stew" by Green Day. I've only been playing bass for four days, and I can play it already. You just stay on the top string and work down from the fifth fret. The guitar part is Denny's favorite. It's nothing but power chords, two fingers, max.

"Wait," Denny says, "I'll tweet the world what our very first song is." Out comes the cell.

"Let's go," I say. All at once, I want to play.

Denny finishes. He puts down his phone. We get our fingers ready on the strings. Pig taps on the hi-hat with a stick. "Two, three, four—"

We all start on a different beat.

"Try again," says Denny.

"What?" says Pig.

"Take your headphones off," I yell.

"What?" says Pig.

I scream, *"Take your headphones off. So we can all hear."*

Pig frowns. He keeps the phones around his neck. Denny adjusts the mike. We get ready again.

"Two, three, four—"

Denny and I start on different notes. It's my bad.

"Two, three, four—"

Denny drops his pick. He stands up and bumps the microphone stand. It wobbles toward the amp. There's another feedback scream. I grab the stand and bump the crash cymbal, or is it the ride cymbal? Pig dives over the toms to grab it. I jerk back. There's a crackle and a *gadump* sound as my bass cord pops out.

We settle again. I plug back in.

"Two, three, four—"

This time we get it—for a little while anyway. The first notes of "Brain Stew" fill the room. They're wobbly but loud, and I think they are music. We get through the song twice. Denny's screams are pretty good. Pig has trouble keeping the beat with his feet, but he starts to get it. Even with only five notes to play, I'm not always sure where to fit them with the drums.

The second time through, Denny tries to solo. This is a mistake with only five strings. Oh, well. Pig and I power on.

Seven: *Bring rubber gloves.*

It's not until everything stops and I pull the tissue out of my ears that I hear another sound. It's weird and high, like Robert Plant screaming on a Zep song. Only it's not Robert Plant.

It's Archie yowling and throwing up in the front hall.

"I think we're an extreme band," Denny says.

We are so extreme we make cats barf. I'm cool with that (except for having to clean up), because I love us. Whatever this is that we're doing is the most fun I've ever had.

Chapter Seven

After three more practices we're way better. You can tell because Arch doesn't barf anymore. Sometimes when I take my earplugs out, I hear him yowling upstairs. When I go upstairs to put him outside, he runs right to the door.

I also know we're better because we can blast through "Brain Stew." We can play "Teen Spirit." We're working on playing it backward too. We've started practicing "Seven Nation Army," and we have a list of songs we're going to learn.

Denny now has all six strings. His screaming sounds good, but he doesn't do many stage moves. That's because the basement ceiling is too low.

Pig and I are getting it together too. On "Brain Stew" I match my notes with the bass drum for those two quick beats every time. At first I couldn't figure out when they came in. Then Pig showed me that I could count along to the beat of the hi-hat.

Pig had trouble because he had to make his left hand play every beat on the hi-hat while his right foot played the two fast beats on the drum. See? It's tricky.

Now I'm checking out websites about bass playing. I got some patterns to practice, and I play bass along to our songs on my MP3 player. I've played so much that my fingers hardly ever hurt anymore. My fingertips are all tough and callused, and I can't feel much with them. It turns out it's a good thing I bite my nails too. Guitar and bass players have to keep them short, especially on the left hand. I'm really getting into this, even apart from the girls. Not that I've forgotten that. Chuck said girls can tell musicians by their hands. I hope he's right. I try to keep mine out of my pockets as much as I can.

"Stage two," Denny says while we're walking down the hall at lunch. We're going to eat outside on the bleachers. "We gotta do the Myspace page, and it's gotta have video." He slings his gig bag higher on his shoulder. "My tweeting is already building a fan base. Now they want more."

"How many followers have we *got*, Den?"

"I haven't checked lately. But I know it's for sure more than my mom. So, what we're going to do now"—Denny pulls the door open—"is ask the girls in the video club to help. And I happen to know that they always eat lunch out here."

"*What?*" All at once I'm not hungry. "We can't just ask them. They'll think we're dweebs, that it's a put-on."

I thought girls would gather around after they heard us. I never thought we'd have to ask them to make a video.

Denny shakes his head and says, "No, they won't. Will they, Pig?"

Pig shrugs. "I'll do the Myspace page."

As we cross the football field, I see the girls in the video club sitting in the bleachers. There's Lucy, from grade school, and Jessica from math, and Alison and Nadia. Oh, man. I see hair and smiles and many round body parts.

"Why don't you text them?" I whisper to Denny.

"None of them gave me their numbers," he whispers back.

Great. It's too late now. They see us coming. Are they giggling about us already?

"Hey, Video Club!" Denny calls. Now they're giggling for sure. I can feel myself shrinking.

I look around for Pigpen. He's bigger, and maybe I can duck behind him. He's gone. No, he's sitting by himself way down the bleachers, opening his lunch. How did he do that? There's no time to wonder.

"You guys still looking for a video project?" Denny asks. He's already climbing the bleachers toward the girls.

"Maybe," says Alison. I feel my face turning red, and I shrink some more. The other girls are still giggling.

"Well, me and Ace have got one for you," says Denny. His grin is a mile wide. "You can record our new band. We need performance video for our Myspace page. Have you been reading my tweets?"

More giggling. "We didn't know you were tweeting, Denny." That's Jessica. I love girls with black hair. In fact I love girls of all hair colors. But I have trouble talking to any of them.

Denny babbles on. "We have this new band, Incoming. It's really turning out cool. There's Pigpe...Jared on drums, Ace on bass—hey, that rhymes! And I'm on guitar and lead vocals." Denny spreads his arms out wide. His gig bag bounces. "We promise to rock your worlds!"

Rock your worlds? If I shrink any more, all that will be left of me will be shoes. There's nothing I can do but send beams of *shut up* thoughts at Denny.

"Where are you performing?" Lucy asks.

I guess Denny doesn't get my message. He blathers, "Well, nowhere yet. That's why we need a video. To get performances. We just started. We're practicing in Ace's basement."

"In Ace's basement?" says Lucy. I think she's been there, at my sixth birthday party.

"Yeah," Denny says. "Hey, you could put Ace's cat in the video! He barfs every time we play. That's how we know we're extreme." Denny hoists his gig bag. "Or know what, *you could all be in it too!*"

"As what," Nadia says, "adoring fans?"

I wish, but I don't say so. I'd have better luck wishing for death.

Denny says, "Sure! But, no, like, we could make something up. Maybe you could all hate us as much as the cat—"

"You mean we have to barf?" says Jessica.

Denny laughs and says, "No, but, like, we play really badly at first. Then you come in and show us how to rock or something. You know, we could make up a story."

"We'll think about it," Alison says.

"Cool," Denny says. "Let us know soon, okay? We have to get this done, and we want to make it really good." He hops down the steps, the gig bag bouncing on his back. I'm right behind him.

"Okay," they call. There's more giggling.

"And check out my tweets!" he calls.

"Okay!" Now they are laughing.

Halfway across the field I say to Denny, "Nice try." He sounded like an idiot, but I didn't sound like anything, did I?

"Nice try?" Denny says. "Are you kidding? They loved it." Out comes the cell. He tweets: **incoming video 4 sure. Watch 4 it!**

Chapter Eight

"Our time has come," Denny announces at our next practice.

This is news to me. A week has gone by. Girls have not called. Denny's little sister did come over to take pictures. She used Denny's cell phone and shot twenty seconds of video too. Denny tried to play guitar behind his head and bashed out the ceiling light. Pig posted the video and pictures anyway on the Incoming Myspace page. Not all of them show our heads. That could make us a mystery band. He has also printed the words *sonic BOOM!* beside the biggest picture of us on the Myspace page. It's a start anyway.

As I finish tuning my bass I say, "Our time has come? I hope it brought pizza."

"No, really," Denny says. "Look at this."

It's a bright green flyer advertising a contest at the youth center. Everyone can play two original songs, and the winners get to be in a show downtown, right outside City Hall.

"Wait a sec," I say. "Original songs? We don't have original songs. We play covers."

Denny says, "So we'll write some. C'mon, how hard can it be?" He picks up one of the old Razorburn CDs. "These guys did it, right?"

"I guess," I say. "I can't remember."

"Then we can do it too," Denny says. "We can all write together. Listen, I already made up a riff and a first line on the walk here."

Denny plugs in and plays his riff. It's pretty lame. It's a repeat of the same note and then one note down: *duh-duh duh-duh, duh-duh duh-duh*.

"That's it?" I say.

"Listen to the words." He plays again and chants: "Don't wanna be what you call normal." Then he stops. "Okay, what should come next?"

"*That's* it?"

"What do you want?" Denny complains. "It wasn't a long walk. Anyway, we're supposed to write this together."

We jam on Denny's riff. It's not hard to do. Figuring what comes next is hard. We call it "Not So Normal" and get as far as this:

Don't wanna be what you call normal
Be the one who barfs at formals
Be the YouTube booger eater
Be the silent farting tweeter

"Then what?" asks Denny.

"Be the shoe with something on it," I say.

"Ewwww," Denny cackles. He really does cackle "heh-heh-heh" like a dirty old man. "That's not very mature, Ace."

"Well, maturity is overrated," I say. "This is a punk song, right?"

"Whoa," Denny says. He hits the riff: "Ma-tur-it-y is ov-er-ra-ted. Okay, rhyme that."

Pig says his first word of the afternoon, "Naked." His nickname fits his mind anyway.

Denny thinks it over. "It's pretty close. Does it fit? Dated? Hated?"

I think of a rhyme, but I don't say it. It's grosser than Pig's suggestion. Instead, I say, "Let's get some juice."

In the kitchen, Denny is saying, "I told you this would be easy," when I hear the front door. Mom comes in. Archie is trotting ahead of her.

"Hi, guys," she says. "Having practice?"

I nod. She opens the kitchen drawer and pulls out earplugs. Then motormouth Denny blows it, big-time. "Not just having practice," he says. "We're writing a song."

"No kidding," Mom says. "That's great. Davey and I used to have a friend who wrote songs."

"Chuck," says Denny.

Mom smiles and says, "That's right. Did you ever meet him? Anyway, I'd love to hear your song."

Denny's eyes widen into car headlights. Pig starts drinking as if he's dying of thirst. I choke and spray juice out my nose.

Mom isn't exactly our target audience.

"We're just getting started," I say. "We'll play it for you when it's done. C'mon guys, we should get back to work." Our footsteps on the stairs sound like a bad drum roll.

"Not So Normal" doesn't sound so great in a whisper.

"It is a good song," Denny says. "I just don't want to scream it right now. My voice is getting tired." He takes off his guitar.

I have a bad feeling. "Den," I say, turning off my amp, "can you think of one girl you'd dare to sing that song to?"

Denny says, "If I scream enough, nobody will know what—"

"If you scream that much at the contest, no one will know what the words are, and we won't win," I say back.

"Won't win if they *do* know what the words are," says Pig.

He's got a point.

"Well…," says Denny.

I say, "Would you sing it to Nadia, or Lucy or Alison—"

Denny says, "In *Chinese*, maybe. If I knew it."

"Lucy *is* Chinese," I say.

"Japanese," says Pig.

"It doesn't matter," I say. "Those girls are smart. They probably all know Chinese *and* Japanese. Don't duck the question."

"Okay. Probably not," Denny says, as he coils his guitar cord.

I say, "The whole idea was to get girls, right? So we gotta start over."

"But it's hard," Denny complains. He picks up the Razorburn CD again.

I nod at the box of CDs and say, "You said if they could do it, we could too. Maybe we should all try to write a song on our own before our next practice. Then see what we get."

Behind me I hear the zipper on Denny's gig bag. "You want to practice Saturday?" I ask.

"Busy till Saturday night," Pig says. He's pulling on a sweatshirt that says *TOP GUN*. Maybe it's a video game.

I say, "Well, Saturday night?"

Pig nods. I look at Denny. He's already picking up his case. "Yeah, yeah," he says.

I raise my eyebrow and say, "Or will you be busy with Lucy and Jessica and—"

"You'll be the first to know," Denny says.

"In Chinese," I say.

"Later," we all say.

Chapter Nine

Now I have to write a song—and I have a math test tomorrow. Writing and studying get in the way of each other all evening. I decide to take my guitar to school the next morning to get more done on the song after the test. I don't know if I look cool. I'm too busy sweating over the math test and the song to think about being cool. No girls rush me though.

At lunch I look for a quiet place to work on my song. Songwriting is hard, especially with math on the brain. Nearly everything I've thought of sounds like another song or like an equation. It's driving me nuts. I don't want to give up though. I've thought of one little bit, and my future with girls depends on it.

As I walk down the hall, an acoustic guitar jangles from the music room. A high voice is humming. I don't take music at school because I don't want to get stuck playing a dweeb instrument like clarinet. I look inside and see a guy with long red hair and a jean jacket. He's got his back to me, playing a guitar. Is it that guy from No Money Down, maybe? There's an open notebook and a pen on the desk beside him. He stops and writes something.

"Hey," I say, "are you writing a song too?" I'm so into the songwriting that the words just pop out.

He jumps a little and turns. Only he's a she. She has freckles and a tiny green nose stud. She is probably my age. I've never seen her before, but it's a big school.

"Yeah, I am," she says. Her face gets pink. I think mine does too.

I start backing away, saying, "Oh. Sorry. I was just…I'm trying to do one for this contest."

"At Lakeshore Youth Center?" she asks.

"Yeah," I say.

"Me too." She brushes her hair back behind her ear. "What kind of song?"

I clear my throat and say, "Um, a rocker, I guess. I have this pattern."

"Show me," she says. "'Cause right now I'm stuck."

"Really? Wow. Me too." I get out my guitar. "See, this is what I've got so far."

I play a pattern of power chords: 8th fret 3rd 6th 1st. *Duh duh duuh duh-duh*

duh-duh, with the last *duh-duh*s a little faster.

It rocks pretty good. All I need now is a melody and lyrics that you can sing in front of girls. I don't say that out loud.

"What are those chords?" She squints at my hand.

I say, "Um, they're power chords. They come out of the bottom two notes." I carefully make an F barre chord pattern. I hate F chords. They take me forever to make on the guitar and they kill my hand.

"Oh, sweet," she says. "Barre chords, I get. I took acoustic lessons. What frets are you at?"

I show her. She works out that the chords are C, G, B-flat and F.

B-flat and F? Wow. Maybe I'm better than I thought.

She plays them, easily, as barre chords.

I say, "Cool. That's good."

"They sound better with the power chords," she says. "Show me again."

I do. It feels good to show someone else music stuff.

She tries the chords and says, "Cool. I've got to learn those. What comes next?"

I swallow and say, "Ah...uh...that's all I've got. That's why I'm stuck." The room starts to feel too warm.

"Oh," she says. "See, I always start with words." She nods at the desk. "I've got a book full of them. It's the other part that's hard for me. But know what?" She flips her hair behind her ear again. "I don't think you need words there. That part should be your hook or whatever. Then you write a song with that in it."

"Oh." So I haven't written a song yet.

This is bad, but the girl is still talking. "It's in C, right?"

"C?"

"It's in the key of C, right?" she says. "'Cause it starts on C."

"Riiiight." Chuck used to talk about keys. There was something about how chords go together. I'm going to have to find out what they are before this girl finds out I'm a moron. Maybe I should have taken music, clarinets and all.

"So," she says, "after you play that part, try a C again and start singing."

I try it. I don't sing out loud, but I keep that *duh-duh duh-duh* beat going. A word pops into my head: *Running running running*.

Is this an idea? It feels like one. Should I run right now? I don't run. Instead I stop playing and say, "Wow. That really helps."

She smiles and says, "Can I try that power chord again? This right? So that would be G. Then in my song it would be…"

She plays a bouncier rhythm: *bum bum-bum-bum-bum, bum bum-bum-bum-bum*, and goes up the neck and sings:

Hey, when you see me
Don't act so dreamy
Hear every word I say...

Wow. She has a killer voice, and it's a good tune too. She stops. "That sounds way better than this." She plays again, with regular chords.

Now it's my turn to watch hands. I say, "Those are G, A and C, right? Try it again, okay? I can see a bass part." I can't play it that fast right off. "Can you slow down a little?" I ask.

We try it again. This time I can play along. She likes it.

"That is so awesome," she says.

I say, "I'm more of a bass player than a guitarist."

"Really?" she says. "Can you show me again? I want to teach that to our bass player."

I say, "You've got a band? What's it called?"

She says, "No Shirt No Shoes No Service."

Niiiiice.

"We're just getting started," she says.

"Us too," I say. "Mine is called Incoming."

"I like that." She does that hair thing again.

"Who are you into?" I ask.

She starts listing bands. I'm nodding when it really hits me. I'm playing guitar, writing and talking with a super-talented girl who has a killer smile, and, well, a whole lot of other things. *And* she knows tons about music.

She says, "Oh, and Sleater-Kinney too. God, how could I forget?"

Who? I can't ask. I'll look even dumber. Suddenly I'm the Incredible Shrinking Ace again. I say, "Well,

I should probably let you…" I turn to put Chuck's guitar away and clunk it against a desk. "Thanks a lot for helping. That was really…"

"Hey, back at you," she says. "Thanks for showing me power chords and the bass line."

My knees practically melt. There is enough of me left to say, "Um, maybe our bands should do, like, a show together or something. We don't make the cat barf anymore."

She gives her head a shake, as if she hadn't heard right. Then she says, "Awesome." She starts to pack up too. "Bell's gonna go. Hey, Facebook me, okay?"

"Sure." Now I'm trying to fasten the snaps on my guitar case, but my fingers aren't working.

"At Lisa Picks," she says.

"For sure," I say. "I'm Dave. But it'll say, um, Ace. It's, like…"

She nods. "Yeah, a nickname. So's Picks."

"Oh. Yeah. Cool. Well…," I say.

"Yup," says Lisa Picks. "Later."

I'm almost back to my locker when I wonder, Did I tell her we don't make the cat barf anymore? Oh, no. I'm shrinking again.

Chapter Ten

"Ohhh-kay, Ace! Lay it on us." It's Saturday night practice. We've just finished listening to Pig's song. Well, actually it was a drum solo. Archie shot upstairs when Pig got going. I can hear him yowling up there somewhere.

Now it's my turn. My fingers are shaky. I pretend to check my tuning. "Okay," I say, "I'm not quite done yet.

It's, like, a road song." I make the C power chord on the acoustic and blow the start. I take a breath and try again. This time I get it. I don't hit all the high notes, and I mess up a couple of chords, but it's pretty good:

> *Running running running it's a thing*
> *that I do*
> *Running running running far away*
> *from you*
> *Running running running is the*
> *thing that I know*
> *Running running running and I have*
> *to go*
> *I'm sleeping in the backseat and*
> *running all the time*
> *Duh-duh-duh-duh-duh duh*
> *Duh-duh-duh-duh duh duh*
> *Duh.*

I stop. "The *duh*s aren't really the lyrics. I haven't got them right yet. But that's the idea."

It's still quiet. I say, "And I didn't hit all the high notes 'cause…" I point upstairs, where Mom might be listening.

It's *still* quiet. Finally, Denny nods and says, "Okay." Pig shrugs and nods.

That's all that they say. I feel like Led Zeppelin with a leak. Geez, all Pig came up with was a drum solo. *A drum solo.* I only said I liked it to be nice.

"It's okay? That's it?" I hear my voice squeak a little.

"Well, what do you want?" Denny says. "We only heard it once."

What do I want? I was hoping for fireworks and these guys falling off their chairs. Then a standing O, a million dollars and Lisa forgetting the cat barf comment and saying I'm cool.

"Want me to play it again?" I say.

"Let me do mine first." Denny grins and pulls out a distortion pedal. "Wait till you hear this," he says. He plugs the Teleporter into it and hits a power chord. The sound crunches through the basement.

"Okay," Denny says. He unfolds a paper with writing on it and lays it on his amp. "This is called 'Got to Rock.'"

"That's original," I say. I fold my arms tight. My pits have gone cold where I've been sweating.

Denny doesn't seem to hear. He starts chopping a rhythm so fast it's practically punk. He sings:

Used to walk but now I run
Used to talk but now it's sung
Used to dock—now I roam
Used to sway but now I rock
Used to groove but now I shock
Got to rock—like a rolling stone

He gets that far, and I already know it's good. It's way better than mine. Even though we're all a band, I feel like I'm doomed. Halfway through, Mom sprouts magically on the stairs.

When Denny finishes, she claps. Then she takes out an earplug and asks, "Is that one that you guys wrote?"

"Well, I did, actually," Denny says. He's grinning like a maniac. "It's for the contest." He tells my mom all about it.

"Wow," says Mom. "That's great. It's catchy. It reminds me of…oh, I don't know, what's that song? What is it, Davey?"

I shrug and I say, "I'm not an Abba expert." My mom loves Denny's song. This does not make me overjoyed.

Denny jumps in, saying, "It sounds a little like lots of songs, probably. That's how you can tell it's good."

Thank you, Mr. Modest.

"I never thought of it that way," Mom says. "You said two songs. What's the other?"

"Ace wrote one," Denny says.

"Later," I say to Mom. I start to fold up my paper.

"Oh, c'mon." she says.

"Later."

Mom shakes her head. "Then later it will be," she says. "Does anyone want anything to drink?"

"A pitcher of draft, please," Denny says.

"Dream on, Denny." Mom laughs and heads for the stairs. "I'll bring down some juice for all of you," she says over her shoulder.

Sunday afternoon, Mom goes to an open house for real estate agents. I promise to do homework. She's happy because I got a B on my math test. (Okay, it was B minus, but it still counts.)

I really do homework, because I can't face music. I know it's wrong, but it bugs me that Denny's song is better than mine, even if it gives us a shot at the contest. How did the guy do it?

I guess there's no reason he couldn't. Except that it's Denny. That means I'm jealous. Of Denny. I never thought I'd be jealous of Denny.

Finally I ditch homework and practice my song. We do get to do two songs for the contest, and my song is better than a drum solo. I sing it again. I hate my voice. Then I have a really bad thought. Lisa is going to like Denny's song better than mine. Oh man, Denny's going to be all over her.

I haven't told Denny about Lisa. I found her on Facebook and sent a friend request. I'd imagined playing my song to her in the music room and her loving it. And me. Now I don't think I want to.

What I have to do is make my song better—except I don't know how. How can Denny write like that when I can't? I sing mine again. I still hate my voice.

I can't help it; I check Denny's Twitter feed: **dr. D writes monster incoming hit 4uall sensstionel.**

I can feel my teeth grind. To get my mind off it, I hunt around for some music to play to. I've left my MP3 player at school. Darn. There aren't many CDs around the house. Mom's are awful.

Then I remember Chuck's. I haven't listened to it in a million years. I go downstairs and grab one from the box. I'm using Chuck's gear, so he won't mind if I listen to his album too.

The front cover says *RAZORBURN: Mullet Over.*

The picture shows a guy's head and back, with a long blond mullet hanging down under a straw cowboy hat. The back of the CD shows the same guy without the hat. He is bald on top. That was Chuck for you. Liked his hats. Usually wore his hair back in a ponytail.

I peel off the shrink wrap and pop the CD in the player. The first two tunes are yawner country rock. We must have listened to this when Chuck was around, but I don't remember these songs at all.

I play along a little. They're boring but easy. I'm getting better at guessing what chords go together. Hey, that means I'm learning my keys. That makes me feel a little better. I skip ahead. The third tune is a horrible ballad. The fourth is more pop. It has a guitar riff that's okay, and the intro sounds familiar. Maybe Chuck used to play it. The singer starts in:

Used to run, but now I walk
Used to sing, but now I talk
Used to dock...

Wait a minute.

Used to rock but now I sway
Used to gleam but now I fade...

It sounds *very* familiar. And all at once I know how Denny did it.

Chapter Eleven

It's lunchtime on Monday before I see
Denny. I've been stewing about the
song rip-off the whole time. I don't
say anything while we eat, because
other kids sit with us. Besides, Denny
is blabbing a mile a minute about the
video club girls. Then we all start
playing Frisbee. One by one the other

guys leave, and there's only Denny and me left. I can't take it any longer.

I've planned it to casually say, "I listened to Chuck's CD yesterday," but now I'm too mad from waiting.

What comes out is, "You stole the song." Then I throw the Frisbee back to Denny. Hard.

"No, I didn't," Denny insists. "Not exactly. Ow!" He shakes his hand and throws back too high.

I jump for it and miss. I walk to get it. I'm not running for Denny. I turn around and say, "You changed the words around and sped it up. Big deal. It's still a rip-off. And you stole one of Chuck's CDs."

Denny laughs. "Oh, come on, Ace. I borrowed it. You can have it back."

I throw the Frisbee back to him, harder. Now I'm almost yelling. "That's not what matters, and you know it. No wonder your song was so good. You cheated. I really wrote a song."

"Hey, not so loud, okay?" Denny says and looks around.

I snap, "What? Are you afraid the video girls might hear?"

"Yeah," he says. His throw goes high again. I have to jump for it. "I've been hanging with them. They're getting interested in a project."

"Right," I say. I throw too low.

"No, they are. Who knows what might happen?" Denny wiggles his eyebrows. He throws high *again*. I jump to my right and miss.

"Don't change the subject. You copped the song. I wrote one."

Denny sighs and says, "Look, Ace, no offence but, which one was better? Huh? I don't mean your song sucks. There isn't time to write a *good* song. The contest is next Friday." He throws. This one I catch, even though it's way over my head.

Denny is as crappy at Frisbee as I am. I'm surprised he doesn't have someone throwing for him. I throw back another worm burner.

"We're going to do your song too," Denny says.

I moan. "Aw, for—"

"My bad," Denny says.

Denny's throw has gone really wild this time. The Frisbee is hanging from a tree branch. We jump for it, but it's just out of reach. We're not supposed to climb the trees at school, but this one is easy and it'll take a second. I start for it, but Denny scrambles up first. He reaches for the branch.

"Look, Ace," he says from above, "we're in this together, right? It doesn't matter who *wrote* the song, as long as it's ours, right? And we're all working to learn how to play it, right? So we're all kind of writing it. With Chuck. We're getting his song heard, and we're making it better. It's not like we're ripping him off for money."

I don't say anything.

"We don't have to say it's mine," Denny says. "It's ours. Okay?"

I look up at Denny. He's got his big goofy grin on his face. "We want to win, right? Video club girls, right?"

I think about winning. Forget the video club girls. I imagine Lisa thinking that I helped write the song.

I nod. Denny shakes the tree branch. The Frisbee drops into my hand like a big fat apple. I look up. Denny's already tweeting.

Chapter Twelve

I get to be Facebook friends with Lisa.
It's stupid, but I am too chicken to ask if
she wants to meet up at lunch one day.
I tell myself she's too busy anyway, that
her band is probably practicing. I'll see
her at the contest.

The contest is coming up fast. We're
supposed to be practicing too, but really
I am the only one who practices.

Pig is "busy." With what? Who knows? His hair is even shorter, and now he wears aviator shades all the time. Denny, Mister Showbiz, is too busy tweeting. All he ever talks about is Alison and Jessica and the other video girls. He's late all the time. Do they care about this, or what?

Meanwhile, I keep working on my song. I mean, how cool would it be if mine got so good that *it* won? Then it wouldn't matter about Chuck's song. I get all the *duhs* out of my lyrics. I decide to call it "Sleeping in the Backseat."

I like my tune so much that I'm almost okay with playing it for Mom. I don't want to tell her that though. Instead I strum Chuck's guitar a bunch when she's around, in case that gives her the idea to ask about my song.

I'm playing guitar in the kitchen on Tuesday when she comes in. She's carrying red flowers—roses I think.

She's all cheery and fussing around, cutting the stems and putting water in a vase.

"There's another math test next week," I tell her. *Strum, strum.*

"Well, I'm sure you'll do fine," Mom says. She puts the vase on the kitchen table and starts to stick the flowers in it.

I say, "Yeah, can't start studying till after the contest though." *Strum, strum, strum.*

"Mm," says Mom. "Is that on Friday? Oh, darn. I hope I don't have to present an offer on a house that night." She doesn't sound very upset. I'm not sure how I feel about that.

I play some more, running through my chord changes. "Well," I say, "guess I should go practice…" *Strum, strum.*

"Okay, sweetie." Mom kisses me on the top of the head. Then she flips open her cell phone. "Just have to check my messages, then we'll talk about dinner."

She heads off to the living room, smiling like summer holidays started. I guess the real estate market is looking up.

I go to the basement and sing "Sleeping in the Backseat" loud enough for Mom to hear. When I finish, I hear her laughing and talking on her phone. Rats. I thought being a songwriter would make me a chick magnet, but right now not even my mom is listening.

Even worse, Denny and Pig haven't heard my tune lately either. They don't know how I've changed it. When we finally practice on Wednesday, Denny keeps messing up the new lyrics. He puts the stupid *duh*s back in instead.

"I'll sing it myself," I tell him as we pack up.

"No sweat," Denny says. I'm surprised. Denny likes being the lead singer. He likes being lead every-thing. "What we really gotta decide,"

Denny goes on, "is what we're going to wear on Friday. I'm going grunge, but with style."

I say, "Such as?"

"New Converse," Denny says. "What are you wearing, Pig?"

Pig shrugs. He's been unscrewing cymbals and stacking them neatly to take with us to the contest. Now he unzips his backpack and puts his drumsticks in. I have to look twice. His textbooks in there are each covered in plastic. Finally Pig says, "What I'm wearing." He's wearing a T-shirt that says *Cleared For Takeoff*. I hope we are.

"I'm going dark," I say. I decide to go with my acid-wash jeans and the tight dark blue shirt. I think dark blue goes with bass. It'll make me look like a serious musician. I'm not going to shave, either. You can tell now when

I don't, kind of, right on my chin. I rub my chin right now. It feels a little prickly. Or maybe it's all of me that's feeling prickly. Thinking about Friday is making me nervous.

Chapter Thirteen

Friday night Pig's dad gives us a ride to the youth center. We have to haul amps and cymbals and the snare and foot pedal for the drum kit, plus the guitars. Pig's dad doesn't talk any more than Pig does.

"There will be beautiful women watching. I know there will be beautiful women." Denny's motormouth is in overdrive. He must be nervous. Plus he's texting or tweeting or something.

Pig's dad laughs. I say, "Yes, Den. And they'll all be watching you." By now my right foot is bouncing like my own rhythm section, and I've got elevator stomach. I'm thinking about a million things at once. Will we win? Will Lisa love my song? Will Lisa love me? Does getting a ride from someone's dad counts as a road trip? It has to count more than moving drums on the bus.

The youth center hasn't changed much. I used to go there to play floor hockey when I was little. The first thing I see is lots of guys in dark blue shirts. Darn. There are parents here too. Luckily, Mom has to present that offer on a house. That's one less thing to worry about.

We haul everything into the gym. It's set up with a low stage with mikes and stands and a drum kit that looks as if it has been attacked by gorillas. A spotlight shines down. The Twisted Hazard guys from Battle of the Bands are setting up.

My elevator stomach jumps twenty floors. We're really going to do this.

I see more kids from Battle of the Bands, but it's Lisa I'm looking for. Then I spot her. She's across the gym, behind another girl and three guys. They seem to be all talking at the same time. I wave, but I don't think she sees me. That's okay. She's busy. I'm busy too—busy being nervous.

We sign in at the judge's table. We are going to be on fifth, out of ten acts. Is that good or bad? I don't know. Denny keeps asking what time they think we'll be on. I don't care about that. "What number is No Shirt No Shoes No Service?" I ask.

"They're right before you," says a bald guy who is one of the judges.

We go to tune up. It feels good to have something to do.

Twisted Hazard kicks off. It's hard to tell about their songs. They pretty much all sound the same, especially with earplugs in. One song is either about *macaroni* or *mayday homey*. But it's not rap, so *homey* doesn't make sense. Macaroni? Who knows. They're loud and they rock though. I look at the judges. They're writing stuff down. Is that good or bad?

The second band is called Death Star. They're pure metal, sort of like Iron Maiden but dumb. One song has the word *troll* in it a lot, and the other is something about hammers. The judges write more stuff down. They can't like troll songs, can they?

Third come two guys with acoustic guitars. I don't catch their names. They play exactly the same thing and take turns singing about a magic potion. They sing so high they squeak.

I'm starting to feel better. I know "Sleeping in the Backseat" is better than these.

Now No Shirt No Shoes No Service is up. I know Lisa's song is good. If we don't win, I want her band to win and us to come in second.

"Let's tune again," Denny says. He's looking at his watch. Then he looks all around. "Beautiful women, beautiful women," he keeps saying. Pig is drumming the wall. He's got his aviator shades on. How can he see anything?

"In a minute," I say. I push forward. A guy is plugging in a keyboard. The other girl is the drummer. There's a guy on bass, and Lisa and the other guy on acoustics. Lisa looks incredible. She's got on soft boots and leggings and this short skirt with her jean jacket. The little green stone in her nose catches the light. She pulls the mike down to her level and looks out at the crowd in front of the stage.

I hope she sees me. I don't want to do anything dorky like wave. She looks my way, and I think she recognizes me. Just then the guitar guy counts, "Two… three…" and they start.

Hey, when you see me
Don't act so dreamy…

But Lisa's song has gone from being a cool indie rocker to a drippy emo ballad. The power chords are gone. The drummer loses a beat. The guy on keyboard messes up a wimpy solo. The bass player uses one string, and none of the bits I showed Lisa. Lisa's voice wobbles with the slow time.

I hang in long enough to clap at the end of the tune. Lisa doesn't look happy. I head back to get my bass.

"They suck," Denny says. He's bouncing on his toes. He has his Teleporter slung on. Pig is still drumming the wall.

Denny's right, but I don't want to say it. "It's a good song though," I say.

"Ours is better," Denny says.

"Ours *are* better," I snap. "Tell me about it." I plug my bass into the tuner as their second song begins. I may sound okay, but my fingers are shaking. Tuning seems to take forever. I slip the bass strap over my head. The patch cord is coiled in my hand. Now I hear clapping as Lisa's band finishes. They announce that Incoming is next.

"Let's do it," says Denny. I follow him and Pig. I almost stumble on the one step to the stage. The amp is heavy. The lights are hot. It takes me two tries to plug in. Then I turn and look out from the stage.

I have to squint in the glare. Pig's shades suddenly seem like a good idea. This may be the youth center, but it feels like Madison Square Gardens. There are a lot of people here. There is also a microphone right in front of me. I'd swallow but there's nothing to swallow. My elevator stomach lurches into a free fall.

Behind me, I hear Pig setting up. He rumbles around the kit and moves something. I fumble out a couple of bass notes. Denny is messing with his distortion pedal. Now he smacks a test chord. From out front there is a buzz of voices. I look at Denny. He's grinning like he lives on a stage. I start to feel it too. We're a team. I *want* this. Maybe I've been waiting for this my whole life and not known it. My stomach stops before the basement. I take a deep breath and run a few more notes on my bass. Pig is still fussing. Now Denny's waving. I look to the back, and coming in the doors are Alison and Lucy from the video club, then Jessica with a camera up in front of her. What the...?

There isn't time to wonder. The judges nod for us to start. As Pig counts us in, I see the girls shuffle forward. Two more people squeeze in behind them. One of them is Mom. She's with a guy, arm in arm. The guy has a mustache and one of those stupid old-guy western-style hats, a long leather jacket and dad jeans. I've seen him before. As we come in on the first beat, I remember where. My place. A long time ago. It's Chuck.

Chapter Fourteen

We rock out. Pig nails the beat. Denny half sings and half screams, and it works. He also bounces, jumps, drops to his knees and flicks a pick out into the crowd. He even plays okay. Lucy and Alison and Jessica are right down in front, filming.

And I hate every second of it. I pretend I have to watch my fingers.

I don't look up once. There's lots of clapping when we finish. Denny does a big goofy bow and before I can stop him, says, "Thanks. We all wrote that, from my idea."

I have to look. Chuck has his dumb hat pushed up on his bald head. He's got his arms crossed, and he's talking to Mom.

Now he's looking at me, standing onstage with his bass beside the guy who just claimed we wrote Chuck's song. It was supposed to be Chuck who had reliability issues.

I know what I have to do. Before Denny can say anything else, I step to my microphone. "Uuuh," I say.

I've stepped too close, and what they hear is *UUUUH* with a huge squeal of feedback. The whole room jumps, including me.

"Uh," I try again. "Uh, actually, there's another writer." My voice sounds like a strangled chicken. Heads lift at the judge's table. I'm not going to look at Denny. I squint at the far basketball hoop. "Our friend Chuck wrote it. He let us change it around and that helped us get started." I point. "He's back there."

Heads turn. Chuck grins and waves. There is more clapping. "He loaned me his bass too," I say. The clapping is still going on. "So, anyway, I don't know if that counts, but we did write this one by ourselves."

I look at the judge's table. This time they're not writing, they're scratching lines right across their papers. Oh, no. I can't look at Denny. I'm not even looking at the basketball hoop now. My eyes are closed. I clutch my bass and play the opening of "Sleeping in the Backseat."

I know I've got the beat wrong even before I sing the first line. Pig and I get out of time. Denny hits a wrong chord and forgets to sing on the chorus.

While we mangle my song, part of me floats above everything. That part of me is calm. It wonders what sounds worse than a strangled chicken. Archie barfing? A sick ostrich? Pick one, it tells the rest of me, because that's how you sound, especially on that high note you can never quite reach—the one that's coming up *now*. Then it tells me that "Sleeping in the Backseat" still sucks. All that *running, running, running* doesn't cut it. Meanwhile, the rest of me feels as if I'm in a train wreck.

There's a trickle of clapping when we finish. Then comes the kiss of death.

Someone at the back is clapping like crazy. I don't even have to look to know it's Mom.

Chapter Fifteen

As we come offstage I know one thing. Now that I've blabbed that we didn't write our good song, no one's going to listen to us again. Ever. Actually I know two things, because I also know that I feel so crappy I don't want to see anybody. Too bad that's not an option. Mom and Chuck are already in front of me.

"Hon, I *loved* it! Why didn't you play that for me before? It's so *sensitive*."

"Thanks, Mom."

Mom laughs. "Don't be sarcastic, you. I had to shuffle a lot of things, but I wouldn't have missed that for the world." Then she says, "And look who I met at an agent's open house last week!"

"Davey," Chuck says, "how are ya?" Chuck is grinning. He sticks out his hand. Mine are full. He sees and laughs. "Know the feeling." His mustache is shorter now. He's thicker-looking. "Man," he says. "Did that take me back! Who'd have thought you guys would still be listening to that stuff? Loved what ya did with it! Make me a million, okay? Hey, we've got to do some pickin'. You still got the guitar too?"

I nod.

"Smokin'," says Chuck. "You're on! Haven't played since I gave up truckin'.

Sell houses now like your mom. I'll be over, okay? Let's do it."

I nod again. I'm still trying to catch up. Mom takes Chuck by his leather-coated arm and says, "We're going to grab a quick bite, hon. Do you want to come with us?"

"I'd better stay here," I say.

Mom smiles and says, "All right. We won't be late."

Next it's Denny and Pig. I see them at the guitar cases. I'm still thinking about my mom's "*We* won't be late." Denny and Pig won't look at me. I know I have to say it.

I put down the bass amp. It's killing my arm. "Look," I say, "sorry, but I saw them come in. I had to."

"Aw, no sweat." Denny shrugs as he snaps his case shut. "Alison said they got good footage."

That makes me feel a little better. After all, it's not as if the whole world was here. "So Pig can post it on Myspace," I say.

"Well," Denny stands and shuffles. Then he says, "It wasn't exactly for that. See, they were just filming me. For a video club project."

"Video club?" I say.

Denny says, "Yeah, I joined, 'cause like, the girls wanted me too. We're making this movie." Denny shrugs and makes a face. He says, "So, like, sorry, Ace, but I have to bail on the band. There's not gonna be enough time for music."

"But—," I say.

"Me too," says Pig, from behind his shades. It might be the first thing he's said all night.

"What?" I spin to him. "You joined video club too?"

"No," Pig says. "I'm in air cadets. Always was."

"*Air cadets*?" I say.

Pig nods and points to his *Cleared For Takeoff* T-shirt. "I'm starting flying lessons," he says.

Suddenly the boots and the hair and the shades make sense. Pig says, "And my brother wants his drums at school anyway." He hoists the snare and cymbals.

"But," I say again, "but…"

It's over. Just like that. Incoming is outgoing.

Pig doesn't stay to watch the rest of the bands. He has cadet training camp early Saturday morning. Denny goes to find the video girls. He says I should come too. I shake my head and put my bass away. There are no props this time.

The next band isn't even finished, and my band is done for good. I have had the shortest music career ever. All that's left is jamming with a bald real estate agent who wears dumb hats and redates my mom.

I sink down by my case and lean against the wall. Music bounces around me, but I don't take it in. I'm staring at the floor tiles when I see the toes of two soft boots. Oh. No. It's the person I least want to see after I've looked like a total idiot.

Lisa sits down beside me. "Hi," she says.

"Hi." I nod to the stage and say, "They're good." As if I'm listening.

Lisa says, "Yeah. We weren't. We sucked."

"Tell me about it," I say back, and shrug. "At least—never mind. I liked your song."

"Thanks," she says.

I wait for her to say she liked mine, but she doesn't.

After a bit I say, "How come you changed your song? I liked it better as a rocker." I did, but I guess I'm also bugged she didn't say anything about my song.

"I did too," she says. "But the band wanted to do it that way. And Grant couldn't play the bass line you showed me."

"That's a drag," I say.

Lisa nods. "Same with yours," she says. "No offence, but your guitar player should have sung, and you could have rocked out on bass."

I nod. "Well," I say, "he didn't learn it, so I had to do it. It doesn't matter. I know I've gotta change the words more. It's still not very good." I wrap my arms around my knees. "And anyway, it *really* doesn't matter. The band just broke up."

Lisa nods and says, "Mine too."

I look at her. "Your band broke up? Why?"

She sighs, then tucks her hair behind her ear and says, "'Cause we sucked and I said so, and nobody but me wanted to practice more so we wouldn't suck."

I think that over as a song ends. Maybe it's my night for saying things. I look at Lisa. Then I look a little bit to one side of her, as if I'm thinking deep thoughts. "We've got guitar, vocal and bass," I say. Deep breath. "Um, maybe we should start a band."

I dare a look at her.

She's smiling. Lisa says, "I think we just did."

Since the publication of his first picturebook, *Puddleman*, in 1988, Ted Staunton has been delighting readers of all ages with his funny and perceptive stories about friends, family and school life. Ted is a frequent speaker and performer at schools, libraries and conferences across Canada and teaches fiction writing at George Brown College. Ted and his family live in Port Hope, Ontario.

orca *currents*

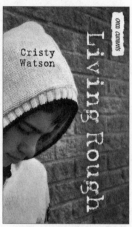

9781554694341 $9.95 PB
9781554698882 $16.95 LIB

In most ways, Poe is like the other kids in his school. He thinks about girls and tries to avoid teachers. He hangs out at the coffee shop with his best friend after school. He has a loving father who helps him with his homework. But Poe has a secret, and almost every day some small act threatens to expose him.

orca *currents*

9781554699100 9.95 PB
9781554699117 16.95 LIB

Fifteen-year-old Maddie has big-city dreams, and she's found her chance to visit New York. An art magazine is holding a portrait contest, and the first prize is an all-expenses-paid trip to the Big Apple. Maddie plans to win, but her mother has different ideas for her: a mother-daughter adventure in organic gardening. Maddie is furious. How will she find an inspiring subject for her portrait amid the goat poop and chickens?

orca *currents*

9781554698202 $9.95 PB
9781554698219 $16.95 LIB

Suspended from school, lonely and bored, fifteen-year-old Zack will do anything for amusement. His mom drags him out geocaching, and Zack finds a CD with the word *Famous* written across it. He puts the CD on his stereo and loses himself in the music. Zack has sound-color synesthesia. He sees colors when he hears music, and the music on the *Famous* CD causes incredible patterns of color for him. Zack becomes obsessed with the girl on the CD and decides he has to find her.

Titles in the Series

orca currents

orca currents

For more information on all the books
in the Orca Currents series, please visit
www.orcabook.com.

shock, too much adrenaline rushing through her bloodstream, even tears. She did none of the expected. He stared into her eyes, his hand immediately going to the small penlight that he kept in his pocket.

"I'm not in shock, Doctor."

Brad pulled the light out, anyway. He didn't have to give her instructions; she immediately looked straight ahead and he checked her pupils. He suddenly smelled coconut, but before he could determine where it came from, she spoke.

"Satisfied, Dr. Clayton? I'm truly not in shock." She turned to go.

He took her arm and turned her back. "You may not be in shock, Dr. Russell, but you are bleeding."

Her hand went to her neck and came away wet. She saw her own blood on her fingers and the color drained from her face. Suddenly it hit her: the man really could have killed her.

Reaction set in. Her muscles seemed to relax all at once.

"Come on. I'll dress it," Brad murmured.

When she looked up at him she *was* in shock.

Mallory couldn't believe she'd nearly passed out. Her legs turned to rubber, and Brad Clayton had to help her to the examination room and onto a gurney. She was never so embarrassed in her life. All because of a little blood. Of all the people in the hospital, why was he here? The E.R. wasn't his usual department. At least not when she was on duty.

"Just relax," Brad said. "You only need a little rest."

"I'm fine. Really," she told him, but she was glad she was lying down. She closed her eyes and allowed the strange feeling of dizziness to subside. She no longer felt afraid. Wayne Mason had scared her more than anything ever had, yet she felt no aftermath of the ordeal. She could return to her duties. Except Dr. Bradley Clayton wasn't having it.

"Open your eyes," he said.

She opened them. "I'm not in shock," she said again.

"I just want to make sure." He took a cotton swab and dabbed at the blood on her neck. Mallory jumped at his touch.

"Did that hurt?" She heard the concern in his voice.

"No," she said. "I wasn't expecting...I mean I forgot..." She stopped, unsure how to finish the sentence. His fingers touched her and she was unaware of her injury, only that they sent a charge through her. Again she questioned why he was in Emergency. If she had to have another doctor take care of her, why not Mark Peterson or Jason Abrams? Why did Brad Clayton have to show up tonight?

"Open your eyes," he said again. Mallory did as instructed. "You're not acting as I expect you to."

How was she supposed to act? She was a doctor. She should know this. Where was her training? All those years of schooling seemed to vanish when she looked into his deep brown eyes.

"Tell me how you feel," Brad said.

How she felt? She'd been at the hospital for nearly a year, and he'd never even looked at her. Yet her first day as a resident, she'd passed him in the parking lot and wondered who he was. He was moody, quiet, sometimes cynical, and he looked right through her, the same way he would look through a ghost.

"I feel fine. I'm just tired. I've been on duty for fourteen hours."

"So you need some sleep?"

"Dr. Clayton, I can go back to work."

Brad took another swab and cleaned away the blood that had trickled down her neck.

"It's only a scratch, right?" Mallory questioned.

"With your skin type there won't even be a scar." His hand brushed her neck. It felt like a caress. Mallory forced her eyes to stay open. She couldn't stop the tingling sensation that streaked through her at warp speed.

She took a deep breath when his hands moved past her collarbone and continued to the bloodstain in the white blouse she wore under her lab coat. Again Mallory's lids swept downward. The sensations that rushed through her at his touch made her want to keep her eyes closed and give in to the fantasies that she often imagined in the quiet of her bedroom.

"I'm sending you home," he said.

Her eyelids fluttered. "Why?"

"Other than you're too tired to keep your eyes open, you've had a really bad shock."

"I'm fine," she insisted.

"And you're no use to the patients in this state." He continued as if she hadn't spoken.

"You can't send me home."

Holding a bandage, he moved around to face her. "Do you think anyone is going to question my decision?"

She thought about the long hours she'd been on duty, the episode with Wayne Mason, the cut on her neck and Brad's authority at the hospital. He was liked, well-respected, a brilliant surgeon, even though he was moody and unpredictable at times. She knew no one would object to his decision.

"Do you live alone?" he asked.

"Why?"

"I want to know if there'll be someone to check on you."

"There isn't. I do live alone."

"Can you call a friend? I don't think you should be on your own tonight."

Mallory hesitated, then said, "I'll call my sister."

Brad gave her an inquisitive look, but said, "Good."

Her sister lived in Atlantic City, an hour from Philadelphia. She was a kindergarten teacher and couldn't come up on the spur of the moment and spend the night with her. There was nothing wrong with Mallory. She didn't need a baby-sitter. Yet if she told him that he would never believe it.

The truth was she had very few friends. She'd only been back in Philly a year, and most of that time she'd spent at the hospital. She'd lost touch with her old friends, and her work at the hospital kept her too busy to make new ones. She'd gotten close to one of the nurses, Dana Baldwin, but Dana was on duty tonight. So she would go home alone. She would be fine. Exactly as she had told the good doctor.

"I'll have someone call you a taxi."

Mallory sat up and swung her legs to the side of the gurney. She felt no dizziness until her eyes met his. They were a deep brown, narrow and piercing. She held his gaze but felt as if he were looking into her mind. "Dr. Clayton, I'm not ill. I can drive myself home."

Brad stared at her for a long time. Mallory wanted to look away, remove herself from those piercing eyes, but she resisted the urge. Finally he hunched a shoulder and took a step back.

"I don't want to see you here for at least twelve hours." His voice was level, yet the command in it was unmistakable.

"If it's any of your business," she said, slipping off the gurney, "I'm off tomorrow. But it's not your call when or how often I work."

Mallory couldn't believe she was saying these things. For a year she'd thought about having a conversation with him, and now she was arguing. It was as if he pushed some long-dormant buttons she hadn't realized she had.

As she headed for the opening in the curtain, Brad Clayton stepped aside. She stopped. "Dr. Clayton." Her throat went dry when she raised her eyes to look at him. He was taller than she was by a head. And he had a powerful presence—the kind of thing they said about people who go on the stage or work as models. There was something about them that caused everyone else to pause and take notice. And he had it. "I apologize," she said. "I shouldn't have said that. I will go home and do as you say."

He smiled. She knew that was rare. She'd stared at him from across the E.R., across treatment rooms, in the operating room and from the back of a crowd of interns on rounds during the last year. He rarely smiled except at his patients. Mallory would have sworn he didn't even know she existed, but she *was* technically his patient. That could be the reason for his smile, but what it did to her insides had nothing to do with a doctor-patient relationship. The man was sexy as hell, and she wasn't feeling like a doctor.

She was feeling like a woman.

As promised, Mallory drove straight home. She didn't call her sister, but instead ran a hot bath, eased into the silky, scented water and promptly fell asleep. She woke up when the water cooled, got out of the tub and dried herself, but had no energy to find a nightgown. She crawled naked into bed.

Brad's keys clinked in the glass bowl where he always dropped them upon entering his house. It was two o'clock in the morning, and he couldn't remember ever being this tired. Still wearing his bomber jacket, he went to the kitchen and opened the refrigerator. The light made his eyes smart. He really needed to sleep.

Grabbing a bottle of water, he twisted the cap off and drank it in one long gulp. Throwing the plastic container in the recycling bin, he closed the fridge, plunging the room into darkness. Mallory Russell's face suddenly entered his mind. He had barely noticed her before but her actions tonight meant everyone would remember her.

She was no beauty queen. On days he did notice her, her hair was often unkempt, knotted on top of her head, with tendrils falling down her neck and ears. She often pushed them back, only to have them work free again. She wore little if any makeup, except some lip color. Her best feature was her eyes. They were large, as deep as an ocean, a dark brown-sugar color and fringed with lashes that were standard issue on girls under ten. By the time they started to curve upward puberty set in and the lashes were left behind in childhood. Mallory Russell had kept hers. Or maybe she just hadn't reached puberty yet.

The phone rang, jarring Brad out of his musings. He realized he was still standing in the dark. Bypassing the phone in the kitchen, he went into the family room and switched on a lamp. The caller ID showed him it was Rosa, his sister, who lived in New York City.

"Rosa, what are you doing up at this hour?" he said without the traditional hello. "Don't cover girls need their beauty rest?"

"You need to work on your lines, Brad. That cliché must be as old as you are," she told him.

"What should I have said?" He took the portable

phone to the sofa and stretched his six-foot length out
on the deep maroon fabric.

"Never mind what you should have said, was it
you?"

Rosa was a news junkie. No doubt one, if not all,
of the local stations, which she got on her Direct TV
connection, had run the story of the "…near killing
at Philadelphia General. Details as they become available."

"It wasn't me."

"It wasn't? It certainly sounded like you. Trying
to save the children. I'm surprised the guy was in his
twenties."

"Rosa…" Brad said sardonically. She was the
youngest in the family, but when she got on a soap-
box there was no stopping her. At 2:00 a.m., after a
knifing and Mallory Russell, he was in no mood to
listen to one of Rosa's rants.

"Okay, okay," she answered.

He could almost see her lifting her hands. Rosa was
a model. When she wasn't on a runway, she talked
incessantly. But Brad loved her and they were very
close. He remembered when she was a child and used
to curl up in his lap and fall asleep. She called frequently now because she was concerned about him.
He loved her for it.

"So tell me what happened."

"What did the news report?" Brad reached over
and picked up the remote control from the coffee table. He switched on the big-screen television and
muted the sound. A costume drama was playing. Red

coats with elaborately ruffled shirts swayed as much as the swords the actors used in the choreographed fight. He pressed a button and the WKYS logo appeared in the corner of the screen. As fate would have it, a photo of the entrance of Philadelphia General appeared behind the newscaster. Brad turned the sound up.

"That a man had held a doctor hostage in the E.R. The doctor disarmed him and had to be treated for minor injuries," Rosa replied promptly.

"The man was on drugs and the doctor was a woman."

"A woman doctor disarmed a junkie? How'd she do that?"

Brad took a breath. He remembered the way he'd felt in the E.R. when he was sure at any moment Mallory Russell would be another statistic in the drug war.

"You wouldn't believe how she did it." He didn't know if he believed it. "She used a maneuver I've only seen in the movies."

"What did she do?" He heard the impatience in his sister's voice.

"She cut off the blood flow to his brain and he passed out."

Rosa was speechless for a moment, clearly in awe. He understood her reaction. He was in awe of Mallory Russell himself.

"I'd like to meet this wonder woman."

"It was an isolated event, Rosa. It happened in the moment. It doesn't make her Wonder Woman."

"She impressed you."

Brad blinked and sat up. He was trying to make the leap of logic his sister had, but missed the mark.

"What do you mean?"

"I can hear it in your voice. You sound different when you talk about her. There's something else in your voice other than admiration and respect."

"Don't read anything into this, Rosa. You're too quick to jump to conclusions."

"No, I'm not." For a moment there was silence. Then Rosa continued, "What were you doing while this man held a knife on the woman doctor?"

"Holding my breath."

"Good sign. Looks like she matters to you."

"Rosa…"

"You were holding your breath because of the woman doctor—"

"Will you stop calling her that? Her name is Mallory Russell."

"Mallory Russell, not Dr. Russell. This is getting better and better. She even has a name. Two names."

"Rosa, I'm going to hang up on you."

His sister laughed, her voice a soft musical trill. "You like Dr. Russell," she taunted gently. "Just listen to the irritation in your voice. At least it's an emotion."

"I feel nothing for her other than what a doctor would feel for a patient."

"Doctors hold their breath?"

"On occasion."

"This has been a wonderful call." Again Brad listened to the sound of her laughter. "Someone has cracked that casing around you. I can't wait to tell the family. It's almost worth a trip down there to meet Dr. Mallory Russell."

"Rosa, it's late and I'm tired and in no mood to try and convince you that you're so far off the mark you could be in China."

"I don't leave for China for months. I know exactly where I am. It's you who's confused." Brad listened in silence. "I'm sure you'll figure it out. Sometime," she added. "Unfortunately, it'll probably take you six months to do it."

Brad hung up a moment later, with his sister's laughter still ringing in his head and Mallory Russell on his mind. He couldn't seem to get her out of his thoughts. The night had been traumatic for everyone in the E.R. He chalked it up to that and nothing his baby sister had said.

Yet Brad wondered if Mallory was all right. She had been tired, overworked, and then that terrible ordeal had played out with her at the center of it. How could she think she could bounce back, with no repercussions? Brad knew bouncing back so quickly was almost never the case. Mallory needed rest and someone to talk to. She'd said she would call her sister. He hoped she had. On nights like this he knew firsthand about needing someone.

He stood up and stretched. The tiredness that had been in his bones fell away like layers of heavy armor. He was wide awake and wondering.

Was she alone?

Switching off the television, he wondered how Mallory was doing. She was technically his patient and he thought about all his patients, although most of them couldn't drive themselves home. Mallory had acted as if her ordeal had been all in a night's work.

It hadn't.

The night was a trauma for most in the E.R., but for her it was an instance of facing her own death. She was probably suffering the after-effects of the episode. Yet doctors really were the worst patients. Mallory Russell had looked him directly in the eye and lied. She had no intention of taking his advice and calling someone to stay with her. Around the hospital she was a loner. And he was sure she had gone home alone and called no one.

Chapter Two

The coma wing took up the entire seventh floor of the Grace N. Clyburn Building, which the staff referred to as Building C. It had been built five years ago, funded by a grant from a man whose wife had died without regaining consciousness. She'd been placed in a long-term care facility a hundred miles away, and he'd had to drive that distance to sit with her. The donated building had a walkway on level three that connected it to Building B. Mallory rarely ever used the walkway, though she worked in Building B, the oldest wing of the hospital.

"I am somebody," she said, standing next to the bed. She leaned in close and spoke quietly. "I want you to repeat it, Jeff." She stared at the smooth-skinned face of a twenty-something young man. He was a drug addict. He'd gone through a nightmarish withdrawal, but something went wrong. He'd gotten more drugs and the overdose nearly killed him. The doctors saved his life, but he'd slipped into a coma.

Mallory thought of Wayne Mason. Her hand went to her neck, where the cut had healed. She could still feel the place where the scab had been. Would Wayne one day be in a coma, or would he die in some gutter before help could arrive?

This patient's name was Jeffrey Amberson. *The Magnificent Ambersons* came to mind, a book she'd read years ago about a rich, dysfunctional family and the effect losing their wealth had had on them. Jeffrey wasn't much different from the fictional George Amberson, at least in age. He didn't come from wealth, that she knew. He'd probably been on the road to becoming a model citizen when he'd taken a wrong turn somewhere and ended up here.

"Say it, Jeff," she repeated. "I am somebody." He didn't move or react in any way. "A very famous man said that. His name is Jesse Jackson. I'm sure you've heard of him."

Mallory touched Jeff's hand, which was cool and immobile but soft. She leaned closer to him and whispered, "Live, Jeff! Fight. Wake up!"

Mallory wanted to scream the words at him, but she kept her voice level. "Jesse Jackson is right, Jeff. You *are* somebody. Sure, you're not at your best now and you've made some bad decisions involving drugs. Maybe there was a reason. You can change that. But you can't do it if you don't live."

Jeffrey Amberson lay quiet. Moonlight streamed

through the windows and slanted across the white bedsheets—the only light in the room. Mallory never turned on lights when she visited coma patients. She didn't think the light would bother them, but it would alert security that she was present, and she didn't want anyone to know. Not even the nurses. They wouldn't understand what she was doing there in the middle of the night.

"You might think there's no one here who cares about you, and maybe that's why you sleep so soundly. The drugs, how you got into them… whatever the reasons for you trying first one and then another, it doesn't matter, Jeff. I care. I want you back. You are somebody and we both know it."

Mallory listened to his quiet breathing. She heard the machines in the room monitoring his vital signs, sending information back to the nurses' station twenty yards away. It was regular, rhythmic and systematic. Like a machine himself, Jeff continued to breath through the use of technology. But that would end. And soon.

"Jeff, you've got to wake up." Her voice was urgent. "You know what's coming. You've only been here three months, but you've been asleep almost a year. The law isn't on your side. They're going to court to have your life support turned off."

Mallory walked back and forth beside the bed. There were other coma sufferers in the room, which was set up as a ward. When visitors came, the patient was moved to a private room. But here several of them slept together, the only sounds were of the incessant machines alternately compressing and releasing air.

"You know, Jeff, I'm a lot like you. No one cares for me, either." She stopped and turned to him. "Oh, there is my sister in Atlantic City, but no one else. When Dr. Clayton seemed to be genuinely concerned about me, I felt..." She stopped. She didn't know what she felt. A warmth settled over her, a comfortable feeling that was unfamiliar to her. "I felt somehow wanted. That maybe someday someone would care about me."

For a long while Mallory was quiet. The words, her words, surprised her. She'd never thought of herself as needing anyone. After her accident and recovery she'd become quite self-sufficient.

"Brad isn't the first man I've been interested in," she murmured. "There were a few in college and one in medical school. But what I felt for them passed quickly. I'm sure I only have a crush on Brad. It will end soon. My work will replace him, just as it did all the others."

She stared at the moon, picturing Brad's face in place of the silvery surface and wishing she could hold on to the feeling for just a little while longer. But she was the ice queen, destined to be alone.

Mallory rushed into Building B the next morning. She was late. It was the third morning this week she'd overslept. She waved at the receptionist who manned the desk at the staff entrance, and headed for the stairs. Few people ever took the steps unless there was a fire drill. Mallory raced up and down them all the time. She'd begun when she'd started talking to the patients in the coma wing. It made getting in and out easier. Now it was routine. She rarely got on an elevator unless she had to go to the top floor.

Her crepe-soled shoes made a sucking sound as she climbed upward, taking the steps two at a time. On the third floor landing she twisted to go up to the fourth, then heard other footsteps. There was no cause for alarm, yet she stopped and listened. The noise came from above her. Looking up, Mallory stared into the dark brown eyes of Dr. Clayton, who was on his way down.

Her heart lurched. She hadn't seen him except for the nights he stole into her bedroom and walked into her dreams. What would he think if he'd known she was dreaming of him?

It should be a law, she thought. No man should be able to look this good with a scowl on his face.

"Dr. Clayton," she said in greeting.

"You look tired," he replied.

"Good morning to you, too." Mallory rolled her eyes and continued up the stairs. She had to pass him to get by. Brad reached for her arm. She felt warmth spread over her. She tried not to react, but that was like trying to stop the Texas heat in August.

"Are you all right?"

"Yes," she said, stepping away from him.

"Do you really have a sister?" he asked her.

"Yes, I do," she snapped. Her voice reverberated in the hollow stairway. "She's a kindergarten teacher in Atlantic City. I couldn't ask her to drive up here in the middle of the night."

"Why didn't you say that? We could have gotten someone to go home with you."

"The hospital was too busy. There was no one available."

"What about a friend? You could have called someone. You must know your condition could have been dangerous."

Mallory glanced up at his face, illuminated by filtered daylight from the skylight above. Of course she knew the danger of delayed stress.

"Let's just say it was too late to call anyone. And I was all right, exactly as I said." She stared directly at him, adding the last in a rush to keep him from asking her anything else.

"You still look tired," he said. "Aren't you sleeping well?"

"I'm fine, Dr. Clayton." She held her hand up when he would have spoken again. "I know about delayed stress—that what happened in the E.R. could result in some kind of physical manifestation, but I assure you, that is not the case." She paused a second, calming herself. "Now if you'll excuse me, I'm late for rounds."

Mallory rushed on up the stairs and through the fourth-floor doorway. Brad Clayton had the most penetrating eyes. She felt as if he were looking into her soul and seeing the lies she was telling. Well, not exactly lies, just some half-truths.

Brad saw Mallory the moment rounds ended. They began and ended on the fourth floor. He'd just finished his morning visits to his in-hospital patients. He came out of one room as Mallory and the others stepped through the doorway. He headed for the nurses' station.

"Did you hear?" Dana whispered. "Another one woke up. And only three days after she was there."

"Who was there?" Brad asked. Three nurses, dressed in hospital blues, huddled together behind the counter. Brad walked in at the tail end of their conversation, several charts in his hands. He placed them back in the appropriate racks.

"The ghost strikes again," Dana said with a smile.

Brad rolled his eyes. "There are no ghosts."

"Well, she was there, and he's awake now."

"And not a moment too soon, either," Renee Crandall added.

"What are you talking about?"

"Jeffrey Amberson woke up."

Brad hunched his shoulders. Sometimes he thought women had a code of their own and only let men in on what they knew for very short intervals.

"Who is Jeffrey Amberson?"

"The young man in the coma wing," Renee answered.

"The one she talks to," Dana added.

"Dr. Clayton, I swear the world could end and we would have to send a child to let you know," Peggy Silverman, the third of the group, said. "You pay attention to nothing that goes on around here except the children."

That had been true in the past, but it wasn't any longer. Since the E.R. incident and his meeting Mallory, he was very aware of things going on now, yet he didn't think he would let these three in on it. "If I did, what would you do?"

Dana looked at him to see if he was joking. She must have decided he was, even though he had no smile on his face.

"It's uncanny," Renee said. "She picks one out and that one wakes up."

"Not all of them," Peggy corrected. "Remember that woman from six months ago? She'd been in a coma since they opened that wing five years ago. The ghost talked to her, but when they pulled her plug, she slipped away within minutes."

"That's not how it was with Jeffrey Amberson or any of the others she's chosen."

"What do you mean, chosen?" Brad asked.

"It's the same M.O. every time," Peggy said. Brad could tell she watched too many detective shows. "The lonely, unloved, unvisited. The ones no one comes to see. She picks patients who have no one else, who never receive any visitors. They're all alone in the world and she's their savior. And it's apparently working."

"Why is that?"

"No one knows," Peggy said. "No one has ever seen her face."

"Millie over in nuclear medicine saw her one night, but only from the back," Renee said. "She was going through the door into the stairwell."

"No one knows how long she's been doing this and no one else has ever gotten a glimpse of her."

"Then how do you know she exists?" Brad asked.

"They tell us."

"Who?"

"The patients. Those who wake up. They want to know who the person was who talked to them," Dana said.

"Since no one knew," Peggy continued, "one of them called her a ghost and the name stuck."

"So you just let this unknown person roam the hospital at will?" Brad asked. "What we need to do is alert security."

"Calm down, Dr. Clayton. She's not doing any harm," Renee said.

"In fact, she's doing good," Dana added. "The court order was already in hand. Jeffrey Amberson was scheduled to have his plug pulled."

Peggy took up the story. "This afternoon when they shut down the machines, he breathed on his own. I'd say the ghost had something to do with that."

"The ghost," Brad frowned. "It sounds like good medicine and a strong survival instinct."

"They'd given up on him. If the ghost had nothing to do with his recovery, then neither did medicine," Dana stated.

Brad didn't agree or disagree with Dana. He turned to leave. He had no patients to see, so he was headed for the doctor's lounge and a cup of coffee. Mallory Russell was approaching the station, several charts in her hands. She didn't look him in the eye. Brad felt a twinge of guilt for their earlier encounter on the stairs.

"Well, Dr. Russell, what do you think of the ghost?" he asked.

She stole a glance at Dana, ignoring Brad. "I was

on my way up and told Cassie I'd drop these off.'' She set the charts on the counter.

"Excuse me, I'm scheduled for O.R.-8," Peggy said.

Renee checked her watch. A small panel light came on, indicating someone in one of the rooms needed assistance. "I'll take it," she said. She and Peggy wedged themselves past Mallory and Brad. Mallory moved, giving them room. Brad smelled the scent of her. He recognized it from that night in the E.R. A vision of them together came into his mind. Quickly, he quashed it. This was neither the time nor the place. But lately, he didn't get to choose the time or place.

Another signal flashed on the panel.

"Will you cover a moment?" Dana asked. "I have to check on this one." She left without waiting for a reply.

He was alone with Mallory, and she was causing him all kinds of fantasies. What was wrong with him? Her hair was up again for work, but it was thick and soft, and he wanted to push his hands through it. Her eyes were wide and bright, light brown.

"Don't you have a patient to see?" Mallory asked. She took a seat at the nurses' station.

"Not at the moment. I was waiting for you to answer the question."

"What question?"

"Do you believe in ghosts?"

She hesitated, keeping her eyes on the light panel. Then she looked at him. "No, Doctor. I don't believe in ghosts…but that's not to say I don't believe in unexplained anomalies."

"Like a patient waking up from a coma after he'd been given up for lost?"

She glanced around, then nodded. "Like that."

"This is interesting." He pulled up a chair and straddled it. "Tell me about the ghost."

"Is that what you all were talking about?"

He nodded. "They believe a ghost helped Jeffrey Amberson wake up."

"And you believe she had nothing to do with it, right?"

"I believe there's a security breach going on here and it's with the knowledge of the staff."

Mallory stood up. She looked Brad directly in the eye. "I find it hard to believe that a man who can have such rapport with children, who can gain their trust in a matter of moments, has no compassion for the rest of society." With that she left him.

Dana came around the counter a moment later. She leaned toward Brad confidentially. "Well, I see you two are getting along just great."

Chapter Three

Dana's words were still ringing in Brad's head later that night when he headed for his car. Mallory Russell did seem to rub him the wrong way. He couldn't think why. She was competent, and he found himself looking for her when he was at the hospital. Yet each time he came in contact with her, the two seemed to be at opposite poles.

Brad opened the door and hopped into the SUV. Automatically, he turned on the engine. The Luther Vandross disk he'd popped in the CD player that morning kicked in right at the place where it had stopped when he got to the hospital.

Brad had stayed late to finish up some paperwork. It was nearly eleven o'clock, and he was wide awake. He didn't really want to go home, but there was no place else to go. If it were earlier he could pick up a game of basketball at the public court he often went to, but at this hour the guys were either asleep or pursuing their women. Brad wasn't friendly with any of them. They were just a collection of guys who played ball together. When they left the court they never saw each other, socially or professionally. But when he was waiting on the sidelines for a place in the game to open up, he often talked with them, and he knew that, for some of them, the pursuit of the opposite sex was high on their entertainment list.

Brad liked them and wondered if their apparent contentment had anything to do with that attitude. He pulled out of the parking lot and headed for home. It wasn't far to his residence, but he suddenly turned and headed toward the shelter on Thirteenth Street. The hospital maintained a clinic there, and he was one of the primary doctors. He would look in and see what was scheduled for morning.

Brad drove through the city, watching the neighborhoods go from well-maintained, to unmaintained, to boarded-up buildings with concrete front yards. The streets were deserted and few cars patrolled the area. Behind these doors, Brad knew, thrived a drug world that wasn't obvious from the outside. He often found himself in places like this, especially on nights he couldn't sleep. This was where he'd thought he would find his mother. Not this exact neighborhood, but one like it. His mom had left him and his brother, Owen, when they were young, and had never returned. Brad believed the reason she hadn't come back had to do with drugs. Yet she hadn't been an addict. The drug story was just something a little boy could cling to for understanding. Brad wasn't a little boy anymore, yet he still thought of her in this kind of place.

He stopped in front of a derelict house with boarded-up windows and no door. Silently he sat looking at it, the car engine running and the lights on. Lots of people had searched for his mother. Child welfare had looked also, but she seemed to have dropped off the face of the earth.

Brad's eye caught something moving in the beams of his headlights. He squinted in the gloom, but could no longer see whatever it was. Time to leave, he thought. This wasn't the best section of town and he didn't need anyone hijacking his car. Putting it into gear, he pulled away from the curb.

That's when he saw her, thirty feet away. A kid. She walked slowly, slinking against the buildings, trying to make herself inconspicuous. Brad pulled up beside her and got out of the car. She didn't stop walking.

"What are you doing here?" he asked, following her on foot. "Where do you live? Do you need help?"

She said nothing. While the buildings were all dark and deserted, one streetlight glowed brightly. In the light he could see she was about twelve. Memories flooded his mind. He'd been abandoned at age nine.

The child's pants were torn and dirty, her blouse

fit poorly and her shoes were too big. One of them was missing a heel, making her limp.

"Leave me alone," she said in a defiant voice. Brad had heard it before.

"I won't hurt you."

"Then go away and leave me alone."

"Do you have someplace to sleep?"

"Yes," she snapped.

"Food?"

She glared at him.

"I'm a doctor. I'll take you to a shelter."

"Do I look like I've lost my mind?"

Brad gazed directly at her. He shook his head. "You look like someone in need of help. I'm offering it. You're too young to be out alone, especially in a place like this."

He took her arm to lead her away, but she screamed. Then things got out of control. Red and blue lights whirled behind him. He looked around to see a black-and-white patrol car roll to a stop. The girl wrenched her arm free and took off as if death was chasing her. She disappeared into one of the abandoned buildings with the surefootedness of practice. Brad knew she'd been there before, but he had no time to think about it. A cop, with his gun drawn and pointing, shouted at him to put his hands in the air.

Drinking coffee to stay awake at three o'clock in the morning was something Mallory had done many times before, but she didn't think she would have to do it tonight. After a year her hours at the hospital had settled into a routine. Most of the time they were predictable and she had plenty of energy after a full day or even a full night on her feet. Tonight, however, she had been bone tired and looking forward to eight hours of uninterrupted sleep. That had been her goal when she'd climbed into bed.

Then the phone rang.

It wasn't the hospital. It was Brad Clayton. He was asking for her help. It wasn't a medical emergency, he told her immediately, but he needed her.

Mallory sat up in bed and looked at the clock. She asked him to repeat himself because she couldn't believe what she'd heard. Brad Clayton, the great and moody doctor asking her for help.

''I'm at the police station,'' he said.

He wouldn't go into why he was there or why he had no car, though he said he'd been arrested. But she hadn't really needed an explanation, she hopped out of bed, dressed and left for the police station.

''I'm looking for Dr. Bradley Clayton,'' she told the officer at the desk when she entered the brightly lit station. The man looked up at her and down at a clipboard, apparently checking for Brad's name.

''He'll be right out.''

Mallory moved away from the glass-paneled area where he sat. As she turned she wondered if it was bulletproof. She'd never been in a police station. It looked exactly as she expected it would. This was an old building, probably built in the 1930s and serving several government functions before being converted into a police precinct. The walls were a drab gray, the furniture old but sturdy. The floors were marble, grooved in places from the thousands of feet that had crossed them in decades of use.

A case with trophies sat across from the officer. Mallory stared into it, not reading the inscriptions, not really seeing what was there. Her mind was on Brad and how he'd come to be arrested. What was he being charged with, and more important, why had he called *her?*

An electronic click that signaled the opening of a door had Mallory turning toward the sound. Brad came out. He was wearing his bomber jacket and jeans. He looked tired. She went to him as if he were a patient about to collapse.

"Are you all right?" She took his arm. Her medical bag was in the car. He'd said it wasn't an emergency, so she hadn't carried it in.

"Let's get out of here." He headed for the exit, and she followed him.

"My car is over there." She pointed to the black Saab across from the station. The car had been a graduation present to herself when she completed medical school. She'd used the last of her inheritance to buy it. If she was going to have to get to the hospital in the middle of the night, she needed to have reliable transportation, and her last car, ten years old, had conveniently died. Mallory had never thought she would need to use it to go to a police station and pick up one of the hospital's upstanding doctors.

"What happened?" she asked when they were in

the car. Brad said nothing. Mallory started the engine, put the car in gear and stared straight ahead. The silence between them stretched until she couldn't stand it. He made her want to scream. Still, Mallory held her temper in check.

"Brad, where do you live?" She asked the question slowly and clearly, as if he were a child and she was trying to coax his address out of him.

"Churchill Road, 1730 Churchill Road."

Philadelphia wasn't a planned city like Washington, D.C. It wasn't laid out numerically with avenues and streets, like Manhattan, either. One needed to know where a street was, which area of the city, in order to find it. Mallory had no idea where Churchill Road was.

"I'll need directions."

He pointed ahead, and she started driving.

"Are you going to tell me why I had to pick you up at a police station at this hour?"

"It was all a mistake," he answered.

Mallory waited for him to continue. She thought he might be angry because of whatever had happened, and she should give him time to recover.

"You missed the turn."

Mallory clamped her teeth on her bottom lip to keep from saying anything. She stopped and made a U-turn, going back to the block where he'd mentioned her error.

"Right or left?" she asked.

"Left."

His tone was cryptic, and Mallory had had enough.

"Who soured you on the world?" she demanded. Mallory was giving him a ride. She was tired. It was four o'clock in the morning and he wouldn't even give her decent directions. The least he could do was tell her what had happened. "Why did you call me?" She was no longer concerned about her tone.

"Because I thought you'd be quiet," he retorted.

"Well, I won't. It's my car and you interrupted my night's sleep. That gives me the right to ask questions."

"I don't want this all over the hospital," Brad said in a more civil tone.

"How do you know I won't tell somebody?"

"You've been there a year and nobody knows a thing about you."

Mallory wondered if that was his way of asking her questions, if people at the hospital wanted to know about her. But she wouldn't go off on that tangent. This was about him, not her.

"How much do they know about *you*, Dr. Clayton?" She paused to glance at him. "You've been at the hospital five years, and I'm the only person you could call in an emergency? I don't need a picture drawn for me."

His jaw tightened, and she felt as if her arrow had found its mark.

"Don't blow this out of proportion," he snapped. "I only need a ride, not a therapy session."

"Maybe therapy is exactly what you need."

"Turn right up here, and my house is the fifth one on the right."

She followed his directions. The street was narrow, with cars lining both sides and no place to park. She slowed the car and pulled up level with the house. Finding an opening she thought was a parking space, she nosed the car toward it, only to see a driveway leading to a garage.

"It's my driveway," Brad said. Mallory angled the car into it and switched off the engine. She turned toward him, staring at him long and hard.

"What?" he asked at last.

"Answers," she said. "Now that you've decided I can be trusted not to tell the staff everything I know about you, can you please tell me what happened?"

He opened the door and got out. Mallory wasn't sure if he expected her to leave or not. Curious, and with her temper piqued by his attitude, she got out in turn and followed him up the steps to the stoop. The prewar-era building was a brick row house, sharing common walls with its neighbors, which helped provide building space for the growing city and conservation of heating fuel.

Brad opened the old-fashioned double doors with etched glass inlaid in their upper panels. He preceded her into the foyer and left her to close the door behind them. If he was trying to dissuade her from coming any farther, he didn't know how stubborn she could be. Her night was already ruined. She wanted answers.

Brad removed his jacket and tossed it on a chair in the living room. Mallory removed hers and did the same.

"I'll have some coffee," she told him.

"You don't wait to be invited, do you?"

"Shall I make it?" She looked around for the kitchen.

He headed out and she followed. "I guess your personality is deceptively hidden at the hospital. Most of us think of you as quiet and docile."

"I am quiet and docile," she agreed, trying to hide her smile.

He picked up an old-fashioned coffee percolator from the stove and washed it out. She'd watched old movies where people used them, but she'd never actually seen one in operation.

Brad filled it with water and measured coffee into a metal filter before putting it on the stove.

"It'll be ready in a few minutes."

He glanced at her, but went to the refrigerator and opened it. He studied the contents for several seconds, then closed the door without taking out anything.

"Milk and sugar," she said, giving him instructions on how she drank her coffee. He pulled the door open again and took out a carton of milk. Then, as if he remembered something, he put it back and took out an unopened carton.

He drinks from the carton, Mallory thought. She smiled to herself, deciding it made him seem a little more human. She watched him as he moved about the small, high-ceilinged room. He was obviously upset about the evening. Mallory stood off to the side, allowing him a measure of privacy even though she was witness to his actions. He opened cabinets and doors, but took nothing from them. She recognized leashed anger. He probably wanted to hit something or hold someone. She couldn't supply him with either outlet.

Going to him, she took his arm. "Sit down," she told him, leading him to a chair. "I'll get the cups."

He didn't argue. He allowed her to take over while he sat in one of the four high-back chairs surrounding the circular table. Mallory found mugs in a cabinet.

"While you're sitting there, why don't you start? What did they pick you up for?"

"Kidnapping."

Mallory whipped around, gripping the cups she had in her hands.

"What?"

"It was a mistake. I was just trying to take a girl to a shelter."

"Back up," Mallory said. She put down the cups and sat across from him. "Start at the beginning."

He told her about his night, about leaving the hospital, feeling restless and finding himself in a run-down district of the city.

"It was late." He relaxed. "I saw the girl and knew she shouldn't be on the street, especially there. I was going to take her to the shelter I help out in. But she screamed and ran away just as the police arrived."

Mallory knew how that could look. Night. A child on the street. A man in a car. The police had all the cause they needed.

"Were you charged?"

He shook his head. "I explained who I was and eventually they reached Detective Ryan."

"Who's Detective Ryan?"

"He's a friend of mine and he knows about me and the shelter. Once they finished talking to him, I was released. But my car had already been impounded, and I can't get it out until morning."

Mallory heard the gurgling of the coffeepot behind her. She ignored it. She wanted Brad to keep talking.

"What about you and the shelter?"

He got up and removed the pot from the stove, bringing it to the table and filling the mugs. He set the pot between them on a metal plate and added both milk and sugar to his cup. When he'd taken a sip he leaned back and looked at her.

"The hospital is associated with the Home Society Shelter. It's a place for homeless children."

Mallory knew of it. She'd also known that the hospital had some association with it, but residents weren't part of the medical team that went there. Her concentration was on her career and the coma patients. She'd forgotten about the shelter.

"I'm one of the primary doctors involved, and I often bring kids there who have no place else to go."

"Detective Ryan knows this?" It was a question, but she already knew the answer.

Brad nodded. "We've both taken kids there for shelter and food." He took a sip of his coffee, but his eyes didn't leave Mallory. She suddenly felt heat rush through her. The sun was beginning to rise, and through the window next to Brad she could see it painting the sky above the rooftops. She looked out, to avoid his gaze and the effect it suddenly had on her.

"Tell me more about the shelter," she said. She really just wanted him to talk. It would get his mind off what had happened earlier and she would learn more about him.

"It's just a place for kids to sleep and get a good meal."

Mallory knew it was more than that. She also realized that Brad didn't waste a lot of words but he often downplayed things. She was sure this shelter must mean something to him, or else why would he be so involved? What was his connection to it? Was he trying to save someone in particular?

"Do you mostly find children on the streets and take them to the shelter?" Mallory kept her voice low.

He looked at her as if she'd touched a raw nerve, but nodded.

"Were you looking for someone tonight?"

"No one in particular. There are so many. They get lost, die, never have a chance at life. I try to get them help."

Mallory listened to the tone of his voice, the inflection as he talked about reaching out and trying to save a child. Most people hurried past the homeless, not wanting to see them, not trying to help. Brad searched them out, trying to give them a second chance.

"What about the little girl?"

"She was about twelve, and dirty. She looked ill, but she was belligerent, the way a lot of them are. They have to fend for themselves, steal food, eat out of garbage cans and avoid the law—often for so long that anyone who extends a hand to them is suspect."

Mallory's heart softened, both for the children and for the man in front of her.

"Do you want to go and search for her now?"

He shook his head. "I'd never find her during the day. These kids are night creatures, hunting in the dark for whatever they can find. During the day they stay hidden in alleys and abandoned buildings. They have a million avenues of escape, and they're agile enough to get away from anyone looking for them."

When he finished speaking Mallory didn't say anything. She recognized the voice of experience when she heard it. Brad might have been searching the streets for homeless children for years, but nothing could put that tone in his voice except having his own life touched by that same grueling education.

"How old were you?" she asked, again keeping her voice as nonintrusive as possible.

"Nine," he answered without hesitation. He was no longer looking at her. His mind had gone back to his childhood, a time when he was a kid on the street. "My brother was eleven. My mother left us one day and never came back. We stayed in the apartment as long as we could. Then we slept on the street, hiding by day, eating what we could find at night. For years I searched for her."

His gaze came back to Mallory—direct, but not

challenging. "But I never found her. I don't know if she's alive or dead, or why she never came back for us." He leaned forward, his hands cradling the empty mug. "And that's the story of my life."

It was obvious there was more to his life than that simple statement. His mother had left him, but he'd gone on to become a doctor. Mallory understood more about his attitude now. The huge chip on his shoulder wasn't for the world. It was for one woman, someone he wasn't likely to find.

Brad touched the coffeepot, testing it for heat. Finding it to his liking, he poured another cup.

"How do you feel now?" she asked.

"Better," he said.

"See?" Mallory smiled one of her rare smiles. "Therapy does work."

She got up and headed for the door. The sun was tinging the sky, banishing shadows. As Mallory reached the living room, Brad called her name. She turned back as he rose from his chair and came toward her. Mallory watched him move. His stride was sure, predatory, catlike, quiet.

She held her breath. She'd never been this affected by a man before. She lifted her head as he got closer to her, imagining her body rising to meet his, her arms clasping his shoulders, her nipples hardening against his chest.

"Thank you," he said.

"What?" Mallory hadn't heard him. She was still lost in the fantasy her mind had created.

Brad looked at her. His eyes were softer than she

was used to seeing them. He must be tired, she told herself. His guard was down. He would never look at her like that if he hadn't had such a bad night. She reached up and smoothed her hand along his cheek. She smiled. He needed a shave.

As she went to pull it away, he caught it and held it. Neither of them spoke. Mallory's throat went dry. For a long moment they stared at each other while the silence screamed.

"Get some sleep," she said, breaking the tension. Then she turned and headed for the chair where she'd left her coat.

"Your turn," Brad said.

"My turn for what?"

"Tell me your life story." He stood across the room where she'd left him.

"That's a tale for another night." If she was lucky there wouldn't be another night for her to share her life with him. She pointed at the coffee cup in his hand. "You should get some sleep."

"Sure." He hunched a shoulder. Mallory recognized the gesture. It was purely male, something guys learned from their fathers or from each other. When they weren't all right they still said they were. Mallory assumed she and Brad had both revealed something of themselves to the other, and it was enough for one night.

"I'll be leaving then."

Something glimmered in his eyes, and Mallory felt that pull, that connection she'd experienced earlier in the night. She turned from it, looking about the living room. The curtains were drawn and the space was darker than the kitchen.

Mallory was struck by the neatness of the place. It didn't smell musty or closed in. There was a coziness about it, like a huge Christmas tree should grace the corner and a family should come down the stairs to mounds of presents. She detected little dust on the tables. There was a huge fireplace with remnants of ashes from a recent blaze. A portrait of several children hung over it and the mantel held several photos of the same people at various ages.

"Family?" she asked, continuing to look at the portrait.

He came up behind her. Mallory felt the heat of him as he stopped.

"My brothers and sisters."

"I thought you only had a brother."

"We were all adopted," he explained.

Mallory turned before she thought about how close he was. They had been together for several hours tonight, but suddenly everything was different. Before, he had needed her. He'd needed someone to talk to, someone to share in the pain of the evening's circumstances. Now he was a male alone with a female. Mallory felt the danger of the situation. She didn't want to start anything she couldn't carry through.

Brad stared at her. She watched his eyes run over her face and shoulders. His eyes strayed downward to her breasts, which tingled as if he'd touched them, before coming back to her face. "Do you have to go in to work?" he asked.

"I'm off today." She should have told him something else. She didn't need to give him any details that said she was free and available. Why, she didn't know. He represented danger, and Mallory was good at skirting danger, staying away from it, away from men who could upset her balanced life. She was grateful that she could return home and resume her night's sleep. She had planned to run errands this morning. The errands could wait now.

"So am I," he said.

Mallory felt her mouth go dry.

"I have to go in and check on a few things this afternoon."

"Good thing," she said, more to herself than him. "You can get some sleep before you have to see any patients."

She picked up her coat. Brad immediately took it from her. She felt the warmth of his hands as he briefly touched her. He didn't hold it for her to put it on, but said, "Thank you, Mallory. I appreciate you getting out of bed for me."

Damn, she cursed inwardly. If he kept saying things like that she wasn't going to need a coat. Her body was already hot, and his comment infused it with a shot of fire that went straight into her bloodstream.

"You don't have to worry about the hospital. I won't discuss this with anyone there." Her voice was slightly higher than normal.

He smiled. Mallory so seldom saw him smile, and it completely transformed his face. She couldn't say he was beautiful. He wasn't, but he was the best-looking man she had ever seen. Mostly she saw him in hospital whites. He was now wearing a shirt that pulled across broad shoulders and tapered to a thin waist. His jeans molded strong legs, and made Mallory want to feel the length of them against her own. She turned away, expecting him to open her coat.

He laid it back on the sofa. She faced him again, but took a step backward. Electricity flared between them, vibrant and alive. Her ears were so hot she was sure they would singe her hair.

"What are you doing?" she asked.

He stared at her, and after a long minute finally said, "Stay."

Mallory weighed that single word, turning it over in her mind. Stay and talk to me? Stay because I don't want to be alone? Stay and let me get to know you? Stay and make love with me? He could mean any of them. She shook her head slowly, trying to make herself believe she wanted to leave.

Brad took a step forward. Mallory closed her eyes and held her breath a moment. It didn't help that she could visualize him even with her eyes closed. It didn't help that the scent of him filled her nostrils and tantalized her. She opened her eyes. Brad picked up her coat and held it out. Mallory didn't move. Relief that he wasn't going to press her rooted her to the spot. It was a short-lived reprieve. Part of her wanted him to stop her. Part of her wanted him to take her in his arms and return her to that dream place she'd been in before.

Brad stepped forward until his feet were toe-to-toe with hers. Heat swirled around them as he put the coat around her shoulders and pulled it closed, imprisoning her. She looked up into his eyes. They were dark pools, reminding her of a midnight sky flung with stars. They were fathomless to Mallory. She felt as if she was going to fall.

She grabbed for his arm to steady herself, but the coat hampered her and her hand found his waist and slipped. She tried to catch herself. In less than a second Brad's arms closed around her. He pulled her to him and his mouth found hers with unerring accuracy, his kiss immediately hot and devastating. Mallory had no time or inclination to resist. She ran her hands around him and gave herself up to emotions that raged out of control.

Mallory had dreamed of being in Brad's arms, had even thought herself there in reality when coming out of a dream. But this was no apparition. Her coat was an encumbrance. Brad took a second to pull it from her shoulders and drop it to the floor. He turned her into his body, resuming possession of her lips in mutual satisfaction. She tasted coffee as his tongue swept into her mouth, causing a riot in her bloodstream. She clung to him, helpless to stop her passionate, almost aggressive response.

She wanted to get closer. She could feel the muscles of his back under her questing hands. Each time she moved them, he groaned. Mallory shifted and her body came in contact with his arousal. Brad's moan held a mixture of pain and pleasure. She pressed even closer and he moved his hands lower, lifting her against him.

Her breath was coming in short gasps, her mind whirling. What had happened to her? To them? She was supposed to be leaving, going home to her own bed. Now she wanted only to get into his.

But that was crazy. Somewhere her mind fixed on that fact and reason asserted itself. She pushed away from him, moving back as far as she could get.

"I…" she began, not knowing what to say. "We can't—"

Reason seemed to come to Brad, too. He moved away. What had they been thinking? They hadn't been. They had been reacting, pushed together by his ordeal and her lack of sleep.

Mallory knew she was rationalizing. She knew Brad had found a way into the locked part of her heart, and she didn't want him there.

Looking at him, she guessed from his expression that he didn't want her anywhere near his heart, either. She stepped forward and picked up her coat. Not bothering to push her arms into it, she headed for the door. Neither of them said a word. Nor did they need to. Mallory knew there would be no mention of this by either of them. What happened tonight would neither be spoken of nor repeated.

Mallory let herself out the door and walked silently to her car. The sun was rising higher in the sky. The city was waking up, ready to begin another day. Mallory knew there would never again be another day like this for her. Brad Clayton had altered her life.

She left his house a different woman than the one who had entered it.

She wasn't sure who that woman was or where her life would go from here, but one thing was certain—no other man had ever rocked her world the way Brad Clayton had. And it didn't help when she looked up to see him smiling from the doorway.

Chapter Four

It was Brad's experience that a secret burned a hole in the jaw muscle. The person holding it just had to tell someone, immediately. Yet Mallory appeared to be true to her word. No mention had been made by the other doctors or nurses of Brad's encounter with the police. Mallory had been off yesterday, but she was due in to the hospital today. With each passing hour he had expected to hear the story, distorted by facts that changed as word of mouth embellished every detail. Yet his secret was apparently safe.

Brad entered the nurses' station on the fourth floor. It was positioned in the center of the floor so only a single one was necessary and anyone coming or going had to pass the station on one side or the other. The circular work space was set up with computers and bright lighting, and a printout of the residents' schedule was posted on a clipboard inserted into a vertical file near the entrance. Brad scanned it as he often did, checking to see which residents would be on his rotation. Before, he'd only glanced at the names to make sure everyone was there when he was ready to begin. Now he specifically looked for one name; Mallory Russell. He wanted to know when she was on his rotation, and if not, where she was.

Her name was missing. Why? he wondered. She'd been off the day after she'd picked him up, so she should be in today. Brad flipped the paper to see if there was another page under it. The brown clipboard stared blankly back at him.

"Dana?" He turned to one of the nurses on duty. Dana Baldwin was reading orders and preparing morning medication for the patients in her care. "Where is Dr. Russell?" Brad indicated the clipboard.

"She left about an hour ago."

"Left? I thought she was off yesterday." He replaced the clipboard in its space and took a step toward Dana.

"She got called in yesterday morning, just after the shift started."

Brad frowned. That would be about the time she'd left his house.

"She's always the first one they call." Dana gave a frown of disapproval.

"But she'd been…" He stopped himself. He almost said she'd been up all night. If she'd just left, she'd been awake more than twenty-four hours.

"Been what?" Dana asked, drawing Brad's attention back to the present.

"Been on my rotation." Half of the residents were male. Some were married. The females were mostly single, but a few had children. Mallory had no dependents. She was composed and efficient and her presence had a calming effect on the patients. The nurses knew that. And Brad was beginning to think they abused it.

"Mallory never refuses," Dana said.

Brad moved to the computer behind the nurse. He pulled up the computerized schedule that the printout had been taken from. Looking at the history, he verified what Dana had said. Mallory was called three times more often than the other residents.

"Well, she's about to get some R and R," Brad stated, his voice low. Dana stopped adding pills to small white cups and stared at him. Brad ignored her. She knew he rarely intervened in the administration of the hospital, but any doctor would be concerned about overworking a resident. "If these schedules are correct, she's been working way too many hours."

"They're correct. I tried to tell her to take it easy, but I think that incident with Wayne Mason scared her more than she lets on."

Brad was keenly interested. "What do you mean?"

"She is tired a lot, more so since the incident than before."

"Some days she's bright and well-rested, and others she's tired and withdrawn," Brad stated.

"Exactly," Dana agreed. "She's my friend, but I'll tell you what I think."

Brad waited for her to continue. He was anxious to hear it.

"I think she's having nightmares about that guy."

It was plausible, Brad realized, and it would explain his own observations. Being a doctor meant having a certain level of fatigue, but Mallory's ups and downs seemed a little more than what was expected. Brad couldn't say he'd noticed any tiredness in her when he'd had her in his arms. But she had been drinking coffee when she picked him up, and at his house they had more. Existing on caffeine wasn't good for anyone. Mallory Russell was burning out.

"Have you asked her about Wayne Mason?"

Dana nodded. "She says she's fine. That she doesn't even think about him or that night." The nurse lowered her voice as if the two of them were coconspirators. "But I'm sure that isn't the truth. How could someone not be affected by a crazed addict holding a knife to your throat?" She moved her hand to her own throat protectively.

Brad saw the logic in Dana's words, but something didn't sit right with him. He'd seen Mallory up close and she didn't appear to be nervous or afraid, traits he would expect in someone suffering from stress.

He remembered holding Mallory in his arms, smelling the scent of her perfume and that indefinable fragrance that was her. Remembered her mouth on his. Her softness as he'd held her…. Quickly he threw cold water on those thoughts. Dana Baldwin was more observant than the other nurses and he didn't want any rumors starting about him and Mallory. Since there was no basis for them.

Do you want there to be? The question came unbidden. Brad didn't have time to think about it now. He went back to the computer screen. He checked Mallory's efficiency level, finding it consistently high. Whatever was bothering her wasn't affecting her performance. According to the computer timetable, the night she'd picked him up at the police station she'd worked three hours past her schedule. Then she'd stayed up all night with him and been called in the next day.

Obviously the woman didn't know how to say no—that is, to anyone but him.

Mallory pulled her jacket off the hanger in the doctor's lounge and pushed her arms through it. She slammed the door to her locker and spun the combination lock.

''Who the hell does he think he is?'' she muttered on the way to her car. A week. She was ordered to stay out of the hospital for a week. What would happen to her patients? Not the ones in the regular rooms; there was coverage for them. But what about the coma patients? She needed access to them. She needed to talk to them. They were alone.

Mallory was still angry when she pulled up in front of the house that, except for medical school and a two-year period, she'd lived in all her life. Since her sister had moved to Atlantic City, Mallory occupied the four-bedroom, red-brick colonial alone. She left the car and started for the front door, but stopped short when she saw Dr. Clayton step out of his SUV.

She stared at his silhouette. The streetlight behind him prevented her from seeing his face, but she recognized the lines of his body. At another time, Mallory would have been glad to see him, but after her meeting with the hospital administrator she never wanted to see him again. She had to pass him to get to her house. If she didn't she would have ignored his presence.

"What do you want?" she asked, hiding none of her hostility.

"I came to tell you why I suggested you take some time off."

"You're not my father. I'm fine. I didn't need any time off. And I don't need your concern." She tried to pass him, but his hand curled around her arm.

"What is it, Mallory?"

She yanked free. "It's nothing. I don't know why you thought there was a reason, but you're wrong."

"The nurses call you three times more often than the other residents and you're always in the hospital. You're wearing yourself out. You need some downtime."

"I don't need you to be my keeper. I'm thirty-two years old, with enough brains to know when I'm in over my head."

She ran up the steps and pushed her key into the

lock. As she'd done just three nights ago at his house, Brad followed her inside as if he were an invited guest.

"If you don't need a keeper, explain what is going on," he asked. "Why can you barely keep your eyes open some days and others you're as bright as the sunshine?"

Mallory went into her living room, keeping her back to Brad. "I do my job." She flung the words over her shoulder.

He stepped up behind her, took her shoulders and spun her around to face him. "Yes, you do, and you're quite efficient at it, even when you're tired. But how long do you think your body can keep going like this?"

"As long as it takes." Mallory stepped back. Brad's hands dropped to his sides. She felt a coldness invade the places they had been.

"I didn't come here to fight with you." His voice was calm, devoid of any anger.

Mallory wanted to tell him why she was tired. She wanted to explain everything to him, tell him about the patients in the coma wing, about herself and what had happened to her, but she couldn't.

"Why did you come here, Dr. Clayton?"

She watched him flinch, as if she'd hit him.

"It isn't often that I intervene in the workings of the hospital, and since word was bound to get to you, I wanted to tell you myself."

"I've heard already."

"Mallory, you need a rest." He stepped forward, then stopped.

"All right, Doctor. I need a rest and thanks to you I'll get it. Five days off. What would you suggest I do?" She turned from him and walked around her living room. This had been her parents' house. She and her sister had grown up here and she was lucky to have gotten into a hospital that allowed her to stay at home. Houses died when people didn't live in them. Hers had sat dormant for several years while no one tended to it. It had taken her ages to instill life back into it.

"Soak in a hot bath and sleep until your body wakes you up," Brad answered.

She hadn't really wanted medical advice.

"You've got dark circles under your eyes." He waved a hand toward her face. "Sleep will make them go away."

His voice was caressing. He moved closer to her. Mallory felt the heat swelling around her. She tried to maintain her anger, but it burned away. She heard his concern. He was looking out for her welfare. She should be thankful for that. Other than her sister, no one had done that for her since her parents died. At least no one she knew. There was someone who'd been pulling for her, someone who came to her in her dreams, but she had no more knowledge of who that person was than she did the substance of moonbeams.

"Brad—" Mallory didn't know what she was about to say, but at that moment his cell phone rang.

He looked at the lighted display before putting it to his ear.

"Dr. Clayton." He spoke into the phone. "Detective." Mallory could hear only one side of the conversation. She assumed it was the detective who'd helped him the other night. Brad's voice was different, professional, as if he'd turned on a switch. Mallory made no attempt to distance herself from his conversation. As Brad listened, she watched his body language. He stiffened, locking his spine and lifting his strong chin. "I'll be right there."

He pressed a button and returned the phone to his belt. "I have to go," he said. "Will you get some rest?"

Mallory nodded. She could use a good night's sleep. She headed for the door, Brad behind her. On reaching it, she immediately pulled it open, hoping he'd go right on through, but she was out of luck. He stopped and faced her.

"I promise," she said before he could give her an order.

He looked at her a long while, his eyes dark and piercing as they had been the time he'd kissed her. Mallory wanted him to kiss her again. She wanted to feel the pressure of his lips on hers, his arms slipping around her waist as passion overtook them and his mouth devoured hers. Brad leaned forward and she knew what was coming.

Mallory put a hand out and pressed it into his chest, stopping his forward motion. She shook her head.

"We seem to have started something that shouldn't have begun."

He retreated as surely as a turtle crawling into its shell.

"I'm sorry," she said. "Call it chemistry. Call it lust. I don't care. I'll take the blame for everything, but I'm not here for an affair."

Brad stared at her.

"You think I'm offering you an affair?"

"It doesn't matter what you're offering," she said. "I'm not going to accept it."

"Does the other night have anything to do with this?"

She wasn't sure which part of the other night he meant—the part at the police station or the part in his arms?

"When I kissed you," he explained.

"Partly," she hedged. "I started medical school much later than most students and I have a lot of catching up to do. I think it would be best if we kept our relationship on a professional level."

"You're right," he agreed.

Mallory was a little disappointed. She hadn't expected him to give in so easily. Her heart sank. Part of her wanted him to fight with her, but the other part, the logical part, told her to stand clear of Bradley Clayton.

"You'd better go."

He said nothing, only looked her directly in the eyes, then turned and went through the door.

Mallory closed it after she'd watched him go down

the steps and head for his car. She stared at the dark wood of the door. Her eyes brimmed with tears, but none fell. She'd chosen her life. She had priorities and goals that needed to be tended to, and Brad Clayton wasn't part of the plan. It was better to stop this relationship before it got started, she told herself.

But her heart didn't believe it.

"What did you find?" Brad asked as he slipped into a booth at the Camden Diner in nearby New Jersey. Detective Simon Thalberg had a cup of coffee he was drinking. In front of him sat a plate with a half-eaten piece of apple pie on it. He slid a folder across the table to Brad.

"What can I get you?" a waitress asked. She was holding a pot of coffee.

"Coffee is fine."

"Anything else?" she asked as she poured the hot liquid into a thick cup.

"Whatever the breakfast special is."

Brad was hungry. One thing he loved about diners was that anyone could have breakfast anytime, and breakfast was his favorite meal. His life had always been erratic. There were times when he hadn't known where his next meal would come from. Even before going to medical school, he'd had to eat at odd hours. And he ate haphazardly to this day.

Simon Thalberg had been a detective on the New York City police force. Until he'd been shot in the left hand, wounded in the line of duty. Unable to continue as a street cop, he'd gone into private investigations. At fifty he had gray at his temples and his hair was thinning across his crown. He was the fifth investigator Brad had hired over the years to find his mother. None of the others had turned up anything. The trail was too cold. No one knew where his mother had gone that day she hadn't come back. The people who'd lived in the apartment complex no longer lived there and no one knew where they were today.

Brad opened the folder the moment the waitress walked away. Inside was a photo of a woman. He looked at it closely. It wasn't a very good picture, and he strained to see some of the mother he remembered from twenty years ago. He didn't recognize the woman. Her hair was dark brown, her eyes twinkling and a wide smile lit her face. Even the poor quality of the photo couldn't disguise the fact that she was absolutely glamorous.

"Is this her?"

The detective nodded. "She goes by the name of Sharon Yarborough. This is her high school yearbook picture. A more recent picture is behind it."

Brad couldn't remember ever seeing his mother like this. Her smile was never this…free. This spontaneous. He recalled the strain around her mouth as if she had been trying to hid something from her son. Brad thought he should say something. He stared at the photo. He was really looking at his mother, Mariette Joyce Randall. He hadn't thought of the name Randall in years—his, his brother Owen's and hers. He'd changed his name to Clayton when he and his brother had been adopted.

After years of trying to find her, here he was, looking at the photo of the woman who was his mother. He'd never truly believed it would happen.

Brad thought he'd have a million questions, and he was sure he did, but right now he couldn't think of a single one. The lump in his throat and the pain in his chest overrode everything logical in him. He'd searched for her for so long and finally here she was, the woman who had given birth to him.

And the one who'd abandoned him to the streets. Anger scored through him like a hollow-point bullet. His hands shook and he dropped the photo on the tabletop. She looked up at him, still smiling. Brad could see his brother in her features. Owen had her eyes, her smile and that happy-go-lucky attitude that carried him through life so differently from the way Brad approached it.

"Where is she?"

The waitress returned and placed Brad's order on the table. He pushed it aside. He no longer had an appetite.

"There's a full report." Instead of Simon telling him the details, he pulled the small folder back to his side of the table. "Eat first."

"It must be a bad report." Brad tried to laugh, but only a grunt came out. He set the loaded plate in front of him and started to eat.

"How are things going?" Thalberg asked.

"You don't have to make small talk for me," Brad told him. Thalberg had worked on this case for five months. Brad hadn't counted on results, and tonight had expected the usual monthly report saying he'd found nothing, but was trying another lead. All the others had led to dead ends.

Over the past five months the two men had started to become friends. At least they were more than acquaintances, and their relationship wasn't really that of employer and employee. Brad liked Simon Thalberg.

"I'm not trying to make small talk. Just prepare you."

Brad stopped eating and stared at him. "Prepare me for what?"

"Is there anyone I can call...?" Simon left the question hanging. He obviously saw the effect the news was having on Brad.

Brad felt like one of the sick children he healed. He could take away their hurt, make them better, heal their physical bodies, but he could do nothing for the ache inside. Sharon Yarborough, his mother. His beautiful mother with a smile on her face and blackness in her heart....

Brad reached for the folder and Simon slid it to him once more. Brad scanned the contents. Sharon Yarborough lived in Austin, Texas. Her current address was at the Austin Rehabilitation Center.

"What's she doing in a hospital?"

"She's an invalid."

Brad slid the more recent photo from the back of the folder. It was a police photo. He laid it next to the high school picture. The difference between the two women was marked. Only the eyes were the same. The woman in the second photo was old, her face bruised, her hair unkempt and ragged.

"The picture is fifteen years old. It's the only one I could find." He paused. "Brad, she's ill. She's been ill for a very long time."

Brad closed the folder and stood up. Simon looked at him.

"Where are you going?"

"I don't know."

The detective stood and took Brad's arm. "Promise me you'll talk to someone before you fly off to Texas?" Brad started to speak, but Simon stopped him. "Don't tell me you aren't planning to go there. I know how long you've waited, but I think you should take someone with you. Someone who can act as a buffer between you and your emotions."

Brad immediately thought of Mallory. He put his hand on Simon's shoulder, squeezed it slightly and headed for the exit. He zipped the folder inside his jacket and felt it burning straight into his heart.

"Hello," Mallory said. "We've met before, but I couldn't come over very often. I'm here now and I'll talk to you." Her compassion welled inside her as she looked at the delicate face of a woman in her forties. She had hair a soft red color and a sprinkling of freckles across her nose. She slept peacefully in her coma world. Mallory knew it wasn't blank inside there. There were dreams, just images that came and went behind a curtain of fog. Outlines could be seen, but images were distorted, unclear and sometimes fearful.

"It's all right." Mallory touched her hand. "I'll tell you some of the things going on in the world. So when you wake up you'll have stayed current with the news. Not the bad news," she amended. "That never changes."

Mallory started talking. She told Margaret Keller about the lost child who had been found safe in Fairmont Park. She told her about the national news, what she remembered of a White House press release. Mallory knew talking about the news was good for Margaret. And she knew she was using Margaret to keep her mind off Brad. She didn't want to get involved with him, but she'd gotten used to seeing him every day, even if it was just as they passed in the hospital corridor. Since the Wayne Mason mess the nurses and doctors looked at her with a lot more respect. Except for Brad.

He taunted her. She knew a lot of it was her own fault. She read things into his actions that weren't there. But each time she saw him, all she could think of was the way she'd felt in his arms. His touch was so much more powerful than she'd ever imagined. She couldn't tell Margaret about that. She couldn't tell anyone.

"I have to go now, Margaret. I'm not supposed to be in the hospital and it's very late. You need some sleep. I'll be back soon."

Mallory let go of Margaret Keller's hand and quietly left the room. She was cautious as she made her way through the dimly lit corridors. She was usually quiet and careful, but she could always give an excuse for being in the hospital. With her current enforced administrative leave, she would have no ready explanation if someone caught her coming or going.

Safely back in her car, Mallory drove home. It was four o'clock in the morning when she slipped the key in the lock. She would skip the bath Brad had suggested and go straight to bed.

Mallory climbed the stairs to her bedroom. She loved the room. It used to be her parents' and it had taken her a while to get over their loss. But she'd eventually moved things around, repainted and moved from her cramped childhood bedroom into this spacious one.

She'd changed into a nightgown and was pulling the covers back on the bed when the doorbell rang. She checked her watch. Who could that be? she thought. It was nearly sunrise. Mallory thought of the sunrise when she'd been at Brad's.

The front door had two oval panels of tempered glass. Mallory stepped to the side and peered through one of them. Brad stood there. He was wearing the same bomber jacket and pants he'd had on earlier that night when he'd left.

"Brad?" she said as she opened the door. "Are you okay? Is something wrong?"

He didn't say anything, but leaned to one side. Mallory thought he was going to lose his balance. She opened the door wide and caught his arm.

"Come in." He stumbled across the threshold and

fell into her. She smelled the liquor on his breath. "You're drunk." She tried to push him back up on his feet.

His arms went around her. "I only had a couple," he said in a slurred voice, leaning heavily on her. His hands moved up and down her back. "This feels good," he said. "Like warm water."

Mallory couldn't stop herself from pressing her body closer to his when his hands smoothed over her back and buttocks. Then she grabbed them and pulled them free. He still leaned against her, so she twisted around to get her arm and shoulder under his.

She helped him into the living room, and he dropped onto the couch as heavily as a sack of cement. Something had happened in the last few hours. He must have gotten a call from Detective Ryan. Brad respected the officer. Mallory had heard it in his voice when he'd talked of him the other night. What could have occurred?

Sitting down on the wooden coffee table, she asked, "Brad, what happened?" She reached over and touched him. He was fast asleep.

Mallory sighed. She leaned back and looked at him. She knew everyone had demons and his had come to visit him tonight. Brad worried about rumors at the hospital. Whatever had happened to him tonight was something else he didn't want to get around. But why did he keep coming to her?

There were rumors about other doctors who'd come in with liquor on their breath. Brad wasn't one of them. In fact, when she'd overhead the discussion, no one had ever remembered seeing Brad drink anything stronger than sparkling cider. So what trauma had occurred to send him to the bottle…and back to her?

Mallory wouldn't find out tonight. She picked up his feet and removed his shoes, then raised them to the sofa. She had never done that before. For a patient, yes, but never for a man, and Brad, even in his alcoholic state, was all man. She looked at her hands, still on his legs. She felt his warmth envelop her as it always did. For a long moment she stared at his relaxed face, reveling in feelings that washed over her just looking at him. Remembering the heat that flooded through her when he smoothed his hands down her body. She sighed, wanting it again.

"What is it about you?" she asked, as if he were one of her coma patients. "Why do you make me feel like…" She stopped. He made her feel like a woman.

Mallory had never been good at relationships. She had secrets. Things she couldn't share with anyone. Relationships meant trust. Someone you could rely on, someone to share everything with. Mallory felt tears rush into her eyes. She was looking at the man she wanted to do that with, but she knew she couldn't. There were things she just couldn't tell anyone.

She got up and went to get a blanket. Holding the blanket to her, she again looked down at Brad. He was wearing his bomber jacket. She had to get it off him. Dropping the blanket on the floor, Mallory unzipped the jacket and opened the front. She saw the folder, and when she picked it up, his warmth and scent came with it.

Mallory drew in a deep breath and opened the folder. The glamorous photo of a woman floated to the floor. Mallory sank down on the blanket and stared at her face. She picked up the photo and glanced at Brad. Then she began to read.

Chapter Five

Brad's feet were cold. He reached for the covers and realized he was wearing his clothes. He opened his eyes and memory hit him. He'd come to Mallory's and that was the last thing he remembered. He looked around the room. It was her living room and he was on her couch.

Sighing, he dropped his head back against the sofa. He was an idiot. What was he doing here? He'd left the diner and driven around for hours. Then he'd gone to a bar. He couldn't remember where it was, only that the music was loud, there were people everywhere and he didn't want anything to do with any of them. When he'd left, he'd driven without a destination in mind and had ended up here.

His mouth felt dry and tasted awful. He wanted

some water. And a toothbrush. Brad started to sit up, and saw Mallory sitting on the floor. Her head was pressed against the sofa and she was sound asleep. He wondered how long she had been there.

She was wearing a nightgown and had a blanket around her shoulders. He couldn't get up without disturbing her. Then he saw it—the folder lying open on the floor by her feet. The face of Sharon Yarborough stared up at him.

"Good morning," Mallory said suddenly. Brad shifted his gaze to her. She was beautiful in the morning. Her eyes were wide and bright and she smiled.

"Isn't it more like afternoon?"

She nodded, pushing herself up straight and frowning as her muscles protested her night on the floor instead of in her comfortable bed.

"You read it?" he asked.

She looked him directly in the eye. He liked that about her. She was a straight shooter. "I read it." She waited for him to continue, not pushing. He knew she was prepared to wait until he was ready, or accept that he wasn't going to talk about it, if that was his decision.

"She left us twenty-one years ago."

"You and Owen?"

He nodded "It's a long story."

"Then why don't I make us some breakfast and you can tell me all about it."

"I need to check in with the hospital."

She pointed to a phone as she stood up. The blanket fell from her shoulders. She wore no robe, only a white nightgown. It was silky and flowed around her body. It looked cool, but Brad had learned that with Mallory looks were deceiving. He had the feeling that if he put his hands on the fabric it would burn him. And his hands ached to try it.

She turned and went out of the room. Brad's eyes watched her as she moved. It had been too long since he'd been with a woman, and his body was telling him so. He pulled his cellular phone from his jacket pocket and checked the screen. No calls. Thank goodness, he thought. No one at the hospital had tried to reach him during his night of self-indulgence.

He checked in, then listened to his messages. There was one from Detective Ryan. He'd picked up a twelve-year-old girl living in the warehouse district. Brad let out a breath. The child was off the streets. Ryan had taken her to the shelter and asked that Brad stop by if he had a free moment. There was no emergency. Brad also called his office. He had no appointments for today, but checked with the answering service. Thankfully, it had been a quiet night.

Hanging up, he replaced the phone in his pocket and looked for a bathroom. He found a full bath just off the kitchen. On the counter lay a set of matching towels, a new toothbrush and toothpaste. He thanked Mallory silently as he pulled the cellophane off the toothbrush, and wondered if she'd been reading his mind.

Several minutes later he walked into the kitchen, feeling more like himself. The smell of bacon made his stomach growl. He'd eaten early this morning in the diner, but had burned off all the energy of that food with alcohol and anger.

Mallory had dressed. She was wearing jeans and a sweatshirt. She didn't have on any makeup and her hair hung about her shoulders. Brad moved toward her, wanting to slip his arms around her waist, but he stopped.

"Can I help?" he asked.

"Can you cook?" She didn't turn around as she asked the question.

"I do all right."

She turned and smiled at him. "Why don't you make some toast? The bread is over there." She pointed to a loaf of wheat bread on the counter.

"I was adopted," Brad began. He concentrated on making toast as if it were brain surgery. "As I told you the other night, I was nine. I never knew what happened to her."

He turned away from the toaster to find Mallory transferring bacon to a plate with a paper towel on it.

"I've been looking for her since she left. I hired five private investigators, but this is the first one who's had any success. I can't believe he actually found her."

"Where is Owen?"

"He lives in Texas. As do my adopted brothers and one sister. My youngest sister lives in New York."

"You said that before." She took an egg from a bowl and held it up. "Scrambled?"

He nodded. She broke the eggs and used a whisk to scramble them.

"Owen and I have the same parents. We lived in Dallas. We were poor, living in one-room apartments and moving often. Owen and I rarely had time to make friends and we went to more elementary schools than I can remember. My mother worked at whatever she could get."

"What about your father?"

He shrugged. "He left right after I was born. Neither Owen nor I can remember him, and my mother never talked about him. She had a job working at a hotel as a night maid. When we got up for school she would be there. One day she wasn't. And she never came back."

"What happened to you two?" Brad heard the surprise in her voice.

Mallory set plates of food on the table. Brad buttered the toast and poured coffee.

"We stayed in the apartment until the police came. Then we ran away and stayed in abandoned buildings." Brad thought of the twelve-year-old and Detective Ryan saying he'd found her and taken her to the shelter. It was the same with Owen and him. They'd been found and taken to foster care.

Mallory listened without interrupting. She ate her meal and drank her coffee while he continued. "We were lucky. We found a couple who loved children and treated us as if we were theirs. Eventually we were all adopted."

"By the same couple?"

He nodded. "Our foster father died and we were

adopted by our mother. She took all six of us. We became a family.''

''You were lucky,'' Mallory said.

He nodded. ''I know that.''

''What do you plan to do with the information you have about your mother?''

Brad suddenly felt claustrophobic. He got up and carried his plate to the stainless steel sink. He set it down and turned back. Mallory swiveled in her chair to look at him.

''I don't know,'' he said. ''I always thought I would rush right to her and start asking questions. But now that I know where she is I'm...''

''Terrified?'' Mallory finished the sentence for him. ''It's like that question you don't want to ask because you're afraid of the answer.''

Brad was amazed at how quickly she understood. He didn't know what to do about Sharon Yarborough. She didn't even have the same name, and Simon had said she was ill.

''You should wait,'' Mallory said. Again Brad had the feeling she could read his mind. ''The report said she's ill, but with nothing life threatening. You don't want to rush into anything. If you don't have rational thought on your side, you could make matters worse.''

''You think there could be a rational explanation for her abandoning us and never finding us in twenty-one years?''

''I know it sounds unlikely, but there is always the

chance." Her voice was soft, wistful almost, as if she was speaking from experience.

"I've waited a long time. More than half my life."

Mallory stood up and carried her own plate to the sink. Brad moved aside to give her space. She put the plate down and looked up at him. "It won't hurt to wait a little longer. You have everything you need to know. If she moves, she can be easily found again."

For someone on the outside, Mallory was extremely perceptive. They were standing next to each other. She faced the windows and he faced the room, but both were looking into the other's eyes. Brad remembered the gown she'd had on. Memories of running his hands over her last night came back to him. His body heated suddenly and her eyes seemed to darken, as if she'd taken a cue from him.

He wanted her, but he remembered what she'd told him. A professional relationship only. And so far he'd broken that rule. "You'd better walk me to the door," he told her.

She moved away and he followed. He picked up his jacket and the folder.

"Thank you," he said in the entranceway. "For more than just breakfast."

She smiled. He leaned down and kissed her forehead. Brad felt her stiffen. He straightened, but ran a finger down her cheek.

"I owe you," he said. "You can sleep on my couch anytime you want."

He went down the steps. His car was parked directly in front of the house.

"Brad," she called as he stepped off the curb. He turned back. "What are you doing tomorrow morning at 4:00 a.m.?"

"Nothing important."

"Meet me here."

Mallory pulled the truck into the parking area of the Flemington Fairgrounds in New Jersey before sunrise. Brad had showed up promptly at four o'clock with breakfast in hand. They'd left immediately, eating on the way. Still, her pickup took one of the last parking spaces. Quickly they got out and Mallory opened the back of the truck. Some balloons were already being blown up. She could hear the burners blowing hot air into the gaping cavities.

Mallory reached inside the truck to pull out the bag with her own folded balloon. Brad climbed inside the bed and tried to lift the basket and burner. "This thing must weigh a ton," he said.

"Six hundred pounds," a voice behind him said. "Morning, Doc."

"Hi, Keith. Greg," Mallory said, turning. They all climbed aboard and the four of them hoisted the heavy basket to the custom lift Mallory had had built onto the truck. It lowered the basket to the ground, where they slid it off.

"Hard to believe hot air can lift that thing," Brad said when they'd finished.

"This is Dr. Bradley Clayton." Mallory introduced him to the men he'd just worked with. "He's my crew for today."

The men shook hands and nodded to each other. "Keith and Greg work the ground for a lot of the pilots and crew members. They help me with the heavy work of loading and unloading the basket and burners and inflating the balloon. They also drive the chase car that picks me up and drives me back to my truck."

"Ever been ballooning before?" Keith asked Brad.

Brad shook his head. The two men looked at each other and walked away. "I'll check your parachute top," Greg said.

"I must look like a greenhorn," Brad commented wryly.

Mallory looked at him, and green was not the color she would choose to describe him. "Don't worry," she said. "It only takes one ride to change that."

"What's the parachute for?" Brad questioned.

"It's not the kind you jump out of planes with." She wondered if he was sorry he'd agreed to this. "A parachute is a sealed panel at the top of the balloon. It's used to help deflate the balloon, so we can land where we want to and not crash the basket."

Mallory had opened the huge balloon and was pulling it so it lay flat. The men at the other end helped her. Brad could see several others had joined them. This effort took a team. Brad grabbed a section near the opening and followed suit. They laid it out on the huge open space.

"How'd you get started doing this?" he asked when they finished.

"My father taught me. He used to take me up be-

fore he died. He was the pilot and I was his crew."
She missed her dad. She thought of him every time
she went up, wondering what he would think of her
now.

"When you were what…nine or ten he took you
ballooning?"

"Earlier than that. I was three the first time. We
didn't go regularly until I turned seven. But I wasn't
the only crew. It takes several people to launch a balloon." She looked around. "There's a fan in the
truck. It's huge and yellow. Would you get it?"

Brad jumped up onto the flatbed of the pickup and
came back carrying the fan.

"I love ballooning," Mallory said. "If you stick to
the rules, it's relatively safe. Today should be a wonderful day for the air."

Brad checked the morning sky. The sun was banishing the darkness at the horizon. "Am I your crew
today?" he asked.

"You're still in therapy," she said with a smile.
"I'm taking you up to give your mind something else
to dwell on."

"Would that be my life?"

She meant him finding his mother, and knew his
comment was a shield to hide his true feelings.

"It will be what you want it to be." Mallory hadn't
intended for her voice to sound seductive, but in the
early morning light, with the dew still clinging to the
grass, it had that quality. Brad must have noticed it,
too. His eyes narrowed in keen observance.

Mallory turned away and resumed her work. "The

envelope needs filling," she told him. "Bring the fan over and we'll fill it."

"Envelope?"

Mallory pointed to the large, rounded portion of the balloon laying flat on the ground. "This is called the envelope. We use the fan to pump cold air into it to blow it up. When it gets to a certain level, we'll switch the frames on and the hot air will force it to rise off the ground."

They worked quickly, filling the balloon with cold air. In minutes the eighty-story nylon circle was billowing like a huge multicolored blanket. Keith and Greg returned for the ignition. Mallory took hold of Brad's arm and pulled him a safe distance away. She gave him a crown line and told him to hold the balloon to prevent it from inflating too fast. Returning, Greg tipped the basket as the two of them turned on the burners. The flames shot thirty feet into the air and the whooshing noise prevented conversation.

Mallory continued heating the air for some time. Then she gave control to Greg and went back to where Brad pulled on his crown line.

"How long does it take to fully inflate?" he shouted into her ear.

"Twenty to thirty minutes," she screamed back.

As the sun began to rise the two of them got in the basket. Mallory took over working the burner, blasting hot air into the envelope's cavity, while Greg got out. The balloon began to rise.

"We'll be airborne in a few minutes."

Mallory glanced at Brad. He looked nervous. She turned her head so he couldn't see her smiling.

Brad smiled and nodded. "Why do people like to do this?" Brad asked, between blasts of hot air.

"Why do people swim or play pick-up basketball?" she countered.

Holding on to one of the secured posts that held up the burner, he looked at her.

"Everyone in the hospital talks, Doctor," Mallory explained. "It's no secret that you like to play basketball."

"Do they know you do this?" He waved a hand, encompassing the balloon and the air around them.

She shook her head. "I don't think it's come up in conversation. And until now I haven't had much time for it." She gave him a knowing look. "But people like the freedom of the air. In a plane, it's not the same. From the beginning man has wanted to soar with the birds. Ballooning satisfies that need. It frees the body from the earth and the mind from things that worry it."

"So you brought me for my therapy?"

"Only partly." She looked at him seriously. "The other part is for the sheer beauty of the flight. Look." She pointed at the horizon. Brad followed her finger. The mountains, emerald-green in the morning sun provided a magnificent backdrop for the multicolored balloons rising all around them. No two had the same pattern or combination of hues. Mallory's balloon had slanted stripes ranging from lavender to deep purple, which from the ground made the balloon look as if it was spinning in the air. Nearby a giant red-and-silver one was shaped like a Hershey's Kiss, and another huge yellow one was shaped like a lion with a golden mane.

Mallory noticed Brad hadn't moved from the spot he'd claimed when he climbed onboard. Ballooning took some getting used to. It was like being at sea for the first time. You had to adjust to the swaying of the basket and the fact that the ground beneath your feet moved. She wondered if he was afraid of heights.

"I never knew so many people did this. I've only seen an isolated balloon now and then," Brad commented in wonder.

"This is a small number. Everyone else is in Albuquerque."

"Albuquerque?"

"They have a huge balloon festival this time of year. Thousands of balloons that take off at one time. It's a real sight." Mallory had been there once for the races. She wished she could go back someday.

"Why Albuquerque? It's flat and brown, nothing like this." He looked at the evergreens blanketing the Pennsylvania mountainsides.

"It has perfect airflow. You can't imagine the feel of the wind sweeping the balloon upward, or the warm currents carrying the basket along. The balloons whirl around like spinning tops and except for the bursts of hot air, all you hear is absolute silence."

"You wish you were there?"

"Every flyer wishes she were there. But some of us have other obligations."

"You're on vacation. You could have gone."

"It's not that easy to leave, Brad. Just because I'm on vacation doesn't mean I don't have things to do." Mallory pulled the lever and hot air lifted the balloon. She hadn't meant to give Brad an opening into her personal life. She headed him off by rushing into speech. "It's flat over the city, but the Rocky Mountains provide a spectacular view."

"This is a pretty sight, too." He was looking directly at her. Mallory felt her body heat under her clothing. There was a look on his face that could only be described as wicked.

"Dr. Clayton, you're smiling." She spoke despite the dryness in her throat. Brad's smile widened even more. "Does that mean your fears of ballooning have been laid to rest?"

"Was I that obvious?"

Mallory shook her head. "Let's just say your heartbeat was visible through your jacket."

Brad Clayton often hid his feelings. He'd probably become so adept that he didn't even realize he was doing so. His scowl was a perpetual expression, except with children. Mallory wondered if she could break through his mask to find the real Brad Clayton.

A pang of guilt shot through her. She had her own masks securely in place. Behind them she helped people, helped them out of their fears, brought them back from the brink of nothingness, helped them to continue living.

Though conscious and mobile, Brad was in a kind of coma. And she needed to talk him out of it as she did the sleeping coma patients. His unique situation was that he could talk back, react, explain. She could watch his body language and interpret his actions.

"It's beautiful up here," he said. He glanced down at the ground. "I've been in many airplanes, but I've never seen the ground from this height. This is so much better."

"You feel freer," Mallory stated. She pulled the burner valve, and a burst of fire shot into the balloon's envelope. Brad had to wait for the sound to die down to speak.

"It is liberating," he said. "I can see why you like it."

He took over the burner then, keeping the balloon at a constant level. Mallory watched him gazing out at the hundred or so other balloons. They reminded her of confetti during a parade.

"When I was a little girl I wanted to be an airline pilot and fly every day," she murmured. Brad turned to her. Mallory thought of her father, her time with him and their mutual love of the sky. That's what had made her want to fly—the hours they'd spent together, just the two of them. Her sister was too young and her mother wasn't adventurous. In the truck, the two of them—Mallory and her dad—would talk for hours on the way to parade grounds and festivals. She still had his old balloon, although it was no longer airworthy.

"What changed your mind?" Brad asked. "Why'd you decide to become a doctor?"

Mallory looked down for a moment. "This is going

to sound very clichéd but I wanted to help people. Being a doctor was the best way.'' She watched his features, wondering if he believed her.

''I became a doctor because of my adoptive father,'' Brad volunteered.

''Was he a doctor?''

He shook his head. ''This is going to sound clichéd, too, but he was there for me when I needed him most.''

Mallory didn't understand what he was referring to, but hoped to learn more in the future. She partially understood, though, because someone had been there for her when she'd needed it most and been unable to ask for help.

''I know my father never amassed the riches that most people equate with success, but he was the most successful man I have ever met,'' Brad stated.

''You said *was*.''

''He died when I was in my teens.''

''My parents died in a car accident,'' Mallory volunteered. ''I was seventeen.'' She rarely talked about her parents. The accident still made her feel raw, mainly because so much of it was a blur in her memory.

An updraft of wind suddenly caught the balloon and pushed it and the basket upward. Mallory's stomach dropped. Brad grabbed one of the braces holding the burners and caught Mallory in a protective hold as she stumbled across the space toward him. She breathed hard as she came up against his chest.

Mallory temporarily forgot about the balloon,

something she'd never done before. She was always conscious of controlling the burners, reading the airspeed, checking her altimeter and generally keeping things on an even keel. But Brad had broken her concentration and she saw only him—his piercing dark eyes, the strong arms holding her against him. She imagined his mouth lowering to touch hers, his tongue feathering against her lips. Mallory felt her body melting. Almost instantly she was swept up in the haze that surrounded them whenever they were together. It was invisible, but as strong and confining as titanium wire.

Pushing herself away, she stood up straight and reached for the burner control. She was suddenly hot and needed something to concentrate on, something other than the tall, dark and gorgeous doctor standing two feet away from her. There had to be a hundred balloons in the air, yet she felt utterly alone with Brad.

Mallory's heart rate returned to normal and she glanced at him, only to find his back was to her. He was looking down. She wondered if he was as affected by her presence as she was by his. The two seemed to come together at the oddest times, yet there was something between them. As much as she gave herself excuses to see him, she silently admitted that she wanted to be with him.

"Are we over the Raritan River?" he asked.

Mallory looked down, then out at the mountains. She nodded.

"I have a cabin down there. It's..." Brad stopped

and appeared to be checking directions. "There it is," he shouted, as if he'd discovered the cure for cancer.

Mallory saw the small building he pointed to. It was on a bend of the river near the mountains in the distance. She fixed it in her mind as a landmark to look for when she flew again.

"I didn't know you had a cabin."

He smiled. "So there are some secrets that are not known by everyone in the hospital."

"Only those you tell to people who can keep a secret."

Both of them understood her meaning.

By the time they set down, Keith and the folding crew were waiting. Five men joined Brad and Mallory to gather and store the balloon and basket. They worked well together and made the work look easy, with no groaning from any of them. Mallory knew her arms and shoulders would be sore in the morning from all the work, but it was worth it. She wished she could fly more often. This unplanned vacation had given her the opportunity, but time off came infrequently.

As the crew started the deflating process, the odor of sauerkraut filled her nostrils. She looked at Brad, then around at the crew. They'd stopped and were all staring at Brad. She knew they'd been waiting for him to say it, to gag on the overwhelming odor that surprised every newcomer after his first flight. It was part of the test, part of the initiation for a new balloonist.

But Brad surprised them. He did nothing, said nothing. He didn't even let on that the odor existed.

"What?" he asked, looking much like the greenhorn he was. One by one the guys slapped him on the back and returned to their tasks. It was a gesture of comraderie. He'd joined their ranks by being here and working through the day. None of them, however, answered his question.

Mallory pushed air out of the balloon, flattening the giant strips of nylon fabric into manageable yards of cloth. "That was the final first-timer's test," she told him. "Now you're a veteran."

Brad smiled at her. "You mean it doesn't get any scarier than this?"

"It can get downright horrific, but if you keep your head..." She trailed off. "Anyway, they accept you." She glanced toward the guys.

"I didn't know I was being tested."

"There's always a test when you do something you've never done before." Mallory remembered her first day at Philadelphia General—a test to see if the nurses would accept her. Would the doctors treat her as one of them or one of the nurses? Would she be criticized for her diagnoses, for everything she said or ordered? She'd run through a gauntlet that day.

Brad had taken the learning process very well. The men had ribbed him from the beginning over his lack of knowledge. Most guys would have clammed up or gotten angry. Brad had taken it in stride, not at all like the doctor she saw in the hospital—the one who had an attitude and rarely smiled. Brad was extremely good-looking, especially when his face wasn't wearing a perpetual frown.

They worked quickly. He didn't make any more comments. Mallory watched him from across the wide balloon. She liked the way he moved. He pulled the fabric up and folded it as competently as the others. Mallory remembered him arms around her and how he'd folded her body into his.

Keith drove them back to the parking area where Mallory had left the pickup. She sat next to Brad, wedged close to his body in the crowded front seat. Mallory tried to keep her eyes straight ahead, but the furnace going off in her body made her want to turn toward him and melt into his flesh. Brad's arm lay across the back of the seat, causing the hairs on her neck to rise as if in anticipation of his fingers caressing them. The drive was short, but it felt like it took forever.

Finally Keith pulled into the parking area. With practiced ease, the crew unloaded and reloaded the balloon and equipment from one truck to the other. When everything was stored and ready, Mallory and Brad joined the others for lunch and champagne. The meal was ready and waiting for them.

Brad stopped and viewed the spread of food and drink that sat on tables with white linen tablecloths.

"Tradition," Mallory stated. She picked up two champagne glasses. "After every trip there's a champagne toast. If there is time we have a meal, too. Today we'll have lunch."

"Is one of those for me?" Brad indicated the glasses in her hand.

"Are you going into the hospital?" she asked.

He shook his head. "I'm covered for the day."

Satisfied, she handed him the glass. Their fingers touched for a moment and Mallory felt the smoothness of his skin. He had a doctor's hands, soft and strong, yet incredibly sexy. She wanted to hold on to them, feel them massaging her neck and back. She wanted to stare into the depths of his dark eyes and know what he was thinking.

Mallory took his arm and led him toward the crowd of other pilots. Several parties were arriving and they waited for them before the toast. Mallory looked at the ground to keep Brad from seeing the flush on her face.

Brad's thoughts had been occupied during the ride in the balloon, but now that he and Mallory were on the ground again and headed back toward their everyday lives, his mother returned to mind. She was in Texas, only a few hours away by plane. She'd been there for years. What could he make of that? Why had she left them and never returned? Why had she stayed close to where they lived and never tried to find them? For twenty years he'd wandered around, wondering where she was and if she was looking for them. And all the time she'd been only a few hundred miles from where they lived.

He'd been back to Texas often. While he'd still lived in Texas he would sometimes visit the old neighborhood, staring up at that apartment in the run-down section. He would scan the faces of every woman walking by. He would walk the aisles of the grocery and convenience stores, knowing at the next turn he might come face-to-face with her and she would open her arms to him, glad to be together again. Whenever Brad ran away from foster homes he would go there. It was where they'd found him the last time he was in trouble, and where his adoptive dad took him when Brad had finally opened up and cried his story out to the Claytons.

He didn't know if Owen ever returned to the apartment. It was something they didn't talk about. But now Brad no longer had to wonder where his mother was. He had an address. He knew where she was. What he didn't know was what to do about it.

To figure that out, he was going to need more therapy.

Mallory pulled the truck into the driveway of a garage Brad didn't recognize. They weren't at her home. The garage door went up at the push of a button, and she pulled the truck inside.

"We're here," she announced in a cheerful voice, opening her door. Brad got out on his side and came around to where she stood. Next to the truck was her car.

Brad was beginning to respect Mallory more and more. Intuitively she seemed to know what he needed. At the moment what he needed was to take his mind off his problems and she gave him something else to think about. He needed solitude to ponder his options, and she drove without speaking and without interrupting his thoughts.

Silently Mallory stepped around to the driver's side and got into the car. The convertible top was up and he couldn't see her.

Brad opened the door and bent down to look at her. "Don't you want me to help you get the basket down?"

"I have someone who does that."

Brad got in. He should have known she was resourceful. The basket and gas weighed over six hundred pounds and it had already been on the truck when he got to her house at four this morning. She was average height for a woman, not as tall as his model sister, Rosa, but taller than most of the nurses and female doctors. Still, she couldn't lift six hundred pounds herself.

Brad's mind drifted back to Texas. He thought of the things he'd done to survive after his mother left. He'd been on his own, he and Owen. Most of the time they stayed together, but when the cops got after them they'd split up and meet back at the apartment later. Brad wondered what Mallory had done to survive and get as far as she had.

Glancing sideways, he took in her classic profile. Her skin was a smooth, even brown, kissed by the sun. Her eyes had smiled brightly when they were in the balloon. He liked seeing her smile at him.

She drove through the streets without speaking. While the air had been sunny and clear in the balloon-filled sky, a slight rain had begun to fall over Philadelphia. By the time they reached her house, rain was coming down in buckets.

Water coursed down in sheets. "There's no way we can get to the door without being drenched," he said, peering out the side window.

"I have an umbrella," she answered.

He turned back to her, hearing the humor in her voice. "But it's in the house?"

She laughed. He did, too, and it felt good. Brad got out and stripped off his jacket. The water splattered cold on his back. He rushed to Mallory's side, and as she emerged from the car, he covered them both with the jacket.

Though the car couldn't be more than ten feet away from the door, they were soaked to the skin by the time they reached the porch. Mallory pushed the door open and they both fell into the foyer as a gust of wind splattered more rain in their faces. Brad pulled his jacket free. It dripped water all over the foyer.

"I'm afraid I'm messing up your floor," he said. Mallory was shaking water from her hands and pulling her wet shirt away from her skin.

"Hang it up there." She pointed to a hook on an old mahogany coat rack. Brad looked at it. He was sure it was an antique, but it had been meticulously cared for.

"I'll get a towel." Mallory disappeared into the back of the house. She returned almost immediately carrying a wad of paper towels. Handing several to him, she smoothed one over her hair and neck.

Brad could only watch as her movements stirred

something inside him. He couldn't budge. Since seeing Mallory early this morning, when the sun hadn't yet tinged the sky, he'd wanted to kiss her, and now seeing her so deliciously drenched in water gave her the look of a summer flower waking up after a refreshing rain.

They stood in her foyer, in the soft, intimate light from the over-the-door window. Brad was losing touch with reality and he knew it. He should be saying goodbye. He should be running in any direction except the one in front of him. Yet he couldn't make his feet move. His eyes bored into her, seeing her body outlined by her rain-soaked clothes. She'd pushed her hair back from her face.

She grew more beautiful to him by the minute. He couldn't tell what she was thinking, but he read her body language, which spoke the same message his was giving. She wanted him, as much as he wanted her.

Brad crossed the space in two steps and stood in front of her, still not touching her. She didn't move, either, but looked up at him. He could feel the warmth of her, smell the rain and that indefinable perfume that was Mallory. He breathed in, filling his nostrils with her scent.

"Every time I get near you I want to take you in my arms," he whispered.

Her eyes opened wider. She looked at him as if she were unsure she'd heard him correctly.

"I don't understand why you drive me crazy, but you do."

Brad touched her then. He took her in his arms and pulled her close. His eyes shut as he hugged her to him, buried his face in her hair. For a long while he just held her, he didn't know why. And he discovered he didn't need a reason. It felt good holding her, but it was more than that. He couldn't explain; he just needed her.

"Is this about your mother?" Mallory asked.

He pulled back and stared for a long time into her eyes. He didn't really know how to answer that question, and hesitated, trying to determine the truth. He had no intention of telling her anything except the absolute truth. Mallory was the only person he'd ever told about his mother. She was the one who came to his side when he called. She was the one keeping his secrets. And she was the one he needed.

"It might be," he finally said. "But only indirectly." Then he lowered his mouth and kissed her.

His mouth was soft on hers, though he only touched her lips briefly before lifting his mouth. Then he tasted her again, tentatively nibbling at her mouth in a manner that shouldn't have caused ripples of sensations radiating inside her to work their way to her toes. A growing weakness made her body slack. She grasped his biceps with her hand so Brad's arms went around her waist and he pulled her into full contact with him. He deepened the kiss. Mallory bent her head back and opened her mouth to the welcome invasion of his tongue.

"We work well together," he whispered into her mouth.

"Is this work?" She could barely manage to get the words out.

"Call it therapy then."

"This isn't part of your therapy." His mouth was on her neck. She squeezed her eyes shut as powerful waves of pleasure rolled through her.

"It's part of yours," he said, and slipped his arms up her back. Brad dipped his head and touched his mouth to hers.

Mallory had never felt like this. It was as if he'd lifted her off the ground and together they floated on a plane of sensation—a place where feeling and emotion were supreme.

Something inside her snapped. Her arms went around his neck as she rose up on tiptoe, pulling his mouth to hers and allowing the waterfall of emotions to pound through her system. She'd never known these kinds of feelings. She could sense her entire body changing. His hands massaged the contours of her back as his mouth worked magic on hers.

He had a power, something dark and delicious that spanned time from the days of dungeons and dragons, magic potions and superstitions. Mallory was caught in it.

Need pumped through her bloodstream like a drug. Rapture so strong it was almost visible took hold of her. She spread her legs slightly, feeling Brad's growing hardness pressed against the juncture of her legs. Her body arched forward, a groan escaping her lips.

He was strong, his body hard, muscular, yet he held her as if he'd discovered in her a priceless object.

Brad's hand moved up, his thumbs gently tracing circles on the sides of her breasts. Mallory felt her nipples stand at attention, craving his hands.

"Brad, I'm burning," she moaned in between the hot, wet kisses he traded with her.

"So am I," he told her. "Where's the bedroom?"

"Upstairs." Mallory didn't have the breath available to form complete sentences. "Top...left."

Brad's hands went to her hips and grasped her firmly. Without removing his mouth or breaking contact with her body, he walked her backward to the base of the steps. Mallory didn't realize they were climbing them, only that she and Brad were like hormonal teenagers, unable to keep from touching each other.

By the time they reached the bedroom door Brad had worked his hands under her shirt. He raised it up and she lifted her arms as he pulled it over her head. Her hair tumbled from its knot and fell around her shoulders. Brad pushed his fingers through it and on down her neck, to her shoulders and waist. Mallory shuddered at his touch. Reaching her hips, he tugged her pants down over them, until Mallory stood exposed, her brand-name underwear bright and colorful in the blurred light. She wore red, never imagining anyone other than herself would see the skimpy pieces of lace, but glad she had them on.

Brad's eyes took her in like a chocolate sundae with a red cherry. "You're beautiful," he said. He pulled her back into his arms. This time his kiss was passionate, steeped in hunger, raw with desire. His mouth devoured hers, his tongue sweeping inside her mouth and tasting her. Mallory felt his touch all the way to her core.

And she wanted him there.

Pulling the snap on Brad's jeans, Mallory unzipped them and pushed them over his hips, just as he had done with hers. She loved the feel of his skin, so smooth and hot against her hands. She could detect tremors going through him wherever she touched, and reveled in the knowledge that she stirred him, not only with her hands stroking his muscled legs, but inside him, where it counted. She knew she'd done so as surely as if Brad had said the words out loud. Some connection had been made between them. She could tell what he wanted and he knew exactly what she wanted, too.

Brad lowered her to the bed. Mallory had lain in this bed hundreds of nights, yet lying there tonight she seemed to feel the sheets for the first time. Her sensitized body was aware of everything—the height from the floor, the depth of the mattress, every fiber that caressed her skin as she lay on it. Brad's hair-roughened skin covered her, his mouth heating her part by part as if his tongue was laced with fire. Mallory expected to combust in seconds, but he wasn't ready to give her the relief she sought.

He began his seduction, kissing her all over, giving her body his undivided attention. Inch by inch he touched her, kissed her, placed his open mouth on parts of her that hadn't ever been touched by a man. Mallory moaned, writhed, dug her hands through his hair. She stretched, arching with the pleasure-pain sensations that Brad, the master of the universe, was evoking.

Mallory's breath was coming in short gasps when he finally worked his way back up her body and entered her. She jerked as a sonic pulse of pleasure shot through her, engulfing her in something so erotic a strangled cry broke from her throat. Throwing off every inhibition, she hugged him close and pulled him farther inside of her, as close as two people could get. Brad set the rhythm hard and fast, and Mallory followed him, then took the lead as her body tasted the pleasure he gave her. She strained against him, fitting herself to Brad as if they had been created for each other.

She relished the closeness, the intimacy, the new world that Brad and she forged out of the fire the two of them kindled. It surged around them, brilliant and colorful, taking on its own life.

Mallory heard a long scream—her voice!—as she finally attained the release she craved. Brad's climax came a second later, then the two of them collapsed against each other. Her heart pounded in her ears as satisfaction overtook her, pulsing waves in a raging sea. Breathing through her mouth, she tried to calm her rapidly beating heart, but was helpless in the moment. Brad had invaded every cell of her body, and extracting herself would take time.

She hugged him closer. Let it take all the time it needed, she thought. Mallory had never been so content in her life, and she was willing to remain where she was for the rest of eternity.

Chapter Six

Through the stethoscope the sound was steady and strong, though slightly fast. Brad listened for several seconds, then moved the instrument several inches and listened again.

"Take a deep breath and let it out slowly," he instructed. The girl in front of him did as she was told. Ellen Grant looked at the ceiling. She held her body still. Brad knew she was scared and was covering it up with belligerence. He should try to help her relax, but he was too distracted this morning. Normally, he would be more talkative. Sometimes the new ones didn't talk back. Ellen fell into that category.

"It's all right," he said in a calm voice. "You're doing fine."

Brad was amazed he could remember a simple sentence, let alone the procedures of a doctor. He was at the shelter, his usual monthly visit to take care of any new arrivals or those needing his care. The girl he'd been accused of kidnapping bit her bottom lip and stared at the floor.

"I am fine," she said.

Brad sat back. "You can get dressed now," he told her. "Your heartbeat is sound, your lungs clear, and I find nothing wrong with you." She hid her face, trying not to let him see the relief there. He didn't push her. She wasn't ready to be pushed, and there was someone else on his mind.

Mallory Russell.

What had happened last night? What had he been thinking? That was the problem—he hadn't been. She'd looked at him and something inside him detonated. Something as strong as a nuclear bomb had gone off in his loins, and his mind had been blown away with it. It was the only explanation he could accept for what had happened.

Brad had rules he lived by. At least he thought he did. That was until Mallory Russell had come into his life. He didn't want to count the number of rules he'd broken yesterday. First, he'd been more interested in Mallory than he should be. He'd gone ballooning with her on what amounted to a date. He'd eaten with her and laughed. And to top things off they'd made love.

"You may go now," he told Ellen. "I want you to make friends with the other kids." She threw him a sarcastic look and left.

When she closed the door, Brad stared at it. He didn't see the opaque glass, the wood frame or the old-fashioned glass knob. He looked back into yesterday's events, into Mallory's eyes. His body stiffened as the memory aroused him. What was happening to him? He should have more control than a fifteen-year-old kid, but that's exactly what he felt like. He couldn't see another patient like this. Thankfully, Ellen had been his last, but Christina Margo, the resident nurse, would be knocking on the door soon, ready to go over his findings. He had to get control of himself, and thinking of Mallory wouldn't allow that.

What was he going to do about her? These feelings?

Still, he couldn't forget their lovemaking. The light had begun to wane when they'd woken in the late afternoon. Mallory's lids were heavy when she opened them. She'd smiled and curved her naked body around his. She was warm and slick against him, with smooth legs and full breasts. And so soft, like cotton caressing his body. She'd kissed his arms and shoulders, stroked his skin with her hands, up and down his arms and across his belly. His reaction to her seduction couldn't have been more immediate if she'd given him an aphrodisiac. He'd wanted her, with a need so strong it scared him, yet not strong enough to prevent him from taking her again.

The first time had altered his conception of a lot of things. He'd thought he knew what lovemaking was all about. He'd thought he knew what having sex encompassed, but their joining had taught him that he knew nothing about how things worked between men and women. All the knowledge he'd gained in his thirty-odd years was nothing compared to experiencing one afternoon with Mallory.

Their second time was even more explosive than the first. She had shown him a world he didn't know existed, a place without hurt or heartache, where lovers spoke a language that required no words. It was a paradise that needed visiting often. And he knew that he could go there with only one person.

Mallory Russell.

"Hi, Dr. Clayton." Brad looked up as a thin, happy voice interrupted his thought. He smiled at seven-year-old Michael Jamison.

Michael always came to see him. When Brad had first found him and brought him to the shelter he'd stayed with the frightened little boy. Mike had lost his family in a fire and clung to Brad as if he were a savior. Traumatized, the child had walked the streets for days, in shock, afraid and hiding. Brad had found him in the early hours of the morning, weaving back and forth like a drunk, or someone going into insulin shock. The child had passed out from hunger. For weeks he hadn't said a word, then one day he'd started to cry and scream for his parents. Brad had stood in as a surrogate until the worst of the trauma was over.

"Hi, Mike. What are you doing here?" he asked him now.

"I'm not sick," the little boy said. "I'm okay."

He emphasized the second syllable. "So I don't need a shot."

Brad laughed. "I don't always come with shots," he told him.

"I know."

"So are you doing all right in school?"

Mike frowned. "I don't like school."

"But…" Brad left the word hanging. They had an agreement about school.

"But I promised I'd try." He hung his head as he said it. Mike had promised Brad he would try his best to do well.

"I hear your teachers have good things to say about you."

"They do?" He perked up as if it were Christmas morning.

"They do." Brad's eyes narrowed on the boy. He was tall for his age and extremely observant. "Mike, how is Ellen doing? Has she made any friends?"

He hung his head again. "She doesn't like anyone. She kicks or screams at everyone who goes near her. I don't like her."

Brad looked at the boy with compassion. "She's been hurt, Mike. Remember when you first came here? You had been hurt, too."

Mike's face transformed as he remembered his parents. "Yeah, but I didn't try to kick anyone."

"She doesn't mean it. She's just scared." He paused to let the words sink in. "Could you try to be her friend? She needs a friend."

"How can I do that?" The seven-year-old frowned.

Brad gazed at him fondly. "Smile at her, even if she frowns at you. Sit with her at meals, even if she tells you to go away. And if she asks you what you want, just tell her you want to be her friend."

Mike stared at him for a long time. Brad wondered if the boy was weighing his words or trying to find a way to back out. "All right," the child agreed slowly and reluctantly.

"Trust me, Mike. She's not a mean person. She's more afraid of you than you know."

"Why's she afraid of me? I ain't done nothing."

"Haven't done anything," Brad corrected.

"I haven't." The child missed the short lesson in grammar.

"Try it, Mike?" The boy looked at his shoes. "For me?"

"All right," he said, drawing out the last word. "But..." He stopped.

"Go on," Brad prompted. "But what?"

"It's nothing." Mike looked at the floor.

"It must be something." He lifted the boy's chin. "You can tell me anything."

"Detective Ryan says you try to save everyone."

Detective Ryan told Brad that, as well. And often.

"It's something you'll learn about as you grow older, Mike."

"Detective Ryan also says you can't save everyone even if you do try."

"That's true," he agreed. "But try with Ellen."

"I will. He also says you have to try, even if you don't always win."

Mike left him with a smile and a grown-up hand-shake. Brad smiled to himself. The child who'd once clung to him desperately now walked away with a handshake. They grow up fast, Brad thought. The street did that. But at least Mike had taken his mind off of Mallory.

And Mallory had taken his mind off of Sharon Yarborough.

Mallory had already started up the stairs when she heard footsteps coming toward her. She pressed herself into the shadows against the wall. Consciously, she controlled her breathing, careful not to make a sound in the hollow stairwell that climbed to the top of the building. She didn't want the person to hear her. The stairs weren't often used, and at this hour she usually had them to herself.

Her heart pounded so loudly she could hear it in her ears. It muffled the approaching footsteps. Who was it? Where was he going? Would he come down to where she stood? She glanced at the door to the fifth floor; there was a station right inside it, she knew. She didn't want to go past it unless absolutely necessary. Mallory wasn't due back in the hospital until Monday, and she would have a hard time explaining her presence here if someone found her.

Don't panic, she said silently, closing her eyes to calm herself. She opened them again. It wouldn't be the end of the world if she were found. She would have some explaining to do, but she wasn't breaking any laws. Maybe unauthorized entry, but that would be a stretch. She didn't want to be found because of her patients. They needed her. They needed her to talk to them, to help wake them up.

The steps were heavy and continued toward her. A man, she thought. She would have to make a decision soon. She looked up. One more floor and she'd have to retreat. She would take her chances going down.

Mallory took a silent step toward the stairs, but stopped suddenly when she heard a door open below her. *Damn,* she cursed. There was someone below her, too. She was sandwiched between them. Mallory had no choice but to go onto the fifth floor. There was a slight chance that the staff on duty would be making their rounds and that the nurses' station would be clear. It was three o'clock in the morning, but remaining where she was wasn't an option. She snapped her head upward as the door on the sixth floor opened. The footsteps above her went silent. Mallory looked down as if she could see through the cement. The footsteps below were slow, but still coming. Quickly she left her place, racing up the stairs on feet that were as silent as feathers. On the seventh floor she peered through the door and checked the halls. It was clear. Mallory slipped through the door and quickly went into the darkened coma wing.

"Hello, Margaret," she whispered, out of breath. Her heart beat so fast it could keep time with "Fascinating Rhythm." "I know I'm a little late. I had trouble on the stairs." Mallory gulped to fill her lungs, then went into her one-sided questions, asking how Margaret was, as if she could answer. Then silence fell between them. Mallory thought of her own concerns. Brad.

She looked down at Margaret, a woman old enough to be Mallory's mother. Maybe if she talked to her, she could figure her way out of what was going on. *If* there was something going on.

"There's a doctor here in the hospital that I'm…involved with." She wasn't sure if that was entirely true, but it was as close as she could get to whatever was going on between herself and Brad.

"At first he needed someone to talk to and I was there." Mallory knew Brad had used her, but it was harmless. She'd listened to him and nothing more. Until last night. "Things have gone a little further now."

A little further. She wanted to laugh out loud. A little further was like saying the Grand Canyon was just a hole in the ground. What had happened between her and Brad was like the earth moving off its axis.

"I don't mean that he's using me. He isn't."

Mallory took hold of Margaret's hand. She herself was the one who needed the touch, the consoling.

"I think I'm falling in love with him." Mallory said it quietly. She stared at the window blinds. Through them she saw the moon and stars. Outside it was cold, but inside Mallory there was a roaring furnace. "I can't be in love with him." She was no longer talking to Margaret Keller. "Falling in love would screw up everything. I have too much to do." She looked around. "Here. These are the people who need me. The poor ones. The ones without family or visitors. Falling in love would mean accounting for my time to someone else.'' She couldn't do it. She knew what it was like to be in one of these beds. She knew the loneliness, the hours of time that passed by slowly and without the kindness of a human voice to fill the darkness. She couldn't condemn these patients to that.

And Brad—he had his own demons to deal with. But he had the most important thing. He had family. People who loved and supported him. He had a mother, even though she'd left him years ago. She was still alive and there was a slim chance that they could now develop a relationship if they both wanted that.

Brad and Mallory had too much to separate them and not enough to bring them together. Then she thought of Brad kissing her, making love to her. She closed her eyes as her mind took her back to the tangled sheets of her bedroom and the hard body that had kept her there.

''There has to be another option,'' she said.

By the time Mallory's week of forced vacation ended and she returned to work, she hadn't seen or heard from Brad. She wondered if he had the same misgivings about their night together that she had. She'd tried to rationalize her actions. She'd tried to tell herself it meant nothing. She'd tried to talk herself into believing it hadn't happened, but then she would remember their lovemaking and her body would heat up to a point of meltdown. Denial was futile.

In the E.R., she picked up the chart of her first patient and read it as she opened the curtain and looked inside.

"Good morning, Cindy." She smiled at a pretty twenty-three-year-old lying in the hospital bed. "I'm Dr. Russell. What happened to you?" Mallory hated that she always had to ask the same question a nurse and sometimes the police had already asked. In Cindy's case there were no uniforms around. Mallory was glad of that. After Wayne Mason, her heart tripped each time she saw police in the E.R.

Mallory visited patient after patient. The E.R. hadn't changed since she'd been away. The morning flew by. Each time she moved about the department she looked for Brad. He didn't have to come to the E.R. often, but she'd gotten used to seeing him there.

She wondered what he'd decided to do about his mother. Had he called his family and told them? Mallory had many questions for Brad. She'd missed him more than she thought she would. But he was busy at the hospital and the shelter. And they hadn't really had a date. She'd invited him to go ballooning because she wanted to be with him. And he'd come to her more than once when he needed someone. It had joined her to him in friendship if nothing else. But she knew their relationship was more than that.

"Hey, how about some lunch?" Dana Baldwin asked, stopping behind Mallory.

"Lunch would be great." Mallory stretched, placing her hands on her back. "It's time for my nap."

Dana laughed. "You take a nap? I'll never believe

it. But I do want to know what you did on your vacation, since you were never home.''

They left the hospital and went to a deli across the street, where a lot of the nurses and doctors ate. The place was mobbed, but Dana knew how to handle crowds. She pushed her way through the maze and ordered sandwiches and drinks. Then they left the noise and chaos for the quiet of Dana's van.

''What did you do while you were off?'' Dana bit into her sandwich.

Mallory knew she had to be careful about what she said. Dana was her friend, but Brad also trusted her. Mallory didn't want anything to jeopardize his trust.

''I went ballooning.''

Dana frowned. ''I don't see how you can do that.''

''You should come sometime. It's beautiful up there.'' The sky had never been so beautiful as it was the last time she went up. Brad had been with her.

''It might be, but it's beautiful down here, too, and I like my feet on the ground.''

Mallory smiled and didn't comment. She knew that ballooning wasn't for everyone. ''How were things around here?''

''It was really busy. We could have used you, but we were ordered not to call you under any circumstances.''

''By whom?''

''Dr. Clayton.'' Dana stared directly at her. Mallory tried to keep her expression neutral. ''I think he really cares about you.''

Mallory was in the midst of drinking from her soda.

She choked on the liquid, coughing to cover her surprise.

"Dr. Clayton!" she said with artificial surprise in her voice. "Why would you think that?"

"The man has an attitude, for sure." Dana raised one eyebrow. "But he's taken an interest in you particularly. The night after the incident in the E.R. he kept asking questions about you, wanted to make sure you had someone to watch over you. Then he found out how often you're on call. He made comments about how tired you look some days, and how rested on others. He never noticed anything about anyone else. And believe me, many of the nurses have tried to catch his eye. To top things off he forbade the staff from calling you after he forced you to take a vacation. His interest in you can only mean one thing."

Mallory had stopped eating. Her ears were so hot she was sure flames were shooting into her hairline. "Gossip," she said.

"Love," Dana countered, dropping her hands to her lap.

Mallory frowned, but the idea wasn't repulsive. In fact, she liked it. She held that inside and felt her heart flutter. She would love to take Dana into her confidence, but she hadn't worked everything out in her own head yet. Until then she couldn't even let her friend know how she felt.

"Can you picture Brad Clayton in love?" Mallory asked. She could very well imagine it. In fact, her body was passionately aware of his lovemaking. Him being in love wasn't a huge leap. Him acknowledging he was in love was a gulf as wide as the Pacific.

"I guess not," Dana finally said with a sigh. "But it was a nice thought. And I still think he feels something for you."

"He doesn't feel anything for me, and if he did, it would probably scare him."

"I'm sure it does. He's been around here for years and never looked twice at anyone until you walked through the door."

"Dana, he never noticed me until that day in the E.R." She couldn't bring herself to mention the incident by name.

"There has to be something that initiates every meeting. Yours was a little unconventional."

"Yeah, we all want to meet during a near-death experience."

"And the hero rushes over to take care of the damsel in distress."

"I was not in distress, and Brad certainly didn't rush over. He only acted like a doctor. There was nothing more to it than that." Mallory bit into her sandwich to avert her eyes.

"I know Dr. Clayton has a lot of problems, but it would do him good to talk them out with someone. And I think the someone he's chosen is you."

"When did you go into psychology?" Mallory wanted to end this discussion. Her feelings for Brad were a little too close to the surface, and if Dana looked closely enough, she was bound to see them.

"Psychology is only human nature, and I've seen

enough of that. They pay me to observe, read what people say and what they *don't* say.'' She stared directly into Mallory's eyes. "Like now.''

"What does that mean?'' Mallory controlled her voice, which wanted to rise an octave. She felt a nervousness in her stomach and wondered if she'd already played her hand.

"It means you're defending him. And that is something in itself. It means something must have changed between you two.'' Dana paused to let her words sink in. "So tell Dr. Dana what it is.''

Mallory was about to burst, wanting to tell someone how she felt, what had happened. But she'd promised Brad she would keep his secret. Dana was waiting for her to say something. She could lie to her, but Dana was smarter than that.

"Dana, is the staff gossiping about Dr. Clayton and me?''

Dana shook her head. "There have been a few comments on his change in attitude toward you, but mostly the talk has to do with the ghost. She was seen last week while you were away.''

Mallory expelled a relieved, yet controlled, breath. The temptation was there. She tried to think of one tidbit she could tell Dana, but anything she said would lead to something else, and soon she would have to tell everything, including Brad's secrets. She knew she wouldn't do that.

"Dana, there is nothing I can tell you that has changed.'' Mallory chose her words carefully.

* * *

This was highly unusual, Mallory told herself for the thirtieth time that afternoon. Since when did a doctor get transferred in the middle of the day, let alone after lunch? And without notice. Yet here she was on the second floor. In pediatrics. Where Brad ruled. He had to have a hand in this, and Mallory didn't like it. She didn't like being manipulated.

Still, it was her job to be cheery, so she put a smile on her face before she went into the room where a little girl, Loretta Emery, lay on a hospital bed. The smile was genuine. As soon as Mallory saw the small child her mouth automatically curved up.

"Hi, Loretta," Mallory said.

The child's eyes opened slowly. She turned her head toward Mallory, but said nothing. The child was alone and Mallory wondered where her mother was.

"I'm Dr. Russell. I'm here to see how you're doing."

"I'm sick." Her voice was thin.

"Can you tell me what made you sick?"

She shook her head. "When I woke up I didn't feel good. Dr. Clayton said I should come here."

Mallory went to the head of the bed. She felt the child's forehead, not so much to check for a temperature as to comfort her. The child looked small and afraid. Mallory consulted the chart where the nurses noted the child's vitals. She had a slight fever and an elevated blood pressure. Flipping through the pages, Mallory noted a previous diagnosis: acute lymphoblastic leukemia.

Her heart sank. The child had been admitted earlier

today. Blood had been drawn, but the lab results were not available yet. Looking further, Mallory discovered the child's spleen had been removed seven months ago. Her prognosis didn't look good.

"Where do you live, Loretta?" Mallory tried to sound happy. Until the lab work came back there was little she could do except stay with the child and keep her from being frightened.

"I'm Lori," she said. "Everyone calls me that."

"All right, Lori, where do you live?"

"At the shelter."

Homelessness in Philadelphia was rapidly reaching epidemic proportions. The foster care system was so overburdened that children stayed in shelters longer than they should.

"How did you get here?" Mallory asked.

"I brought her." Mallory jumped at the sound of Brad's voice. She steeled herself to look at him. She hadn't seen him since the night they'd made love. She didn't want their reunion to be here, over a sick child. She wanted to see him someplace outside the hospital, where she could run into his arms and feel the strength of that magnificent body.

When Mallory turned to look into his eyes what she saw turned her blood to ice. There was no warmth in them at all. She could tell he'd crawled back into the shell he presented to the world. Mallory had thought she'd cracked it, broken it open, but the look in his eyes showed her it was solidly in place. She knew the words. She'd heard them before. *Forget we ever had anything together.*

Brad moved to the side of the bed and ran his hand over Lori's hair. The child tried to smile at him, but she was too weak.

"I'm still waiting for your test results," he told her. "I want you to get some sleep."

Lori closed her eyes and settled into the pillow. Brad had a talent with children. They loved him and he had a genius for showing them he cared about their well-being. Mallory was exactly the opposite. She could cope with any emergency, but to see children suffering tore at her heart.

"Dr. Russell?" Brad had called her name twice before she heard him. She looked up. "Come with me."

Outside the child's room Mallory's composure came back. She walked along with Brad as they headed down the hall.

"I see you went back to the Bradley School of Charm in the last few days."

"What?" He stopped.

"Your attitude is back. What happened to you? I haven't seen you since..." She paused, remembering their night together and their morning. When he'd left her she would have sworn he was a changed man. "I thought you'd act more human."

"Human?" Brad looked around. A couple of people were staring at them. They quickly looked away when his eyes settled on them. Grabbing her arm, he pushed her down the hall to his office. Closing the door, he turned to face her. "We need to talk."

"About what?"

"About us."

"There is no us. You've already decided that."

Brad looked at the floor, then back at her. "I'm sorry things got out of hand at your place, but they can't spill over here."

"Things didn't get out of hand at my place. They changed after you left. After you had time to think about us. After you saw how good we were together. It scared you, didn't it, Brad?" She waited a moment. "It scared me, too."

"This is pediatrics, Mallory, not psychiatry."

"You won't acknowledge it. You're so wrapped up in trying to save every child, trying to find that child who was lost on the street, you can't even see what you're doing to yourself."

"And what am I doing to myself?"

Mallory wanted to hit him. He was mocking her. "You're trying to find yourself. It's too late, Brad. The kid that was you is not out there. He's in here."

"What do you know of it? You grew up in the well-ordered world of people who loved you from the day you were born. You weren't left to fend for yourself, eating out of garbage cans and never knowing who the next bully would be who wanted to take you out."

"You're right, I don't know. I don't know life on the streets. But I do know what it's like to be alone and afraid and feel as if no one understands you." Mallory drew in a deep breath. "I also know what it's like to have a mother abandon you."

With that she pushed him aside and opened the door to leave.

Chapter Seven

Brad's eyes snapped open. The dimness of his bedroom revealed familiar objects as the cloud of dreams in his mind vaporized. His heart drummed inside his chest. He swung his feet to the floor, sitting up and dropping his head in his hands. He hadn't had that dream in years. And now he'd had it three times in one week.

It was raining hard. Water ran in rivers down the gutters and lightning flashed over trash cans in back alleys. He'd been running, jumping over fences, skidding around corners, the police on his heels. But he knew the alleyways, knew where to find unlocked doorways, vacant buildings and the maze of tunnels that offered sanctuary or escape. Brad had been alone. He didn't know where his brother was, but Owen and he had a meeting place.

Brad didn't give any further thought to Owen. He concentrated on running, getting away from the cops behind him. His breath came in short gasps and his feet pounded the ground with the same rapid cadence as his heartbeat. His lungs burned from exertion and he thought his legs would burst into flames at any moment. Still the cops followed. He searched his brain for a way out, a place he could go that would throw them off, slow them down, but he couldn't think.

He sucked in air and remembered to breathe through his nose. The rain soaked his clothes. Water squished inside his sneakers as he ran through puddles in his quest to remain free. He wasn't going to make it. He could feel the cops getting closer. What would he do if he was caught? Where was Owen?

Brad hopped the fence, bending both knees and angling his agile body sideways. Surefooted, he hit the ground, continuing his escape without missing a beat. Sweat poured off him and he was hungry. That's how he'd gotten into this foot race: he'd stolen a candy bar. He hadn't had anything to eat all day and didn't think anyone would see him. He'd been nearly through the door of the convenience store when the cop came in. Chaos broke out and he took off, focused solely on escape. He could usually lose the cops within a block or two, but whoever was behind him this time dogged him like a shadow.

Brad pushed himself on, despite his burning lungs and fiery legs. The rain did nothing to cool the heat in his muscles. He kept going, but he could feel the hand behind him. It was close. Soon he would feel it on his collar, yanking him back. He feared that hand more than he feared going without food or never seeing Owen. There was something about it that would change his life, if not end it. He had to get away.

He ran as fast as he could, but it wasn't fast enough. He was slowing already, allowing the man behind him to shorten the distance between them. Suddenly he felt the hand on his collar.

And he opened his eyes.

Brad drew breath into his lungs. He took long, deep gulps of air, filling his lungs as if he'd been a drowning swimmer who reached the surface in the nick of time. Relief spread through him. He was in his bedroom, safe. No one was chasing him. The wind outside was thrashing rain against the windows....

That had to be it, he thought. Rain was the trigger that had caused the dream. It took a while for his heart rate to return to normal, but the feeling in his stomach told him something was utterly wrong.

The clock dial read one o'clock. He'd only been in bed for an hour, yet he knew his night's sleep was shot. The dream always disturbed him. Growing up in a secure environment after he'd been caught and sent to the Claytons didn't negate the time he and Owen had been homeless.

Brad grabbed his clothes and dressed. Water pounded at the windows as if someone was trying to get inside. Brad ignored it. He would go for a drive. He wanted to go to Mallory. Talking to her made him feel better. But he'd insinuated himself in her life too much and he didn't want to go deeper. Last week he'd crossed the line. Hell, he had obliterated it. And today in pediatrics, she'd been right on the mark.

He wouldn't go near her. He would just go out for a drive.

"Dr. Clayton, I didn't expect to see you." One of the night nurses at the pediatric station stood up when he stepped off the elevator. She inclined her head at a questioning angle, obviously curious about his presence.

"I just wanted to check on a couple of patients." He took a step toward Lori's room.

The nurse stopped him. "Dr. Clayton." Her voice was soft, but commanding. Brad turned back. He could tell by her expression Lori was gone. The woman didn't have to tell him. He could see it in her eyes, hear it in the unspoken communication that reached across the silent corridor.

"When?" he asked.

"Twenty minutes ago. We've had several power surges due to the rain. The wind scared a lot of the children. We've only just gotten them calmed down. I was about to call you."

Brad felt the emptiness inside him. He glanced at the door to Lori's room. It was closed. No light came from under it. He knew she'd already been moved. The cleanup crew had gone in, sanitized everything, remade the bed with clean sheets and replaced all the pitchers and cups. The drawers to the nightstand had been cleaned, the floors mopped, the tray table sterilized. It was as if Lori had never been in that room.

"It was quick," the nurse said from behind him. She must have moved, for her voice sounded closer. He didn't turn to look. "She slipped away in her sleep. There was nothing we could do. No warning. Suddenly the machines buzzed. We tried to resuscitate her, but it was too late."

Brad turned then. "I understand," he said as quietly as he could. He hadn't thought she would last through the night, but he'd hoped… "I'm all right," he told the nurse, who looked at him as if he needed medical care. She waited a moment, then returned to the desk.

Brad felt sick. He had to get out of there. He pushed open the door to the stairs and went through it. With his back against the wall and his hands in tight fists, he took in long breaths. Lori was so young. She'd come to the shelter only three months ago. She and her mother, both ill, were apparently too late for care. Her mother had run away from an abusive husband and had gone to the shelter. She'd been beaten badly. Christina, the shelter nurse, had called an ambulance and the paramedics had brought the two of them to the hospital.

The arriving siren had stopped Brad as he was on his way out of the hospital. He couldn't go home after he'd seen the child. She was bruised, pale and afraid, and all around her people had been barking orders and using instruments that were scary to a child.

They had taken her mother to surgery immediately,

but it was too late. She had died before she ever got to the O.R. And he had discovered Lori had leukemia.

Leaning his head back against the cold cement wall, Brad closed his eyes and practiced his breathing. It was a calming effort. He did it to bring down his stress level. He knew he couldn't save the world. How often had Owen, Digger and Luanne said that to him? Still he wanted to try. Lori had been a beautiful child. In her short life she'd known few pleasures. He'd wanted to make her feel that she could laugh before she died. He'd known her time was short. There was nothing they could do to arrest the cancer, but he'd wanted her to lose the wariness, be content that no one was lurking about, ready to pounce on her if she let herself feel happy.

Brad hung his head and opened his eyes. He would be forever sorry he couldn't help Lori.

Somewhere, his brain registered something else— a faint sound. Brad latched on to it, wanting something to take his mind off the little girl. Then he heard them.

Footsteps.

He looked up. It was her.

The ghost, he thought.

Brad pushed away from the wall, trying to see better. She was wearing the outfit the nurses talked about—everything white except a green scarf that hung from the pocket of her pants. Brad had seen that first, but he hadn't seen her face. He assumed she'd seen him and retreated. He started up the stairs. There were few places she could go. He would bet she'd get out on the coma floor. It had the least amount of people on it at this hour, and she could use the bridge to get to the other building.

Brad rushed up the stairs, bent on discovering the identity of the person who'd broken more hospital rules than he could count. His footsteps echoed in the stairwell and in his ears, but he kept his focus. He had something to keep him from thinking about Lori. He would find the ghost.

On the seventh floor he yanked open the door and stepped inside. He looked up and down the empty corridor. There was no sign of the ghost anywhere. Still, he knew she couldn't have disappeared into thin air. He sprinted for the ward. Breaking through it without slowing down, he caught the hand rail of the next set of stairs to slow his speed.

His labored breathing obliterated any sounds. Forcing himself to hold his breath for a moment, he heard the cadence of footsteps below, and raced toward them. He saw the green scarf as the woman swung around a corner. He ran on, rushing down the steps toward the ground floor. Finally he was going to see who this was. She was only one flight away, and even if she reached the door, the only thing outside was the parking lot. He could easily catch her. There was no place to hide.

Brad reached out. His hand closed over her white-clad arm. She resisted, but he held tight. Pulling back, he forced her to slow down. Possessing a greater strength than the woman fighting him, Brad whipped her around.

Just then the lights went out, plunging them both into absolute darkness.

The blackout was surprising, but it gave Mallory the opportunity she needed. She had known it was Brad chasing her. She'd seen him standing in the stairwell and had panicked. Then the hunt had begun.

She recovered from the sudden blackness before he did. Yanking her arm free, she dropped to a crouch, grabbed his ankles and pulled him off balance. He went down hard on the concrete floor.

Mallory heard Brad cry out in pain, but knew he hadn't hurt more than his pride. Sitting might be difficult for a day or so, but he would be all right. She fled.

She was accustomed to darkness and stairwells. She knew exactly which landing they were on and how many stairs she had to descend in order to reach the exit. Counting to herself, she agilely negotiated the steps, her feet as sure as if she'd grown up climbing mountains.

With only a second to spare, Mallory went through the door on the ground floor as the emergency generators kicked in and the lights came on. There were no patient rooms or nurses' stations on the first floor. The space was designed for admitting and discharging patients, giving information and directing visitors. The emergency room was on the other side of the building.

Brad wouldn't be far behind her. There was an exit only a few feet away. Mallory turned toward it; that

was the logical place for her to go. She opened the
door wide, but instead of going through it, she let it
swing shut, and ran along the corridor instead. All
elevators in the hospital automatically returned to the
first floor when not in use. She pushed the button and
the doors opened with a silent whoosh of air.

Mallory got in.

She laughed as she drove away from the hospital
long minutes later. She'd escaped. She'd escaped
from Brad. He would love to find out who she was,
who the ghost was. He was adamant about turning the
intruder over to hospital security. She would have
loved to have seen his face when he discovered it was
her.

Her laughter stopped. It would be awful if he did
catch her. What would happen to Margaret Keller?
She hadn't wakened. She still had no visitors. And
the other patients? The ones Mallory hadn't gotten
to?

Tonight she'd had a close call. She couldn't let it
happen again. And she knew security would be tighter
from now on. Brad would make certain of that.

Her phone was ringing as she came through the
door. Mallory ran for it, shrugging out of her coat and
picking up the receiver.

"Hello," she said, sure at this hour it had to be the
hospital.

"Mallory."

"Brad?"

Nature dictated that the oldest had more experience
and was therefore the wiser. But there were excep-

tions to every rule, and Brad and his older brother, Owen, constituted an exception. Brad had been the one finding food and places for them to sleep after their mother left. He'd eluded the police and come up with the meeting place in case the two of them got separated. Brad had taken care of Owen instead of the other way around. But they loved each other, bonding by blood and circumstance. No one could separate them and they would never abandon each other.

Owen had long ago come to terms with their mother's disappearance. Or so he'd led everyone to believe. He played the happy-go-lucky role, but Brad understood his brother well and knew it was only an act. Still, how Owen would react when he learned their mother was alive and living only a few hundred miles away was an unknown.

Brad's own reaction to the news had been unexpected. He'd always sworn that if he ever found out where she was, he would be there in no time, confronting her, accusing her, demanding to know why she'd left them, why she'd stopped loving them. Why she'd allowed them to spend the last twenty years living in limbo, not knowing if she was alive or dead. Yet he hadn't done it. He'd kept the information to himself. He hadn't called Owen or his adopted brothers and sisters. He hadn't flown to Austin to confront her. He hadn't told a soul. Only Mallory.

He missed seeing her, holding her. As much as his reaction—rather his nonreaction—to his mother's situation had surprised him, his reaction to Mallory was

an equal, though pleasant, surprise. He'd gone to her
on several occasions when he needed someone. And
he wanted to keep going. He liked the way he could
talk to her, tell her his secrets and not find them on
the lips of every nurse in the E.R. He liked the way
she felt in his arms, the way she handled a hot-air
balloon. He liked everything about her. He needed
her.

Earlier tonight he'd almost driven to her house. After learning the news about Lori's death and then
chasing and missing the "ghost," he could only think
of going to see Mallory. He wondered about her all
the time. Yet when he saw her he wouldn't let on that
she was anything more to him than one of the hospital
residents.

But she was more.

Much more.

He knew he was acting like jerk. Owen would be
the first to tell him so. Brad had called her from the
police station, had gone ballooning with her and had
spent the most wonderful night of his life in her arms.
Still, he couldn't let Mallory think that their night
together meant anything more than two adults needing sexual gratification. He couldn't let her see that it
meant more than that to him.

It was his way of slowing things down before they
led anywhere. He didn't often find himself in this position. He stayed away from entanglements with
women. Those he slept with were one-night stands or
women who weren't looking for long-term relationships.

But with Mallory it was different. It hadn't started out being serious. It had just happened. And he couldn't let it go any further. Every woman he'd ever been close to had left him, starting with his mother.

Sharon Yarborough. Thinking of her reminded him of Owen. Brad needed to tell him.

He reached for the phone....

Brad's deep baritone voice came across the line. Mallory froze. Had he known he was chasing her?

"Are you still my therapist?" he asked.

He was sending such mixed messages. He'd stood over Lori's bed and virtually told Mallory to steer clear of him. And now he was on the phone asking her to be his confidante. If he were someone else, she would have thought he was playing head games with her, but the tone of his voice said something else.

"Of course," she heard herself saying. She sat on a kitchen stool, apprehension causing her heartbeat to accelerate. "Are you in need of therapy?"

Mallory wondered what kind of therapy. It was the early hours of the morning. Did they need a session tonight? Would she see him? How she hoped so. She wanted him...in her bed.

"I'm sorry, Mallory. I don't need to involve you in..." He left the sentence hanging.

"Has something happened?" Mallory asked, genuinely concerned.

"Lori died tonight." His voice was strained. Mallory could hear the pain in it. Like cold water, his words instantly doused the fire that had ignited inside her, and she also felt a little guilty for her thoughts.

"Are you at the hospital?"

"No, I'm home."

"I'll be right over." Mallory hung up and grabbed her coat. She didn't give Brad time to refuse her offer. He was concerned about all his patients, but since she'd found out about the shelter, she'd discovered he had a special connection to the children who came from there.

She was almost out the door when she remembered where she had been tonight and what she was wearing. Backtracking, she removed her white uniform, and hid the key hanging from the green chain in her pocket and changed into jeans and a sweater.

Morning rush hour hadn't begun yet. The wind had died down and the storm had passed over the city. Power lines were down and tree branches scattered the road. Mallory wove her way around them and drove to Brad's.

"I'm so sorry," she said when he opened the door. "I know Lori had a special place in your heart."

"You didn't have to drive all the way over here. I'm all right."

"I know you are. I'm the one who needs therapy." Mallory rushed into his arms. In a second she felt Brad's arms encircle her. He pulled her close, burying his face in her hair and holding her almost as desperately. They stood in the doorway taking deep breaths and drawing what they needed from each other. Mallory let Brad take strength from her. She took the comfort of his arms, even knowing that there was no future for them.

When he finally loosened his hold, he kept his arm around her waist and closed the door. Together they walked into his living room and sat on the sofa. The lights were off, leaving only a wedge of illumination coming from the hall.

"When your residency is over, are you going into psychiatry?"

"I gave it some thought," Mallory told him seriously.

"Many of the nurses have said you're very easy to talk to. It seems like a natural direction for your career to take."

Mallory smoothed her hands over Brad's. "Tell me about the kids at the shelter."

He took a deep breath and rested his head against the back of the sofa. "Lori had only been there a few months."

"Not the shelter here," she murmured. "Tell me about the shelter you and your brother were sent to."

He untangled his fingers from hers and leaned forward.

"There wasn't a shelter for us. We were sent directly to foster care. And we ran away after the first night."

"Didn't the family care for you?"

"They weren't really interested in us. They were in it for the money, but that's not why we left."

Mallory waited in the darkness.

"Owen and I were sure our mother was coming

back. If we weren't there she wouldn't know where to find us. But she never returned.''

''And you and Owen eventually found a happy family and grew up to be a doctor and an architect.''

''We were lucky.''

''About Lori...''

''She wasn't so lucky. She'd been abused, not properly cared for. She was afraid of anyone who came near her.'' He turned then and looked over his shoulder. Mallory knew he couldn't see her features. ''Except you. She trusted you immediately.''

''Her counts weren't good. There was nothing you could have done.''

In the dark his head bobbed up and down. ''I know.''

Mallory recognized something else in his voice. ''Was there anything you wanted to say to her that you didn't get to say?''

He shook his head. ''I didn't want her to be afraid.''

''Of dying?''

''She wasn't afraid of dying. She was afraid of being hurt. So little in her life had been pleasant. I wanted to do something for her.''

''You did,'' Mallory told him. ''You made her laugh. Do you know how powerful that is? For a child who has nothing, laughter is the first sign of trust. You gave that to Lori.''

Brad was quiet. He would need time to let it sink in, time to believe he had done something truly worthwhile. Perhaps bringing laughter to a patient wasn't considered hard to do, but to a child who'd been abused, his efforts amounted to a miracle.

"Are you sure you're not going into psychiatry? Because you're very good at it," he finally said.

"The mind does interest me, but I'm more interested in its physiology than its psychology."

"Brain surgery?"

"Yes."

"You are full of surprises. Had I been given a list, that is the last one I would have chosen."

She hunched her shoulders. "Looks can be deceiving."

"You've proved that more than once."

"We're not talking about me. This is your session. Why don't you tell me about Owen?"

She needed to get his mind onto other things.

Brad sat back again. He didn't take her hand, but he smiled. Mallory heard it. "He's the best architect in Texas."

"I suppose he says that."

"All of the time. But he is good, exceptionally good."

"What else does he do?"

"He collects marbles."

"Marbles? Why marbles?"

"When we were kids he was the champion marbles player. He had all kinds, cat's eyes, clear, steelies, aggies. He has a whole room in his house where he has them on display. You'd be amazed at some of the designs he's made with them."

"And what do you collect, Brad?"

"Nothing."

"Don't you? What about children?"

"I don't collect—"

"Ellen Grant, Michael Jamison, Barbara Correy, Kadeshia Speer." She listed them. "They're all at the shelter because you found them on the streets and took them in."

"I couldn't leave them out there."

"That's not the point. The point is you didn't just happen upon them. You went looking for them."

"They needed someone to look for them."

"They needed the police or social services. They didn't need a doctor out scouring the streets, getting arrested for kidnapping, or a worst fate. You have important work in the hospital to tend to. There are lives there that depend on you. Working all day and combing the streets at night will burn you out, and then you'll be no good to anyone."

"I can handle it."

"No, you can't." She paused for effect, and to take the sting out of her words she grasped his hands and held them. "If you could handle it, you wouldn't have called me."

"All right, I admit it. I collect homeless children. Is that the first step in curing me?"

"It's not a joke, Brad."

His fingers squeezed hers and quickly released them. He didn't want her to know that her words really affected him. And she was about to increase the pressure. "You're not looking for homeless children. You're trying to find yourself. Don't you know they're all you? That each one of those kids represents a piece of you.''

''Is that what you think? That I'm out there trying to find myself?''

''Can you tell me different?''

''Sure I can.'' He got up and pushed his hands into his pockets, pacing back and forth.

''Brad, you're a very talented doctor. If something happens to you, medicine would lose, and all those children you're trying to save won't have you as their advocate.''

He stopped pacing. Mallory remained quiet. Her voice was only a whisper in the dark. After a while she stood up. It was time for her to go. Brad needed to be by himself. He needed to think about some of the things she'd said to him.

At the door she turned. ''Get some sleep. And for a few hours try to forget everything that's going on,'' she said.

Brad nodded. He stared at her for a moment, making her uncomfortable. Then he took a step forward, reaching out to take her in his arms.

Mallory stepped back. ''Don't,'' she said. ''It's not that I don't want you to, but our lives don't connect.''

Chapter Eight

Rumor spread like a plague through the hospital. Rosa Clayton, star of billboards, subway posters and magazine covers, was in the building. Brad knew there was nothing he could do about it. Rosa couldn't help the disturbance she caused. She was beautiful and Brad was proud she was his sister. Tall and slender, with hair that swung in direct opposition to the wiggle in her hips, she naturally drew attention. Brad had seen many a guy glance in her direction. An equal number had to contend with him and Rosa's other brothers.

People had seen them together, and since her arrival, a steady stream of doctors and nurses gawked at them in the public cafeteria. Rosa had clear brown skin with undertones of yellow. She wore a yellow scarf today, enhancing even more her perpetually happy look the camera loved.

"Why can't we go somewhere else and eat?" Brad asked with irritation.

"And miss all these nurses staring at you?" she said sardonically, her mouth forming a mischievous pout.

"They're not looking at me."

Rosa Clayton glanced around and smiled. She raised her hand and waved her fingers at a first-year resident who couldn't keep his eyes off of her. Brad wasn't in the mood for his sister's antics today.

"And where is this lady doctor? I want to meet her."

"Rosa, let it go. There is nothing between the two of us."

Rosa opened her eyes wide, "It's been months," she told him. "Even you should have made a move by now."

"Rosa..." There was a warning in his tone. At that moment Mallory walked into the room and Brad couldn't help reacting. Whenever she was around his eyes were a slave to her. He looked away abruptly, becoming supremely interested in his half-eaten sandwich.

"Is that her?" Rosa turned around, following Brad's line of sight.

Not only did Rosa's gaze go to Mallory, half the people in the room swung around to look at her. Brad could see the expression on her face. She wanted to back out of the cafeteria. He wouldn't blame her if she did. But she wasn't going to get the chance. Rosa Clayton was on her feet and moving toward her.

Brad couldn't hear what Rosa said or what Mallory answered, but his sister returned to the table and Mallory went to the food line.

"She's going to join us."

"You know you aren't too big to be spanked. And that little act warrants a walloping."

Rosa raised her eyebrows. "You?" she said. "Hit someone? You'd just as soon cut off your right hand."

Brad didn't like living in a fishbowl. If he was sure Rosa would behave herself he would leave the two women alone and return to work. But he wasn't sure what either of them would say.

"So when are you going home again?" Rosa's change of subject caught him off guard.

"It just so happens I have a conference in Dallas, and I'll be going next week."

"Wonderful," she said. "We can make a reunion of it."

"I'm not going home for a reunion."

Rosa halted abruptly. It was her way of getting attention. Her entire body, which could be as fluid as water, turned to granite. He supposed it had something to do with her having to stand still for photos.

"You're not going home and not seeing anyone." She stated it as if it were an order.

"I have to go to a conference. There isn't time for visiting. As soon as it's over I have to return to work here."

"Bradley Randall Clayton, I will put your business all in the street if you try some foolishness like this."

He wished he hadn't told her. This trip to Texas would be different. He had a specific purpose that involved family. Not the family he'd grown up in, but the one he'd been denied. He needed to see his birth mother. And he didn't need to have the entire Clayton clan looking over his shoulder.

Brad didn't have time to think of a reply to his sister's threat. Mallory approached the table and sat down.

"You're causing quite a stir," she told Rosa. "I think everyone at Philadelphia General knows you're here. And they all want to meet you."

Rosa had that effect on people. She largely ignored the stares, but it made Brad uncomfortable. "Rosa likes the limelight," he said.

"Only at times," she corrected. "But it makes Brad crazy, so I particularly love to play it up when he's around. Do you know when he was a kid, he'd hide whenever anyone we didn't know came to the door?"

Mallory glanced at him as she raised a soft drink from the tray.

"I did not hide." He spoke to Rosa, but his eyes were on Mallory.

"No, he just left the room."

"Rosa…" he said warningly again.

"Your brother tells me you live in New York City." Mallory changed the subject and Brad wondered if she did it for his benefit. She seemed to be able to tune in to his feelings without him being aware of it. The fact that she could tell what he thought and felt made him both uneasy and elated. There were so few people who had been able to understand his sudden mood changes. He knew he perplexed some members of his family. But not Rosa.

"I do. It's convenient for work, but I really like small towns. What about you? Do you like living in a big city?"

"I've lived here most of my life."

"Mallory lives in a house that her family has had for generations," Brad interjected. Rosa turned her attention to him and he knew by her look he'd stepped right into her trap.

"You've been there then?" The question was delivered with a raised eyebrow that Brad knew meant she was searching for answers. He finally realized why Rosa had suddenly appeared for lunch. She was probing, prying into his life. She thought he was too much alone and that he needed to find a wife. He hadn't mentioned Mallory to her since the night of the emergency room incident with Wayne Mason, but Rosa obviously had not forgotten it.

"Brad met me one morning and we went ballooning."

"Brad went up in a balloon? A hot-air balloon?" She shifted her gaze from Brad to Mallory. "With you?"

Before Mallory could answer, Brad jumped in. "Rosa, I know what you're doing. Stop it."

The two women glanced at each other. He could

see the conspiracy in their look. They didn't know one another, but there seemed to be an unspoken communication and understanding between them—unlike anything he'd ever seen among men.

"I'm not doing anything."

"You're trying to find out if there's something between us. Let me answer directly. No."

Rosa said something, but Brad didn't hear it. He was staring at Mallory. The impact of his words on her was obvious. She seemed to crawl inside herself.

He regretted it as soon as he realized his mistake. There *was* something between them. She'd mentioned the ballooning trip, but he remembered their afternoon after that trip. The long day in bed with her wrapped in his arms and his body filling hers.

"Rosa," she said in a voice that was lower than he'd ever heard it. She cleared her throat. "It was very nice meeting you, but I have to go back to my patients now."

Rosa glanced at Mallory's tray. Her food was only half-eaten. Both of them knew she was lying. She hadn't been paged or beeped. Her lunch hour wasn't over for another forty minutes. Yet she stood and smiled and walked away.

"How could you be so insensitive?" Rosa asked. "There's something so obvious between you that it's almost visible. And I'm sure your denial hurt Mallory's feelings." She leaned closer to him and lowered her voice. "But it scares you to death, doesn't it, Brad?"

"Rosa, stay out of my business."

They both stood up then and started for the same exit Mallory had taken. "Brad, you have to go after her."

"Leave it alone."

"But you hurt her feelings," Rosa insisted.

"Whatever I did or didn't do is no concern of yours."

"I know you didn't mean to do it. You're afraid she'll leave you like all the others."

Brad sighed heavily. He didn't want to talk about this. Rosa and the rest of his family knew about his mother and the two other serious relationships in his life that had ended miserably. The women from both relationships had moved, leaving him holding his heart in his hand.

He didn't want to be reminded that whenever he let someone in his life they eventually left him. Rosa concentrated on his relationships, but it had started with his father, his real father, not the man his mother married. His dad had left him before Brad was even old enough to know him. Then his grandmother died and his mother never returned. He refused to think about how devastated he was when the woman he'd been about to ask to marry him decided she was ending their relationship, not for another man, but for an out-of-town job. She hadn't even talked it over with him.

"It's been years since they left," Rosa pointed out. "Love is something you have to be willing to take a risk on. I can see you have serious feelings for Mallory. And she has feelings for you."

"Suppose it doesn't work? What then?"

"Then pick yourself up and try again."

"You say that with such ease."

"Words are easy. Look, brother dear, I know this is hard, but in the long run it could be worth it. But you'll never know if you run away every time a woman gets close. You saw how Digger shut down after Josh died and Marita left him. Then Erin came into his life and opened his heart. You know how happy they are."

Brad did know. His brother, who'd sworn he would never marry and have children again, who'd never even wanted to be around kids, had married last year and adopted a little girl. Digger did nothing but smile and talk about his new wife and family now. Brad envied him.

He looked back at his sister. She turned her big brown eyes on him.

"I'll go talk to her."

At the entrance to the hospital Rosa hugged him and said goodbye. "I'll see you in Dallas. Now go talk to Mallory," she urged.

Brad watched the tall, thin woman walk toward her car as if she were on the runway of some Paris fashion house. He waved as she continued out of view.

Where would Mallory be now? And why had she acted as she had earlier? The last time they had been together, she'd told him their lives didn't connect, that they weren't on the same plane. Yet he'd seen the hurt in her eyes at his comment just a few minutes ago.

When they were together it was incredible. He liked her, liked talking to her and making love with her. Rosa had said what they had between them was obvious, almost visible. Brad knew he liked being around Mallory, but his feelings weren't that deep. And he wasn't scared. Or was he? Could Rosa be right? Did he really have a deep-seated fear? Was he so entrenched in the past that he didn't even realize it? Ruled by a fear that made him push women away so he couldn't be hurt by them? So he would be left alone again?

Of all the women he'd ever known, Mallory was the one most in tune with his feelings. Yet they weren't a couple; both of them understood that.

Didn't they?

Mallory received a message from every nurse and doctor in pediatrics that Brad wanted to see her. She ignored them all, retreating to the coma section. There was no medical emergency. She was aware of all her patients' conditions. He could only want to talk about their conversation during lunch. She didn't want to.

Mallory went straight to Margaret Keller, taking her hand and pouring out her emotions to the serene sleeper. Brad had told her exactly what she meant to him: nothing. And she didn't need for him to elaborate. She didn't want to be involved with him, either. She knew that, had known it from the very start. Yet she'd been pulled in by his charm, the compassion that seemed to be reserved for her and the children he cared for. She'd let herself fall victim to a false sense of promise. Without realizing it, she had hoped that Brad was falling in love with her.

She'd reluctantly let him into her life, into a vulnerable part of hers. She'd listened to his problems and hoped she was helping him work through them. She'd also hoped she was more than just a therapist or friend, but she knew the hard, cold truth now. A single comment to his sister told Mallory everything she needed to know. She was nothing to him and never would be. Brad Clayton was an island unto himself. He was not planning to sail away from it or to invite others to join him there. He was content, happy to be the master of his world, happy to control it as it was and as he wished it to remain.

There was more to the complicated Brad Clayton than the nurses knew. He wasn't just a moody doctor with a huge chip on his shoulder. He was a man who didn't like change. And Mallory represented change.

"It's all right," she said to Margaret. "I shouldn't have let him get to me." She held the woman's hand, knowing being in the coma wing at this time of day would be suspect if she were discovered. "I wonder why he has that effect on me?" She looked at the silent coma patient. "Was there someone like that in your life? Sometimes I hate him and other times…" She stopped. What was she thinking? At other times, what? She loved him?

Mallory shook her head. She wasn't in love with Brad. He was too moody, had too many problems. He didn't need her or want her. No, that wasn't the truth. She and Brad had made love, and if he didn't want her he was the best actor in the world. She'd never felt so alive as when they were together.

She couldn't be in love with Brad. It would screw up everything. She looked again at Margaret. She wasn't the only one reaching out to people. Brad had his own kind of coma wing. He took care of children by day, at the hospital and in the shelter, but by night he prowled the streets, looking for lost ones to save. Mallory channeled her efforts into reaching the sleeping.

She stared at Margaret, listened to her breathing, watched the steady rise and fall of her chest. The woman slept on, oblivious to Mallory and her dilemma. After a long pause, Mallory finally admitted it. She *was* in love with Brad.

"Aren't you the lucky one?" Dana Baldwin's bright smile greeted a sleepy Mallory as she entered the hospital the next morning.

"What are you talking about?"

"The neurology conference in Dallas. The handsome Dr. Clayton is going to go with you."

Dana made it sound like an enviable proposition. Mallory didn't feel that way, especially after her afternoon with Margaret and her sleepless night thinking about what she'd discovered about herself.

"He's not scheduled to go." Mallory was presenting a paper at the conference in Dallas. She and several doctors from the trauma unit were attending, but Brad was not one of them.

"Plans have changed," Dana said. Her flippancy

grated on Mallory's nerves. "I heard the good doctor requested to go." Dana rolled her eyes. "I'll bet his decision has something to do with you."

"You'd lose that one."

Mallory didn't know what to think. She wavered between excitement at spending days with Brad and fear that she wouldn't be able to conceal her true feelings if she was with him for any length of time.

"By the way, you should steer clear of Dr. Allen today. She knows about you and Brad and she has designs on the man." Dana recaptured Mallory's attention. What did the nurse mean about her and Brad? Mallory wouldn't ask. She was in no condition to argue. Instead she thought of Dr. Stacy Allen, who made no secret of her attraction to Brad. But from what Mallory had seen, the affection wasn't returned.

"There is no me and Brad. If she wants him, he's hers." She didn't sound convincing even to herself.

"I think *he* might have something to say about that. Obviously he's chosen you."

They reached the doctor's dressing room. Dana left Mallory with a smirk. Mallory opened her locker, putting her purse inside, where she kept a change of clothes and several pairs of shoes. She found the greatest drawback to being a doctor was the strain it put on her legs and feet. Changing shoes several times during her shift helped.

She closed the gray locker and spun the dial on her combination lock. Thoughts of Brad returned to her. He was going to Texas with her. Did he want her there when he met his mother? Mallory had acted as his therapist, first as a joke, though later he'd appeared to take it seriously. Was that the reason for him attending the conference?

Mallory saw her first patient moments after she left the staff room. From then on she had no time to think of anything except medical care. There were plenty of sick children in the pediatric department. She visited the ones she needed to see and kept to the busy schedule. She had no time to think about Brad until her lunch hour. When she walked into the cafeteria he was ahead of her in line. Unlike the day Rosa chose to visit, the place was nearly empty.

"I've been looking for you." He said it casually, as if they frequently met for lunch and she was slightly late for today's appointment.

"It's a lot busier here than it was in the emergency department." Mallory kept herself busy, trying to avoid running into him, but she had to see him every day for rounds. After that she would disappear into one of the children's rooms or the playroom to help someone. She also spent her share of time in the operating room.

Brad had a sandwich and a container of yogurt on his tray. He added a cup of coffee and paid for both their lunches. Mallory didn't protest. She didn't want to cause another scene. When Rosa was here with them, they'd caused a stir by sitting together. Mallory followed him to a table and sat down. "I hear you're attending the conference next week."

He nodded, choosing his coffee over the other items on his tray.

"Why did you request to go?" she asked immediately.

He stopped and looked directly at her. "I'm going to tell my family about my mother and I'm going to see her. I want you to be there with me."

Mallory forced the food in her mouth to go down her throat. Inside her something melted. She thought it was her heart. Brad had captured it. No matter that he didn't want it, he held it nevertheless.

"Am I your therapist or moral support?"

"A little of both."

"You don't need me there. From what you've told me, you have a large support system with your family. One of your sisters is a psychologist."

"It's not the same." Brad reached across the table and took Mallory's hand. His fingers were warm and firm, and the effect the simple act had on her senses was devastating. "They're too close. So many emotions are involved there. I need someone impartial."

"And you think that's me?" She hadn't meant to say it aloud. The words were out before she could stop them. She was far from impartial.

"Yes," he replied. They stared at each other across the table.

Mallory wanted to pull her hand away. She wanted to put her palms to her ears to try to calm the blood rushing through them. His voice had a unique combination of desperation and need in it. She was a doctor, sworn to take care of the sick. Brad was ill. He'd been sick a long time and finally there was a treatment for his particular disease.

Mallory knew it wasn't a cure. At least not yet. This disease had metastasized. It would take a while to clear it from his system. But it was curable.

And she had to be part of the cure.

The air in Texas had been thick and hot ever since Mallory got off the worst plane ride of her life. The flight had been smooth and the service excellent; the problem was Brad. She'd sat next to him throughout the three-hour trip. He'd been silent and uncommunicative. Despite her effort to draw him into a conversation, he'd appeared irritable and distracted. She tried to understand his mood, but frankly she was a little tired of it. The passing days hadn't changed him, they'd only made him worse.

Mallory stood in her fifteenth-story hotel room, looking at the windows of buildings across the street. Brad was in the room next door. The clerk at the desk assumed they were together and had given them rooms with connecting doors. Mallory had kept her side locked.

She was sure Brad hadn't been to see his mother yet. Mallory had seen him at most of the seminars she'd attended. She had the feeling he wanted to talk, maybe apologize, but time passed and he said nothing.

Had he called his family? Did they even know he was this close to them? His plans to come had been sudden, but from what he'd said about them, she'd assumed there would be a delegation of relatives at the airport complete with welcoming signs and balloons. But the group from Philadelphia General had gone to the taxi stand and on to the hotel without incident.

Mallory turned and stared at the connecting door. She wondered if Brad was in his room. The only time she was sure he was there was when he showered. Their bathrooms had adjoining walls and when the shower was on she could hear it. Not that the image in her mind was unpleasant, but the thought of that strong, healthy body lathered with soap, covered in cascading water, sent her senses into overdrive. There was no doubt in her mind that she was attracted to him. She had been since their first encounter. But if she was to list the qualities of her ideal mate, she would never choose someone who focused so inwardly. She needed someone to talk to her, share with her.

Crossing her arms, she acknowledged there was no chance of that. Brad had apologized for their one night of pleasure. Had said it was a mistake. She knew that, too.

She looked at the connecting door again, as solid as a brick fortress. Mallory had no intention of going over there, but she found herself standing in front of it, unlocking her side and knocking lightly on the tan-colored wood panel. She could hear the low rumble of voices and assumed he had the television playing.

She heard the lock being turned and the snap that told her it was open. Her breath caught and fear gripped her. Her heart hammered furiously and suddenly her hands had no place to go. Heat burned in her ears again as if dragons had breathed fire at her.

Brad opened the door. While Mallory still wore the suit she'd had on at the seminar, he had on shorts and was pulling a golf shirt over his head. His feet were bare. Mallory swallowed. Every coherent thought left her.

"Are you coming to my lecture?" She said the first thing that came into her mind.

Brad checked his watch for the date. "It isn't today?"

Mallory shook her head. "Tomorrow." She crossed the threshold and stepped into his room. It was a mirror image of her own, with a soft rose carpet and flowered bedspread. Brad had the curtains thrown back and October sunshine flooded the room. Mallory wondered if the cheery light had changed his attitude.

"Are you going out?" she asked.

"I thought I'd go for a run."

"I can come back later." She took a step in retreat. Many people used exercise to work out their problems. She liked to swim, and often in the quiet fluidity of the water she could let her problems dissolve. Maybe Brad needed to run off his anxiety at meeting his mother and telling his family of her existence.

"You're here now. The jog can wait." He led her farther into the room. Mallory sat down on one of the wing chairs in front of the windows. Brad busied himself scooping ice into two glasses and filling them with bottled water. He handed her one and straddled the desk chair facing her.

She noticed his muscular legs. The sight aroused her. She remembered the feel of them against her own legs. For the first time she thought knocking on that connecting door had been a mistake.

"I'm not planning to stay past tomorrow," she started.

"Why?"

"This was always the plan. The conference is over tomorrow night. I head home on a midnight flight."

"I didn't know." He lifted his glass and drained it, then got up to refill it.

Mallory drank some of her water. "When are you planning to see your mother?"

She watched his back stiffen. "I don't know if I'm going to."

She remained quiet, not knowing what to say. Could he go on now without seeing his mother? Even absent, she'd obviously had a huge influence on his life, dominating his choices and behavior, and now that Brad was within a stone's throw of closure he was shutting the door.

Mallory got up and went to him. She stood close behind him for a moment. "Brad, have you given it enough thought? You came here to see her. You've let her rule your life for twenty years. Don't you deserve closure?"

Brad said nothing. Mallory waited so long she didn't think he was going to answer her. Then he suddenly whirled around and grabbed her, dragging her close to him, crushing her body against his and burying his face in her neck. Mallory had no time to react. Brad practically lifted her off her feet.

"Mallie, I'm afraid." She felt him shudder against her. Her arms came up and she caressed him.

He'd never called her that before. It was as sweet an endearment as she'd ever heard. She nestled in his arms for a moment, feeling her rioting emotions straining for free rein. She held them back. "You have support, Brad. There is a solid network of people out there on your side. They love you. All you have to do is call them."

"I want you." He lifted his head and looked into her eyes. His were bright and wet. She could see desire in their depths. Her eyelids fluttered down. She had no willpower where Brad was concerned. She laid her head on his shoulder and burrowed into him. "Please stay," he whispered, his warm breath feathering her ear.

His lips touched the skin under her ear and a volcanic fissure opened in her heart. In an instant Brad's hungry mouth engulfed hers. They battled for dominance in an attempt to get closer to each other. It had been too long since they had made love and the need to feel him inside her overwhelmed any rational thought Mallory might have. She'd come to discuss his mother, she'd believed, but now she knew this was the real reason she was here. She wanted to be in his arms. She wanted his mouth on her, all over her. She wanted to feel his hands as he undressed her, the solid weight of him as his body covered hers, and the shattering experience of their mutual climax as their worlds collided and merged.

Brad pulled the jacket from her arms and let it fall to the floor. Cool air made her skin prick for only a moment before the heat generated within her warmed her through and through. Mallory's breasts were crushed against Brad's chest. There was no tenderness in his hold on her, rather desperation, frightening and exhilarating at the same time.

She found the hem of his shirt and ran her hands up his back, her nails gripping the skin of his shoulders and holding on as if she could somehow climb into the throbbing body that pulsed against hers. Brad found the clasp on her skirt and freed it. Pulling her arms down, he made short work of the buttons on her blouse and then let the white material flutter to the floor to join the rest of her clothes. She wore only her sexy underwear and her shoes. She knew she looked like a wanton woman, and that's how she felt. It was who she wanted to be right now. She wanted no restrictions, only the wild sexual ride that Brad promised.

Lifting his shirt, she kissed his skin from navel to nipple, feeling the tremor that flashed through him at her ministrations. Her hands went to the pull-cord of his shorts while her mouth was still prisoner to his. She loosened the cord, running her hand inside the fabric to touch him in the most intimate way. Tremors changed to quavers as her hand moved with deliberate slowness over him. He moaned against her mouth, taking her hand and pulling it away.

"That feels too good," he said, his voice as raspy as the winter wind. He kissed her again, moving his lips down her neck to the tops of her breasts. He released the hook of her bra, taking the tip of one nipple in his mouth. It was wet and wonderful. Mallory raised her leg and encircled Brad's. He pushed the bra aside, his hands holding her as if taking full possession of a treasure.

When his mouth touched her breasts again she felt her whole being turn to liquid. Brad carried her to the bed. Her body slid down until her feet touched the floor. Tiny electrical currents sparked her blood as she moved. Running her fingers inside his waistband, she pulled his shorts and underwear down in one movement. His body was powerful, dark and fully aroused. He was male, primitive, in the throes of mating, and he wanted *her*.

Mallory flowed like the sea as he entered her, with rippling tides and rushing waves. Pleasure drenched her like crashing surf on the beach. The two of them swam in their own private ocean, a place inhabited by no one else. Mallory couldn't believe the freedom she felt. There would never be anyone else who could take her to this level of ecstasy except him. She closed her eyes and followed him. She absorbed the waves, loving the way they crashed into her, the way Brad's hands held her, supported her and loved her.

She was turning into pure sensation as he rode her, flew with her, took her to places neither had been before. It was wild, exhilarating and radiant. Mallory felt the burning, the liquefying of her body. She hadn't thought it was possible to burn in water, but she burned for Brad. Being in love changed her perception of lovemaking. She wanted to give him all she had, every part of her—body, mind and soul. She told him so in a thousand ways. In the touch of her hands on his body, her lips on his, the way her thighs gripped him. Only in words did she not say it. But the cry of release that was forced from her throat as they both reached the pinnacle expressed all she was feeling.

Together they collapsed onto the bed, sated, out of breath, satisfied. Mallory couldn't speak for fear she'd say the words or cry out again. Neither was the right reaction. So she encircled him with her arms and ran her hands over his naked skin.

Chapter Nine

Brad recognized experience when he heard it. And Mallory's speech revealed someone who'd been there. He sat in the darkened amphitheater listening to her present her paper on coma patients and their treatment and healing. She'd co-authored the paper with Dr. Holt Carter.

When Mallory first came to Philadelphia General she'd been assigned to the coma wing. Holt's report said she'd showed great promise and a keen interest in the field of neurology. At the last minute he hadn't been able to attend the conference, and Mallory had to give the presentation alone. It was highly unusual for a first-year resident to do so, but she looked relaxed and at ease. She had that ability, but underneath Brad knew a cauldron bubbled inside her. They'd made love throughout the afternoon yesterday. He couldn't get enough of her no matter how hard he tried. Mallory Russell had something that complemented him body and soul, and each time they made love it was an electrifying experience.

He pulled his mind back to the room and her presence at the podium. She wasn't repeating things she'd heard or read. Her words were original, taking him inside the mind. This woman had known the comatose state from inside, from the place where life hangs in the delicate balance between being alive and being dead.

When had that happened, and why had he never known about it? Had he been so wrapped up in his own problems that he hadn't been able to see anyone else's? Brad was attuned to a lot of things about Mallory. *He* changed whenever she entered a room. She didn't have to do anything, just be there, and she became the focus of his thoughts. So how had he missed this?

The audience was applauding. Brad joined them.

"Thank you, Doctor." The afternoon's moderator was speaking from a microphone on the other side of the stage. "I'm sure all the doctors have learned a lot from your presentation." Brad shifted his attention to the audience. "If there are any questions, we have a few minutes."

The question-and-answer period was very lively. Brad sat forward in his seat, which was situated in the last row of the amphitheater. Mallory couldn't see how intensely he concentrated on her.

After ten minutes the moderator broke in. "We have time for one more question."

There was one Brad was burning to ask. He couldn't decide whether to wait until they were alone or ask it in front of the forum. Other hands were already in the air. Deciding his query would give greater credibility to her presentation, he called, "I have a question."

The moderator looked up, squinting toward the back. Brad stood up and stepped into the aisle. He walked down two steps until he stood under one of the few lights left on for emergency purposes.

"Yes, Dr. Clayton."

As Brad formulated his question, he realized there had to be volumes about Mallory Russell he didn't know. More surprising was how much he wanted to discover it all. She fascinated him. Every time he heard her speak or saw her in a hospital corridor, he wanted to know what she was thinking, what secrets she harbored.

"Dr. Russell, your paper points out not only the neurological areas of the brain common to coma patients, but also some insights into the psychological effects on the body and well-being of the patient."

Mallory nodded. "Yes, it does."

"It would seem to me that you could only speak of this from personal experience. Were you ever in a coma, Dr. Russell?"

Many people in the room gasped. Brad felt as if he'd confronted her with being a prostitute or beating children, something criminal and unacceptable.

Mallory stood her ground, unflinching. She waited for the rustle of movement to subside, then she spoke directly into the microphone, her voice strong and sure. "I was in a coma for two years."

The room was quiet for a long moment. Then someone stated, "So, Dr. Russell, these are not only your observations, but a personal account?"

"Yes."

The lecture broke up then and immediately Mallory was surrounded by doctors asking questions. Brad got close enough to hear them complimenting her on her lecture and asking if they could consult on her findings. One doctor asked if she would be willing to join his hospital's team.

Brad had achieved the desired result for her, but he wondered if it was in fact the right thing to do. He didn't want Mallory to leave or to be angry at him. When he finally caught her eye, those dark orbs bored into him like the point of a diamond drill.

Anger burned in Mallory as she stepped off the elevator on the fifteenth floor. She walked to her room, stomping along the plush carpeting. She closed and locked her door, then got her suitcase out of the closet and threw it on the bed. She was leaving Texas as soon as possible.

"Mallory."

She whirled around. Brad stood in the connecting doorway.

"You've got a lot of nerve," she said. "What were you trying to do?"

"I was trying to help you."

"Well, I don't want your kind of help. I authored that paper without you, and if I wanted the world to know I'd been in a coma, I wouldn't need you to stand up and ask the question."

"It gave validity to the paper. Look at what happened after the lecture."

She scooped up clothes from a drawer and put them in the suitcase. "How do you know that wouldn't have happened anyway? It was a good paper, a damn good paper, and I didn't need to open an artery to make it work."

Mallory skittered about the room, gathering jewelry and shoes, pulling slacks and blouses off of hangers.

"What are you doing?"

"Nothing that concerns you, and I'd appreciate it if you'd leave my room."

"Mallory, why are you so upset?"

She stopped and stared at him. "Suppose it was your lecture and I stood up and asked how many kids you'd stalked in abandoned buildings and down alleyways."

"That's not the same thing and you know it." She could both feel and see the stiffness in him.

"You're right. It isn't the same. It's what you do, and you have a good reason for doing it. Don't you think I have a good reason for doing what I do?"

"You mean for breaking in and out of the hospital many nights to talk to coma patients?"

She felt the color drain from her face. Her entire

body tingled as if there was an electrical field surrounding it, ready to shock her.

"You know?"

"That you're the ghost?" He nodded.

Mallory snapped out of her frozen state and started moving again, this time even faster. She wanted to get away from Brad, away from Texas.

"Stop, Mallory." He started toward her, and she shrank back toward the wall. "I won't stop you from leaving. Just talk to me. Tell me why you secretly go into the coma wing."

"No," she said. "You never talk to anyone. You keep your feelings bottled up inside you, making everyone jump as your moods come and go. Well, it doesn't work on me. You told me once you didn't want anything but a professional relationship. I'm sorry the rules were broken yesterday. It won't happen again. I'm leaving Texas and as soon as I get back to the hospital I'm asking for a transfer." She pulled the business cards she'd collected out of her pocket and dropped them onto the pile of clothes in her suitcase.

Brad looked at them, then moved so fast she didn't have time to react before his hands had pulled her into contact with his body. "This is a rash decision," he stated.

"It may be rash, but it's mine." She yanked her arms free of his hold.

Brad sighed. "I apologize," he said. "My intention was to help you, not anger you."

Mallory moved away from him. He was too powerful when he was close. He had a greater power over her than he knew, and she didn't want that revealed along with her identity as the ghost. Going into the bathroom, she checked that she'd retrieved everything. "Well, you should have checked with me first."

"Please stand still and talk to me," Brad said.

Mallory dumped the things she'd gathered on the bed and turned to face him.

"Can't we sit down and talk about this?" he asked.

"Brad, I don't want to hear what you have to say. I'm leaving."

"You're running."

"Okay, I'm running."

"Why?" His voice was so soft she barely heard it.

Because I'm scared, too. She was afraid of him, afraid falling in love would change everything. She could no longer be the doctor she wanted to be. And he wasn't the man she wanted to fall for. But life didn't give her the choice.

She felt Brad's arms go around her waist and she leaned into him. "I never meant to do anything but help you," he whispered into her hair. "I would never hurt you."

It was too late, Mallory thought. She was already hurt.

"Please don't go." His hands combed through her tresses. "I need you to stay. I want you to stay."

Night had fallen. Windows in various offices across from the hotel were lit up, part of the glittering cityscape before them. Brad and Mallory occupied her bed, along with her open suitcase and the collection of items she'd dropped there in her haste to pack and leave. She hadn't left. Brad had stopped her. They sat up against the pillows, holding each other and watching the windows. They hadn't made love. They had talked, not about the day, but about everything else.

Finally Brad shifted, aligning himself against her. "Tell me about the coma."

Mallory knew he wanted to hear about it. Tonight, it seemed, he wanted an account of her entire life, minute by minute.

"It was an accident. I was seventeen and angry with my parents. I wanted to go to the movies. It was opening day for a popular film and all of my friends were going. My parents insisted that I go with them to my father's company picnic. On the way we had an accident. My parents were killed. My sister was put into foster care. I hadn't been wearing my seat belt and I suffered a head injury that sent me into a coma."

She remembered those days. They were painless, and she could still recall the floating feeling that she was someplace safe, inside a warm, moist holding place. She'd had no desire to leave it or to find out what it was. It was just a nice, pleasant place where there was nothing to worry about.

"Then the voice came."

"What voice?"

"I don't know. It was a woman's voice, soft, melodic, soothing. She talked to me. I couldn't hear any words at first, at least none that I remember. There was a sense of time passing, although—''

"Time passing?" he interrupted. "Coma patients don't—''

"You're being a doctor," she stated, cutting him off. "Coma patients are aware of time, although not the same way conscious people are aware of it, in hours and minutes. It's daylight and darkness that defines time passing.''

"You knew there were days and nights?''

She nodded, but realized he couldn't see her. The sun had set and the room was dark. "I was aware.'' She went on with her story. "I couldn't distinguish single days or know how often the voice came, but there was a regularity to it. I could sense she would be there and I looked forward to hearing her.''

"Did she come for the entire two years?''

"I believe so. I don't know how long I'd been in the coma before I heard her voice. But once I heard it, she continued to come and talk to me.''

"When did you recognize words?''

"You don't recognize words until you wake up. When I woke up I remembered her like a dream. Someone would say something to me and it would trigger the memory.''

"Didn't you ever ask who she was?''

"No one knew. She was like a ghost.''

"And that's why you do what you do now?''

"There are worse things I could do," she told him.

"I didn't mean—''

"I know," she interrupted. "The people I talk to

are like the children you save. They have no one else.
No visitors come to see them. Nurses and doctors
monitor their vitals, but there's no caring, no one to
touch their hand.'' She reached over and took Brad's
hand as if to demonstrate. ''Or caress their face.
They're in a void, and all they need is a voice to help
them return.''

''Why do you keep it secret?''

''It affords me freedom. I don't have to answer to
anyone. There are no statistics. No one is monitoring
the number of patients who wake up versus those who
don't.''

''But they are. The hospital knows. The nurses talk
about it every time one wakes up or someone dies.
You appear to be providing a valuable, life-affirming
service.''

''I don't need accolades, and I don't need people
looking over my shoulder. I do it for the patients and
no one else.''

''You surprise me all the time,'' Brad murmured.
''Anyone else would want to make front-page news.
You're content to stand in the background and do
what you think is right.''

Mallory smiled to herself. He got it! She was glad
it was dark in the room, although the glow coming
from her could probably light several candles.

Brad was quiet for a while, the two of them lying
side by side, taking in the twinkling lights of the city.
Mallory felt this was as close as she would get to
paradise. She slipped her arm around Brad's middle.
She'd been so angry with him earlier, but if she was

honest with herself, she'd have to admit his question had probably helped her presentation. The audience had taken her paper seriously enough, but the addition of a personal connection to the psychology of coma patients turned a corner for her with the doctors in residence.

"Brad," she said, "I owe you an apology."

"For what?"

"For this afternoon. My anger. You were trying to help me. I understand that now. It's just that I'm not that forthcoming with my private life and…"

"I know." He didn't let her finish. "Until that day in the emergency room, few people had ever noticed you. Only Dana knew anything about you. Then they went overboard. I admit I did, too."

She looked up at him. Their mouths were so close she could feel his breath on her lips.

"I called you to bail me out. Then I called you when I needed someone to talk to. You saw that I was upset over finding my mother and you stepped in. I let you play the therapist every time I needed one."

"Brad, I didn't mind."

He dropped a kiss on her lips. "I know you didn't."

"But had you known I was the ghost, you wouldn't have asked for my help?"

"I wouldn't have added to your burden."

Mallory moved away slightly to see him better. "You're not a burden."

"You had enough on your plate. You didn't need me."

"Now that's where you're wrong. I do need you."

She moved closer to him and pressed her mouth to his. She needed him more than he would ever know.

Brad crushed her to him, deepening the kiss as one hand smoothed down her body, over her breast and waist to her hips, before returning the same route. Then there was no more talk. His leg accidentally kicked the suitcase, and her belongings toppled to the floor. The two of them barely heard the thud as it landed. They had other sounds ringing in their ears.

"What did you say?" Owen glared at the brother he'd smiled at only a few moments ago as he came through the hotel room door.

"She's alive." Brad stood on the balls of his feet, his weight evenly distributed as if he were a tennis player who would have to move in one direction or the other as soon as his opponent struck the ball. "I have a report from a private investigator." He looked toward the desk. The manila folder was inside his briefcase.

Owen turned his back to Brad and walked across the room. "You just couldn't leave it alone, could you? You had to keep picking at it, over and over. You're a doctor, Brad. Why couldn't you just keep to the business of healing children?"

"I did, Owen. We were children and we haven't settled this."

"You're wrong. I'm completely settled with it."

Owen spread his hands in his I-don't-have-a-care-in-the-world gesture.

"You say that, but it's not true. It's never been true." Owen didn't turn around. Brad watched his brother's back, watched the movements of his muscles as his hands curled into fists and relaxed again. Brad waited. This was a twisting knife in an old injury to Owen. Brad had had time to get used to the idea of their mother being alive. Owen hadn't had time yet to digest the news. Brad had spent months thinking about her. And he'd had Mallory to hold him, to help him through the trauma. She had been there to keep him sane.

He wished Owen had someone like Mallory, but his brother played the field. Brad thought their mother was the reason. While Brad had openly searched for her, Owen had hidden the effect she had on him behind a mask, so no one could see the real harm. But Brad knew. Their mother was the reason he didn't settle on one woman. He was afraid she would leave him, just as their mom had done.

"Where is she?" Owen asked.

"Austin. She goes by the name Sharon Yarborough."

"All this time. For most of our lives she's only been two hundred miles from me."

Brad nodded.

"I don't want to see her." Owen made a snap decision. He didn't usually do that, certainly not in his work as an architect. Brad knew it was the hurt—the deep-seated, heartbreaking hurt at what she had done to them and the fear of finding out that she'd really never wanted them—that made him say that. It often manifested as anger or some other emotion, but it was the kind of fear every child knew. Neither Brad nor Owen had ever addressed or released that fear. Silently, Brad thanked God again for Mallory.

She was in the next room, waiting for him to finish talking to his brother.

"I want to go and see her," Brad said.

"So go. No one is stopping you."

"I want you to go with me."

"Not on your life. She left us years ago. She wasn't concerned if we lived or died. I'm returning the favor."

"You don't know that," a woman's voice said.

Both men turned to see Mallory standing in the doorway of the connecting room.

"Hello, Owen. I'm Dr. Mallory Russell. I work with Brad and he's told me about your mother."

She extended her hand as she came into the room. Owen took it and quickly shook it. Even when he dropped it he made no comment about how she looked or how attractive she was. Brad understood that meant he was truly distracted. Owen was always ready to compliment a woman.

"There could be many reasons why your mother never got in touch with you. Not wanting you is only one of them."

"Such as...?" He left the sentence hanging.

"You have to go see her and ask."

"Psychiatrist?" He looked at Brad.

"Friend," Brad answered. Mallory stared at him. He thought she was happy that he'd addressed her as such.

"Brad admitted he was afraid of what he might hear," she murmured. "I imagine you are, too." She held her hand up when he started to protest. "You don't have to deny it. Whatever the reason is—that you need to know why she left, you want to tell her off, or just get closure in your life—you owe it to yourself to put it to rest."

"You said she wasn't a psychiatrist."

Brad smiled. "She's going with us."

"Is there something here I should know about?" Owen moved his finger back and forth between them.

"No." Mallory answered, without giving Brad a chance to deny it.

The Austin Rehabilitation Center was a single-story brick building that sat on seventeen acres of wooded land a half mile off the highway. The name called up visions of wealth, of uniformed nurses pushing wheelchair-bound patients around the grounds. In reality it was a state-supported nursing home. The building looked tired. Its roof sagged along the end and the windows were gray and coated with dust. Brad couldn't imagine the last time they'd been cleaned. The side of the building, under the trees, had green moss climbing its face.

He got out of the car and expelled a long breath. Brad was hot, but it had more to do with what waited for him inside than with the unusually high temperature.

Owen must be apprehensive, too. He'd gotten out of the car and stopped just as Brad had. Both of them wanted to go in, but both were afraid of what they would find.

The unassuming building seemed like a dungeon to Brad. Inside lay all the answers. Questions he'd asked himself in the dark of night and on a sunny street when he thought he saw someone who looked like her could all be laid to rest. All he had to do was walk thirty feet and cross the threshold.

Their mother didn't know they were coming. Brad hadn't called, and Owen hadn't had the time or inclination. Brad glanced over at his brother, who stared back at him. Half a head taller and looking a lot like him, Owen stepped around to his side.

Mallory hung back. She'd been quiet in the car, too, letting them relive old times, a mechanism they used to avoid discussing the present and the possible reasons their mother would leave them.

But now they had only two options, go in and ask the questions or leave. Brad couldn't leave without knowing. He had to find out. He'd prepared himself for the worst—that she just hadn't wanted two kids around.

Mallory slipped her hand into his and he looked down at her. Contact made him feel better. She also took hold of his brother's hand. She glanced back and forth between them, as if she were a conduit or a pipeline through which the two of them communicated.

"Ready?" she asked.

Neither spoke. Owen cleared his throat and Brad nodded. The three of them walked toward the glass entry door, hands still linked.

"I'll wait here," she said after they'd spoken to a receptionist, who told them Sharon Yarborough's doctor would see them first. They were shown to a waiting room with walls painted a muted blue, dusty and in need of fresh paint, and furniture several decades old.

"Stay with us." Brad took her arm and pulled her to her feet just as a short man in his sixties, with thick, graying hair and glasses, came through the door. He wore khaki shorts, an open-collared shirt and sandals. Brad thought he looked more like a beach bum than a doctor. All three pairs of eyes focused on him.

"I'm Dr. Diaz. You asked to see Mrs. Yarborough."

"Yes." Owen spoke first.

"I'm Dr. Brad Clayton. This is my brother Owen. And this is Dr. Mallory Russell."

"Doctors?" Diaz's eyes, behind his glasses, revealed his curiosity.

"We're in town for the neurology convention." Mallory looked at Brad.

"Is that your field?" the doctor asked her.

"That's my wish. I'm a first-year resident at Philadelphia General. My interest is in coma patients."

He smiled. His teeth were even and too white to

be natural. Even with the products on the market to produce white teeth, his gleamed like a toothpaste ad.

"And you, Mr. Clayton? What do you do?"

"I'm an architect," Owen answered cryptically.

"I see," he said enigmatically. Then he stated, "Mrs. Yarborough has never had any visitors. Are you relatives?"

The brothers looked at each other. Brad still held Mallory's arm. He felt the tension inside himself and tried to relax, wondering if she could feel it, too. He could also see tension in Owen. Mallory raised her hand to cover his. Her touch told him it was all right.

Owen spoke again. "We believe she's our mother."

The doctor looked at Mallory. "I think we should sit down," he said. He gestured toward a group of chairs in front of a black coffee table strewn with old magazines. They took seats in tribunal fashion—the three of them on one side, facing the single doctor on the other.

"Mrs. Yarborough has been with us for nearly fifteen years. She speaks to no one."

"Can we see her?" Brad asked.

"I think it's only fair that I tell you something about her first and you tell me something."

Brad glanced at Owen, then murmured, "What do you want to know?"

"Why are you here now?"

"We found out only recently that she was alive and living here. I live in Philadelphia, my brother in Dallas. We wanted to see her."

"I'm afraid she won't recognize you," Diaz murmured.

"Can you tell us how she got here?" Mallory spoke for the first time.

"I can only relate what I've been told and what's in her records. But before I do that, tell me—when was the last time you saw her?" He swung his glance between the brothers.

"I was nine," Brad said.

"Eleven," Owen stated.

"Did you come here to confront her?"

The question took them by surprise.

"You don't have to answer. I can see it in your faces," the doctor said. "I won't have it. I don't know the reasons for her actions, but she was severely traumatized, and I won't have her accosted in my hospital."

"Dr. Diaz…" Mallory spoke softly. "That is neither Brad's nor Owen's intention. They were abandoned by Mrs. Yarborough, and while they do want to know why she left them, they would never deliberately cause her any harm, or even agitate her in any way."

"We may not be able to help that, however," Brad added. "If she sees us and knows who we are—"

"I don't think she will." Dr. Diaz cut in. "She was very agitated the first few months she was here, but after that she lapsed into a remote state. She's never asked anything of anyone. She crawled inside herself and there she lives. I've tried everything short of surgery to get her to respond to the world around her, but she stays where she's comfortable.''

''Coma?'' Mallory asked.

He shook his head. ''There is no medical term for her condition. She's just…lost.''

''What is her physical condition?'' Brad asked.

''She's healthy, suffers from mild high blood pressure and has arthritis in her knees and fingers. She's got a strong heart and clear lungs. Other than needing medication for the blood pressure and arthritis, she's rarely ill. I'd feel better if she got more exercise, but she passively refuses.''

''Then she's really fine?'' Mallory said.

''She was abused badly before she came here. We haven't been able to get the full story.''

''Physically or sexually?'' Owen asked.

''Both,'' the doctor said. ''She was beaten, and I'm afraid there is some indication of brain damage.''

''Indication?'' Brad asked.

''Because we can't get her to do anything except sit in her chair, it's difficult to assess if she is not responding because she can't or simply because she won't.'' The doctor opened his hands in a helpless gesture.

''Can we see her now?'' Brad asked again.

He nodded. ''I need to warn you that the abuse left her face scarred.'' He stood up and the three of them stood, too.

''I believe you should go in one at a time. Since she's never had a visitor I'm not sure how she will react to you.''

"I'll stay here," Mallory said.

"Actually, I think you should go first, Dr. Mallory. If she is only hiding inside herself, seeing her sons might cause shock or distress," Dr. Diaz said.

Brad looked at Mallory and nodded. "You can tell her we're here."

Mallory came out of Sharon Yarborough's room and headed down the corridor. She stopped when she saw Brad standing there. He'd probably been pacing, too restless to stand still. She went straight into his arms, hugging him close as if he were a child and needed to be prepared for what was to come.

His arms encircled her and she felt the safety of them. Mallory hoped her arms made him feel safe, too.

"How is she?" he asked.

She leaned him back and looked into his eyes. "Her face is disfigured, but she's not grotesque. She's listless and incommunicative. I told her you and Owen were here and that you'd be in to see her. She didn't act as if she'd heard or understood me." Mallory didn't want to sound like a doctor. Brad needed a friend, and she was trying to play that role.

He stepped around her and faced his mother's doorway. Then he took Mallory's hand and pulled her with him.

Mallory felt helpless. Brad had spent his life trying to find his mother and she'd retreated long ago from everything and everyone, including her sons.

* * *

The door clicking closed registered in Brad's mind, but his heart did double-time as he saw the woman who was his mother for the first time in decades. He held Mallory's hand, his cold fingers gripping her smaller ones in a painful grasp.

Dr. Diaz's description had not prepared him for what he saw. He didn't think he could be prepared even if ten doctors talked to him before allowing him to come and see for himself. The woman across the room was old. Her hair was gray and wiry. Her eyes looked out vacantly as if the world around her had no reality for her.

"I told her you were here," Mallory whispered, as if the situation warranted soft voices. "She didn't react. Her stare remained unchanged."

Brad took that in. His medical training had him looking deeply into her eyes, noting the grooved lines around them and her mouth, the scar that covered most of one side of her face. Her skull was misshapen and her jaw looked as if it had been broken and not set. A wave of anger went through him at seeing her in this condition. What had happened? he wondered. His hand went automatically to his waist, where he kept the pocket flashlight he used to check fluid pressure on the optic nerve. It wasn't there. He wasn't wearing a lab coat. He wasn't here to examine her or to prescribe treatment.

"Mom." The word felt foreign to his tongue. He studied her for some kind of recognition. She gave none. She sat stoically, almost, as if she were alone in the room, alone in the world. The fact that two other people occupied the room was immaterial to Sharon Yarborough.

Brad wanted her to wake up, wanted to force her to focus on him. He'd spent more than half his life looking for her, searching for answers to questions that invaded his dreams and shaped his actions. Was this all he would get, a catatonic old woman so lost inside herself that she might never find her way back to reality?

He crossed the sterile institutional room, softened only by a vase of dying wild flowers. Brad had never thought much about flowers. They were a staple in hospitals. He'd seen so many of them that he was desensitized to their presence. Yet he wondered about these. Who'd sent his mother flowers? A woman who'd had no visitors for fifteen years had flowers in her room. It didn't fit.

"Sharon." Brad hunkered down to eye level with her. She stared blankly into space. "Sharon, it's me, Brad. Do you remember me? I was smaller, only a boy. Owen is here, too."

He realized he was talking as if she were a child.

"Do you hear me? Do you know who I am?"

He might as well have been talking to himself. Sharon didn't answer or acknowledge him in any way. Brad straightened up and glanced at Mallory, who stood quietly where he'd left her. He returned to her, twisting back to look at the woman who'd commanded so much of his life.

"I'm ready to leave," he said. It had been a waste of time. Whatever he wanted to know was locked up inside her, and she wasn't about to release a single bit of news. They turned to the door.

It opened before they reached it. An older woman stood there with flowers in her hands. She looked from one to the other in surprise and suddenly smiled.

"Are you here to see Sharon?" Not giving them time to answer, she went on. "That is very nice. She never gets any visitors. She has two sons, but they never come to see her. Just like my son."

"Mrs. Seleig," the duty nurse said, coming in behind her. "This isn't a good time. You can come back later."

The woman looked at the nurse. Mrs. Seleig was in her seventies. Her face was scored with lines and wrinkles, but her smiling eyes sparkled with life.

"Oh." She put her hand to her mouth as if she'd done something wrong. "Well, I'll just put these in the vase and I'll be off." She walked spritely for a woman of her age. Dropping the dead flowers in the trash, she laid the new ones on the table and took the vase into the bathroom.

"She's another patient," the nurse told them. "She attends to Mrs. Yarborough as if they were sisters."

Mrs. Seleig returned from filling the vase with fresh water. She smiled at the small grouping waiting for her to finish. Taking her time, she arranged the flowers, then turned around. Slowly she walked across the room.

Stopping in front of them, she looked at Mallory. "I don't know you." Her comment could have been a statement or a question. Brad didn't know which, but what she said next, as she turned to him, nearly knocked him off his feet. "Are you Bradley or Owen?"

The three people in the room stared at her in astonishment.

"Mrs. Seleig, how did you know who this was?" The nurse had taken a step forward. She stood next to Brad and Mallory as if they were all part of the same family.

"I may be seventy-eight years old," the woman scolded, "but my mind is as sharp as a twenty-year-old's." She stood up as straight as she could. Brad could see the start of osteoporosis curving her back, but she must have kept herself in shape as long as she could or it would be much worse by now.

"I'm sure it is," Mallory told her. "We're just a little surprised. Mrs. Yarborough hasn't spoken to us, and no one here in the center thinks she's talked in years."

"She talks all right," Mrs. Seleig contradicted. Then she looked down. "At least she used to. I haven't heard her now in a long time." She glanced up with a sad frown on her face.

Brad understood she felt as if she'd lost a friend. His heart opened to her. Mrs. Seleig crossed the room and put her arm around Sharon's shoulders, who sat unmoving in her chair. "I know she'll talk again. She's just resting right now. So which one are you?"

"I'm Bradley."

Chapter Ten

Mallory and Brad had only been in Sharon's room ten minutes, yet the nurse felt her patient was tired. Before Owen went in she wanted her to rest for a few minutes. They used that time to interview Mrs. Seleig.

"Why didn't you tell us she'd talked to you?" Dr. Diaz asked.

"You never asked." The logic of it all made Brad want to laugh. The simplest questions were often overlooked.

The doctor appeared exasperated. He probably had to deal with Mrs. Seleig on many levels. "Is there anything else I never asked about?"

"You never asked where the flowers come from."

"They come from you. The florist delivers them every Monday and you bring them here."

"That's wrong," she declared firmly, pointing her finger in the air. "The flowers are from her daughter."

"She doesn't have a daughter," the doctor said. Brad had told him her only children were Owen and himself.

Mrs. Seleig looked at Mallory. "Doctors," she said conspiratorially. "They never know anything." The older woman turned to Brad and Owen as if she were bored with the doctor and his questions. "Why didn't you stop?" she asked Brad.

He didn't know what she meant, and wondered if her age was causing senility. "Stop where?"

"In the airport."

"We drove, Mrs. Seleig," Brad said.

"Not today." She frowned as if they just weren't getting it. "Back then. When you were running and she called you?"

Brad looked at the doctor. He shook his head, and Brad thought she must have gotten him mixed up with someone else.

Mrs. Seleig got up then and headed for the door. "I have to go now," she told them. "I'm late for my television show."

"Is she all right?" Owen asked.

"Sometimes she gets mixed up," Dr. Diaz answered.

"Mrs. Seleig," Brad called before she reached the door. "Is there anything else you haven't told us? Anything at all?"

She cocked her head to one side and thought a

moment. "I don't think so." She pulled the door open
and left them.

"Do you believe her?" Mallory asked.

"Believe what? That she saw me in an airport?"
He shook his head.

"Not that. The part about a sister."

Both brothers looked at each other. In unison they
shook their heads. But the seed had been planted. Dr.
Diaz said their mother had been sexually and physically abused. She could have become pregnant from
sexual abuse, and since they hadn't seen her in years
they really had no way of knowing.

Could Mrs. Seleig be believed? Brad could see
signs of dementia and absentmindedness, and he
wasn't sure she had a real grip on reality.

The door opened again and they all turned to see
Mrs. Seleig stick her head inside.

"I remembered something else," she announced.
"Sharon Yarborough isn't her real name. It's Mariette
Joyce Randall."

"What is the daughter's name?" the doctor asked.
Brad was too stunned to say anything.

"What daughter?"

It was after three o'clock in the morning when Mallory stole into Brad's room and climbed into bed with
him. He wasn't asleep. Owen had been there until
two, and Brad hadn't turned off the light that filtered
under the door. She saw it was the bathroom light.
Brad lay on the bed wide awake.

He put his arm around her and pulled her close.

She took in the scent of him and let it fill her nostrils. His arm across her was heavy, but she craved its pressure.

"How do you feel?"

He sat up then, crossing his legs and sitting Indian style on the flowered coverlet. "I don't feel anything."

"You and Owen spent hours talking in here and you feel nothing?"

"I thought I would feel something, anger mostly. I realize now that all the time I've been looking for her it was due to anger. I wanted so badly to fight with her, accuse her of being a bad mother, of leaving us to fend for ourselves, but when I saw her... When I saw the shell of a woman she's become, there was nothing there. It's like all the fight went out of me when I saw that poor woman. I couldn't equate her with my mother. The person I knew wasn't in that room."

"Then why did you and Owen stay up practically the entire night?"

"I think we both feel a little guilty."

"Why?"

"We don't know what happened to her. But she was somewhere being abused while we were blaming her for leaving us. Yet when I saw her all I saw was another patient. Someone in need of care."

"I don't believe that." Mallory sat up. Brad was a much more sensitive person than the one he was describing.

"It's true."

"Are you going back to see her?"

"Owen and I thought we'd go tomorrow. Then we have to tell the family."

"Why are you going?"

"What do you mean?"

"If all you feel is that she needs medical care, and she already has a doctor who appears concerned about her, why are you going back?"

"She is my mother."

"Do you love her?"

"Love her?" He thought a moment. "I don't know."

"Are you going out of duty? Honoring thy mother?"

"I don't know why I'm going." He levered himself off the bed and stood. She followed.

"Of course you do." She knew she was badgering him, but there were times when people needed badgering. "You feel sorry for her."

"Sure I do. How could you not feel sorry for someone who..." He stopped.

"Who what?"

"Who took care of you!" he practically shouted.

"Who loved you."

Mallory didn't have to see the glimmer in his eyes to know it was there. She went to him and he pulled her into his arms. His hold was so tight she could barely breathe.

"Oh, Mallie, she looked so pitiful. I never expected that. I kept seeing her the way she was the last time, smiling, full of life. She was almost dancing around the room as Owen and I left for school. She blew us a kiss. She did that every morning before we left. That's why it was so hard to believe she'd left us.''

"Maybe you can find out what happened to her.''

He released her enough to look into her eyes. Mallory took in a full breath, glad to be able to breathe again.

"There must be records," she continued pensively. "We know her real name and some minor details. We can find out where she came from before she was sent to the nursing home, and work backward from there.''

"What about work? You were planning to go home today.''

"I'm here for as long as you need me,'' Mallory stated.

Brad stared at her for a long while. Then he lowered his head and kissed her. It was the tenderest kiss she'd ever received and it brought tears to her eyes.

Brad woke with Mallory in his arms. He'd only awakened this way a few times, but he loved having her there. She was a calming presence for him, and he was thankful that she was here to keep him sane. Yesterday had been traumatic. Mallory had instinctively understood. He and Owen had talked, but Mallory had forced him to open those feelings he held inside and look at them. Deal with them. And go on.

He couldn't go on yet. There was a lot left to do here. He had to find another place for his mother to live, a place where there wasn't concern over budget cuts and staff reductions. He hoped he could find a doctor as caring as Dr. Diaz. And he hoped he could rest at night.

Mallory stirred and he pulled her closer. He kissed her shoulder—the bare area where her nightgown met clear brown skin—and the warm body in his arms turned hot. Her bottom burrowed into him and instantly he was aroused. A single thought of her could turn him to fire. Her presence could render him unable to speak coherently, and making love to her took him to places he'd never known before.

He kissed her arm down to her elbow before moving up to her mouth. His hand roamed across her belly and up to her breasts. He heard the tiny intake of air when his thumb smoothed the fabric over her nipple. He loved that sound. She made it when he touched a part of her that drove pleasure sensations through her.

She reached out and linked her fingers with his. Pushing them down, running their joined hands up and down his leg caressingly. He always loved it when she touched him—the feel of her hands as they moved across his skin, the light rasp of her nails as she ran them over his back, that boneless way she melted when he kissed her.

She turned over, her gown catching under her and pulling tight, outlining her body. She had a beautiful figure. As a doctor he appreciated it. As a man he worshiped it.

Her mouth sought his and liquid heat poured from his body into hers. A hunger so strong it scared him rushed through him. He wanted her now! He lifted her gown over her head and dropped it on the floor next to the bed, leaving her totally unclothed. Almost reverently he swept his eyes downward, from the tips of her extended brown nipples, past her softly defined waist, to legs as long as the Rio Grande.

"You know you drive me crazy," he stated. His voice was lower than normal and tinged with a quiet desperation. Brad didn't know what was happening to him, what happened every time he was near Mallory. He just knew he wanted to go on being around her.

"I'm making it my life's work." She rolled closer, pressing against him, rubbing her leg up and over his. Pleasure burst and ricocheted inside him until he thought he'd die from her touch.

He groaned. His body covered hers. He took her nipple in his mouth and felt the tremors passing between them. He continued his benevolent assault, aroused by the actions and reactions of her body, spurred on by the sounds she made and the way that long body grew even longer as she stretched under him.

Brad moved away to discard his boxers and slip on a condom. The hotel room air was cold and sterile, but together they'd formed a cocoon of warmth where desire was king and control didn't exist. She cupped his face and drew his mouth to hers. Explosions went off in him as her tongue dived into his mouth. Mallory was different from any woman he'd ever known. She instinctively fit well in every aspect of his life.

He felt the wave of desire as he slipped inside her.

The soft gasp from her that accompanied his entry was like a bomb going off in his pleasure zone. He set the rhythm, fast and hard. Frenzy took over quickly and the two of them rushed toward ecstasy. Brad lost all sense of time and place, driven by a need so elemental he had no control over it. He'd never been this free, this uninhibited, this untamed.

And he cried out when she took him to heaven. Her voice joined his as they rode through a new universe on stellar waves that took them higher and higher until they crested in a zone so full of pleasure that they burned in the glow of euphoria.

Brad was out of breath as they fell back to earth, and sweat poured from him. His temples pounded and his body was spent. Mallory did this to him. No one else ever had or ever would.

He realized it in that moment. With his body still joined to hers in the most intimate way, he knew why his world moved every time she was with him.

He was in love with her.

When Mallory got out of the shower she could hear the deep voices of the two brothers in the next room. She didn't disturb them. She had her own feelings from this morning to ponder, and she relished the time alone. She and Brad had made love before—twice before—and he'd kissed her on several occasions, but this morning something was different.

They'd both abandoned all reserve. She couldn't be restrained when he was playing her body like an instrument. He drew out so much in her, gave her so much pleasure, that denying any part of it never crossed her mind. She had no inhibitions where Brad was concerned.

Drawing the thick robe around her, she sat on the chaise-style chair, leaned back and closed her eyes. She relived the morning, thinking about how good it had been with him.

Mallory couldn't believe the many facets to Brad. At every turn she discovered something new and different about him. Though he'd been raised by foster parents in a happy home, he'd grieved the loss of his biological mother all these years, and now he'd found her. Some might suspect that seeing Sharon Yarborough yesterday had been the reason his lovemaking was so intense, but Mallory didn't. She'd never believed in the life-affirming theory that having sex after a trauma restored balance. Sex might help ground a person, it might relieve stress, but she and Brad hadn't just had sex. They had made love.

She smiled.

Suddenly, she felt a hand touch her face and she snapped her eyes open. "Brad," she sputtered, gazing up at his somber expression. "What's wrong?"

"Owen and I are going to the police station."

"Police? Why?"

He bent down and kissed her forehead, then sat on the chair with her. She moved slightly to accommodate him. He was warm against her. "It's nothing to worry about. Owen read the detective's report last night, and we're going to the police station to read the official report of what happened to…Sharon."

Mallory noticed the hesitation in his voice. He didn't call her by her real name or by any of the terms most children call their mothers. She'd been estranged from him so long Mallory wondered if he thought of the woman as "Mom" or as "my mother who abandoned me." "Sharon" was easier to say.

"Do you want me to go with you?"

"You're not dressed." He looked at her in the white robe. "We won't be long." He kissed her then, slowly and deeply. Mallory didn't have far to go to reach the aroused state she'd been in shortly before. Brad's kiss took her there. She leaned into him, the robe falling open at the top, and kissed him back.

He smelled like soap from the shower, a distinct male scent.

"No," he moaned against her lips. "You have got to stop doing this to me." The deep note in his voice told her the exact opposite.

He stood up then and ran his hands down her jawline. "Owen is driving, so I'm leaving the car if you want to go out." He kissed her gently, one last time. "I won't be long."

Mallory heard the promise in his voice as surely as if he'd said he couldn't wait to get her into bed again.

When he disappeared through the door and left she felt alone and restless. She dressed quickly in shorts, a shirt and sandals. The weather was unseasonably warm for this time of year, but Mallory had no complaint. She would be back in Philadelphia soon, where fall was giving way to winter, with the prospect of snow for Thanksgiving. A few days in the sun were to be relished.

Checking her watch, she decided Brad and Owen probably wouldn't be back for at least an hour. She took the keys and left the room to go for a ride. Half an hour later, Mallory turned into the driveway of the Austin Rehabilitation Center. Dr. Diaz was on duty and spotted her as she walked through the door.

"Dr. Russell, I didn't think we'd see you so soon."

"I thought, if it's all right, I'd like to visit with Mrs. Yarborough for a few minutes."

He smiled kindly. "I'm sure she'd like that."

They started toward the back of the building, heading for the hall that led to her room.

"Did she show any reaction after we left yesterday?"

"I'm afraid not," he said with obvious disappointment in his voice. "I thought if anything was going to draw her out of the state she's in, it would be her children. That is most times the case. But with Mrs. Yarborough it didn't work."

They'd reached her door. It was blue like the walls, and like all the hallways, it needed to be repainted. Mallory stopped and turned to face Dr. Diaz. "Why do you call her Mrs. Yarborough?"

"According to her file, when she was admitted to the hospital after the police discovered her, she weighed only eighty pounds. Her brain was damaged and she was unable to speak or write. When she was transferred to this facility she was very agitated and made many sounds, but nothing coherent. One of the nurses thought she said her name was Sharon, and so they began calling her that.''

''And her last name? Yarborough?''

''Same thing. 'Yarborough' sounded like what she was trying to say when she tried to speak.''

''Actually, Sharon is her grandmother's maiden name,'' Mallory provided. ''She might have been trying to say that for a different reason.''

The doctor's frown made her go on and explain how she knew that information. ''Dr. Clayton hired a private investigator to find his mother. I've seen the report from the investigation. He discovered her here by going further back into her family tree and using combinations of names she might have used. He discovered the Jane Doe in the hospital and then the transfer here under the name of Sharon Yarborough.''

Dr. Diaz nodded. ''Since we know her real name now, we'll change her records and begin calling her that.''

Mallory smiled as he left her. She opened the door, hoping to find Brad's mother in an alert state. But with her coma patients, she was often disappointed in discovering them exactly as she had left them.

Brad's mother sat in the same position, in the same chair, with the same blank expression on her face that had been there twenty-four hours ago.

The moment Brad recognized the rental car he and Mallory had used since they arrived in Texas, his blood started pumping. He knew why she was here: to see his mother. She seemed to be in a comalike state, and Mallory was an expert on comas. Had she talked his mother into coming back from wherever she had hidden herself?

When he and Owen opened the door, Mallory looked up. None of the surprise he expected her to display was in her eyes, only a reserve he'd seen time and time again, starting with the Wayne Mason incident in the emergency room.

"Hello," Owen said.

Mallory shifted her attention to him and smiled. "Hello," she replied.

"We know what happened to her," Brad murmured. Mallory came toward him. Together they walked back to the waiting room where Dr. Diaz had talked to them yesterday, and sat on the government-issued furniture.

"The police report had the details listed under 'Jane Doe.' No one knew her name, and even when she got here her real name was never discovered."

"That's why no one ever contacted you or your brother."

He nodded.

"What about fingerprints? Wouldn't they try to identify her using those?"

"Her prints weren't on file anywhere, but even if they were, with the state of government and the cost associated with what was essentially a closed case, I doubt it would have been done."

"Closed case?"

"No. They'd found her raving in a house on the outskirts of Austin. It was little more a shack, apparently. She'd been held there for months, by a crazed man who'd repeatedly raped and beaten her. She was delirious for weeks after they found her, and when eventually she woke up, she could tell them little."

Mallory shuddered at what she must have gone through. Brad tried to keep his voice steady and sure, but there was a rage inside him that needed an outlet.

"The man holding her was shot and killed trying to escape capture on an unrelated charge. He'd been running toward the house where my mother was." Mallory took his hand and kissed his knuckles, then kept it close to her. "They took her to a hospital, but one day she just walked out. No one knows where she went. They assumed she lived on the streets for several months. Then she was involved in a traffic accident and was taken back to the same hospital. One of the nurses recognized her as the Jane Doe from the previous visit."

"The man was her first husband, Dawson Armstrong."

"How do you know that? Did she talk to you?"

Mallory shook her head. "Mrs. Seleig told me the story. I had to keep her on track. She wanders a lot, but I got the details out of her."

"What else did she tell you?" Owen spoke from the doorway. He came all the way into the room and took a seat in the chair across from Mallory.

"The day she left for work he was waiting for her. She hadn't seen him in years, but he apparently had been stalking her. He kidnapped her and took her to a house not far from here. He kept her there for months. She didn't know how long it was, but it felt like years, and all the while she wondered what had happened to you two. She stayed alive for her sons.''

Mallory swallowed. Brad saw the workings of her jaw. She was giving them a moment to let it sink it.

He wanted to hit something. All the while he'd cried in the night, alone and wondering, his mother was being abused and thinking of him. All the times he'd hated her for never coming back, it wasn't her fault. She couldn't return. And when she did, they were gone.

''The police found her and took her to the hospital. She ran away from there to try and find you. But she couldn't talk. Her vocal chords were swollen from a rope that had been tied around her throat to keep her in the cabin when Dawson Armstrong wasn't there. She couldn't talk and she couldn't write. So she went to find you.''

''The state had already taken us away.''

''Not quite.''

Brad looked at Owen, then they both stared at Mallory.

''She saw Brad.''

''Me! When?''

''You were running. She ran after you, trying to call your name, but she couldn't speak. There was a cop chasing you and you went over a fence. She was too weak to keep up with you, but she tried. But when you ran across a street and she followed, she was hit by a car and woke up in a hospital. After that she was moved here.''

"I thought she said she saw me at the airport."

"It was the Airport Road," Mallory corrected.

When Mallory finished, both brothers were quiet, astounded by the story and too stunned to move.

"I can't believe it," Owen finally said. "All these years I've hated her, hated her memory, hated her for leaving us, and all the while she was trying to reach us, trying to return to us."

"Don't beat yourself up over that, Owen," Mallory said. "You were a child. It was a natural reaction. You felt alone and abandoned. But what matters most now is that you both know she loved you and would never have left you of her own accord."

"Why won't she talk?"

"I don't know why she only talks to Mrs. Seleig. Her speech is very impaired. It's hard to understand her, Mrs. Seleig says. One reason she remains silent might be fear."

"Fear?" Brad asked. "Why?"

"She saw you being chased by the police. Owen wasn't with you. She couldn't protect you and she was afraid something might happen to you if she talked to the police, so she told no one."

"Except Mrs. Seleig."

"Mrs. Seleig is her voice in the dark."

Brad understood what that meant. He was sure Owen didn't.

"Dr. Russell spends a lot of her time with coma patients," Brad explained. "She talks to them, usually in the dark." He looked at Mallory and smiled. "She's had a lot of success in getting them to wake up. Mrs. Seleig was there to talk to…Mom." He'd said it. He cleared his throat. "Or to listen to her when she talked."

"So why won't she talk to us?" Owen repeated.

"If she didn't react yesterday when you two went in the room…" Mallory trailed off.

"She's not likely to?" Owen finished.

"Not likely to what?"

Mallory immediately stood up. Mrs. Seleig stood inside the door. Next to her was Brad and Owen's mother.

"Mariette," Mrs. Seleig said, and looked at the gray-haired woman. "I can call her that now?"

Mallory nodded.

Brad and Owen got to their feet. Each of them moved slowly, as if there was a heavy hand on their shoulder.

Mrs. Seleig looked up at the two tall men who stood in front of her, straightening her stooped shoulders.

"She wanted to see you," she stated.

Every eye in the room was trained on Mariette Joyce Randall.

Chapter Eleven

Cobblersville, Texas, was a pretty little town thirty miles east of Austin where two of Brad's siblings lived. And they were all waiting to hear the news Owen and Brad had to tell them.

"It's about time." Rosa greeted them without preamble. "Why didn't you tell me the real reason you were coming here?"

"Hello, Rosa," Brad replied. He took Mallory's hand and pulled her forward. "You remember Mallory?"

Rosa smiled at her. "It's good to see you again." She threw a glance at her brother. "I'm not finished with you."

"Hi, Uncle Brad." A small child of about six bounded over to them. Brad stooped down and scooped her into his arms.

"Look at you," he said, that wide smile reserved for children on his face. "You are so big."

"I am six years old," she told him proudly.

"Oh, that is really old. I guess you'll be getting married soon."

She giggled. "I'm not old enough for that yet."

"Well, you be sure to tell me when you are. In the meantime, let me introduce you to Dr. Mallory Russell. Mallory, this is Samantha Yvette Pierce Clayton."

"Are you a children's doctor, too?" she asked.

"No, I'm training to be another kind of doctor." She knew the word *neurology* would mean nothing to the child.

By the time Brad set Samantha on the floor, several other people had joined them. He introduced her to his family. Digger and Erin were the child's parents. His sister Luanne was a social worker, and her husband, Mark Rogers, was an oil geologist. Owen and Rosa she'd already met. Dean was a film student, away on location, so he was missing from the gathering.

"Sit down," Luanne urged them.

"I'll get the kids busy in the playroom," Erin said. "Don't wait for me. Digger will fill me in."

"All right," Rosa insisted. "Tell us."

Mark and Luanne passed out glasses of iced tea as everyone settled around the large kitchen table. In the center was a dish of tortillas and a bowl of jalapeño dip.

Owen told them the story of finding their birth

mother, the detective Brad had hired, the report, the police department, everything right up to her walking into the waiting room and looking at them.

Everyone sat silently while he talked. When he finished, they appeared spellbound.

"Did she say anything?" Luanne asked.

"She tried." Brad picked up the story. "Her eyes focused on us and she tried to say something, but only a low sound came from her throat."

"Dr. Diaz examined her and said he could see nothing wrong in his preliminary examination, but he'd have to run some tests."

"But she knew who you were?" Rosa asked.

Both brothers nodded.

"How did you feel?" Luanne asked.

"Numb, like an eleven-year-old," Owen said. "I wanted to laugh and cry and shout all at the same time."

"Brad?" Luanne looked at him.

"I wanted to apologize."

She placed her hand over his. "You have nothing to apologize for. And don't go playing the 'if only' game. You did what you could. You were nine years old. And there was nothing you could do to stop what happened."

Mallory immediately liked her. She was the social worker, and Brad seemed to take her words seriously. He didn't show it, but then he never did. Only when Mallory was in his arms did she know his true feelings.

For several minutes more they talked about Brad

and Owen's mother, asking what the two planned to do now and when they were going to tell their foster mother about her. Mrs. Clayton lived in Dallas and rarely traveled anymore.

Owen said he knew of several nursing homes near Dallas. He'd have Mariette moved as soon as possible and get her better care. With luck she'd recover and resume her life. It seemed she had been waiting for her boys to find her, and now that they had, she could return to the living.

Eventually the conversation moved on to other things. And finally it came around to Mallory. "They have these little powwows all the time," Mark said to her. "I'm sure Brad has mentioned them."

"He said his family was very supportive." And they were. From what Mallory had seen, they were concerned about each other, always ready to pitch in and help if needed. She wished she had the kind of support they shared. She and her sister had only each other, and while they would do anything for one another, it wasn't like having a large network to fall back on.

"You two work at the same hospital?" Luanne asked.

"We do," Brad answered for her. "She's a first-year resident and she's not planning to be a pediatrician."

"Well, you only need one in a family," Rosa interjected.

Mallory was uncomfortable. His family had assumed they were a couple. She was in love with Brad, but she had no indication he felt the same. Mallory had no idea what would happen when they returned to Philadelphia. This was a little like being on a ship, but they had to return to land soon and resume the lives they had there. They worked at the same hospital and she already had one secret to keep.

Mallory left Brad in Texas. He took her to the airport and kissed her goodbye, but he stayed to take care of details regarding his mother's new living arrangements. Mallory felt bereft without him, but knew she had to get used to the idea of being without Brad. His family was close and supportive, and she wouldn't be surprised if he used this time to find employment in a Texas hospital.

"Margaret, you should have seen his face." Mallory told the coma patient everything that had happened at the conference—her discovery that she was in love with Brad, his birth mother's recovery and his family's welcoming support. Despite their closeness, Mallory thought she and Brad were as far apart as two people could get. "I'm really scared, Margaret. There's nothing holding him here. He has family in Texas. He can go home anytime. And then what would I do?"

A week had passed, and Brad hadn't so much as called her. Mallory went through the motions of the day, doing her job without thinking about him. She had a lot to do—even more with filling in for him—but in those minutes between patients she had time to miss him, and in the darkness of her bedroom at night she ached for him.

Mallory cut her visit to Margaret short and headed for home. She didn't exactly feel at her best tonight worrying that the longer Brad was gone, the more he would want to stay there. He had family, and now a mother who needed him. He'd want to be with her. Mallory couldn't fault him for that. If she had the chance to be with her mother again wouldn't she want to go wherever she was? Mallory was anchored in Philadelphia. Her sister lived only an hour away. She would be at the hospital for the remainder of her residency. Even if she wanted to go she was committed to staying here.

She pulled her car into the garage and closed the door. She didn't bother with lights. She started for her bedroom, dropping her purse on the kitchen counter as she passed through it. Halfway up the stairs she heard the doorbell ring. She stopped. It was three in the morning. Who could that be?

Brad! Her heart jumped into her throat as she rushed to the door and looked through the side window. He stood there.

Yanking the door inward, she jumped into his arms. Brad's arms closed around her and she felt safe. "I missed you," she whispered, her voice so reverent she could be praying.

"I missed you, too." He kissed her, pushing her into the house and closing the door.

It felt so good to be back in his arms. Mallory tugged his jacket off and heard it hit the floor as her own arms tightened around his neck and she went up on her toes. His mouth devoured hers and she reveled in the feel of him. In seconds a hot frenzy seemed to flash through them both and they rained wet kisses all over each other. Mallory tried to discard his clothes without separating from him and he tried to do the same to her. Slowly they moved toward the stairway dropping garments as they went.

At the base of the stairs Brad stopped, his hands cupping her breasts, his mouth drugging hers with a long, languid kiss that robbed her of the strength to stand. He lifted her, carrying her up to her bedroom. They crashed onto the bed like teenagers having their first sexual encounter and afraid their parents would come home and catch them.

It had been a week, a long, lonely, solitary week, during which she missed having his hands on her, having him kiss her and make love to her. Her body ached for him, burned in the most intimate places, wanting his to satisfy her, free her from the need that gripped her.

Rational thought seemed to leave her whenever she saw him. She went on instinct, following an urge that had no origin in her well-ordered world. She was in love and love commanded her actions. Love made her forget everything except the pleasure that flowed through her like a river.

Brad's hands smoothed over her hips, traveling over sensitized skin until they reached her breasts once more. She moaned with pleasure as he touched her—inside and out, and cried out in ecstasy when he once again took her to the stars.

Afterward, Brad held her close as their ragged breathing mingled. It felt like a century since she had made love with him. She had never been so aggressive, so uninhibited. Every time they made love she lost control, but tonight some deeper element in her being had been released.

She slipped off of Brad, but remained in his arms. She never wanted to be anywhere else. And never wanted this night to end. She'd like them to stay this way forever, in each others arms, surrounded by the afterglow of a love so pure and sweet it seemed to fill the whole room.

Mallory closed her eyes and listened to the beating of Brad's heart. "Welcome back," she murmured.

He kissed the top of her head and pulled the covers over them. She looked up at him and he dropped a kiss on her mouth.

"What happened this week?"

Other than letting out a long breath, nothing changed about Brad. He still held her lightly in his arms. His hand rubbed across her back and down her hips, yet she knew something inside him shifted.

"We found her a rehabilitation hospital in Dallas. She was moved last Thursday. Her recovery will be slow, but the doctors believe in time she can return to a normal life."

"Is it close to Owen's?"

"Yes, the hospital isn't far from his office. He'll be able to visit her often and monitor her progress."

"And you?"

Brad released her and shifted away. He got out of bed and pulled on his boxer shorts. His pants were somewhere on the stairs or the floor outside the bedroom.

"I'm moving back to Texas."

Mallory was stunned. She'd thought of it. In the back of her mind probably known this was coming. He'd searched for his mother most of his life. Now that he'd found her it was natural he'd want to be close enough to see her regularly. Mallory would have wanted the same thing if it were her mother. Yet when Brad had said the words they were the last thing she expected to hear.

Her hand came up to her breast, hiding the rift in her heart she was sure he could see. They had become a couple although there was no spoken commitment between them.

"What are you thinking?" Brad asked.

Mallory sat up, holding the sheet against her. "I'm thinking you've already made a decision." She didn't bother to keep the anger out of her voice. "You made up your mind before you ever got on the plane."

"Mallory—"

"Don't Mallory me." She got out of bed unmindful of the fact that she had no clothes within reach. "I can't believe you've come to this decision without even talking to me about it." She snatched up her abandoned clothes and headed for the bathroom. "Rosa told me about the woman who left you. Not your mother," she said as she shrugged into clothes that protested her treatment of them. "The woman you wanted to marry. She decided to leave you without a word." Mallory went to the door. She hadn't bothered to look in the mirror. Her hair hung over her shoulders. She quickly pushed it out of the way. "Well, you're no better."

"Mallory, I am talking it over with you."

"Are you?" She stepped farther into the room. "Look me in the eye and tell me you haven't already decided to go. That you haven't already told Owen and Rosa and...and..." She groped for the names of his other brothers and sisters.

Brad looked directly at her, but said nothing. Her point was taken. She'd wanted it to be different. She'd wanted him to say the words, tell her that he hadn't made up his mind, that he wanted to weigh his decision, look at it from all the angles, and get her input, but it wasn't to be.

"Don't think about me. Don't consider the hole you will leave in the hospital, all the residents who respect your talent despite your mood swings and grumpiness. Don't think of them and don't think of the children in the shelter who've come to trust and rely on you. Think about yourself. Because in the long run that's what it comes down to."

"Stop it!" Brad shouted, and took a step toward her. For a moment Mallory was immobile. She stared at him, stopping his approach with a withering look. Hostility hung in the air like loose wallpaper. Then she swept past him and headed for the door. She was close to tears and she wanted to get as far away from him as possible. She stopped in the doorway and held it open. It was the last time she would see him.

Her voice was quiet when she spoke. "Good bye, Brad."

A numbness surrounded Mallory as she went through her duties at the hospital the next day. She hadn't had any sleep. She knew Brad would be turning in his resignation, and while she felt as if she had a knife sticking into her chest, she would still have to see him on the floor every day until he departed.

Life was not fair. Mallory repeated the cliché to herself. She knew it, had dealt with the fact often. Life threw you curve balls and lemons to make it interesting, except this wasn't interesting, it was devastating. She'd vowed to steer clear of men, but Brad had touched her heart in a way no one else had. He'd gotten through to her by finding the cracks in her system and slowly slipping through them. Now he was entrenched in her life. When he left, she would be so alone.

"You must have heard the news," Dana said when she joined Mallory in the cafeteria.

"What news?"

"Dr. Clayton resigned this morning."

"I know." Mallory lifted her head as if the revelation meant nothing to her. "He's a fine doctor. Wherever he goes children will benefit from his care."

"Mallory...!" Dana called in her I-know-there's-more-to-this voice. "What happened in Texas? I thought you two were on the road to coupledom."

Mallory looked at her closest friend. She knew she and Brad were the subject of gossip at the hospital, and today she didn't care. She decided to confide in her friend. "To tell you the truth, I thought so, too."

"I hear the reason is he's found his mother, who's been missing for twenty years."

"I understand about his mother. I'd feel the same way if I were in his situation."

"Mallory, you could go with him."

She stared straight at Dana. "First, he hasn't asked me, and second, I have three years of residency to finish here. I can't go."

"If he asked you, would you go?"

Mallory hadn't considered that option. She didn't think it was open. If Brad had wanted to ask her he'd have done it last night, when he had her in his arms. Instead he'd gotten out of bed and put distance between them. Brad was a loner. He liked being alone. Like his other relationships, she was only a short interlude in his life.

"I don't think there's much chance of that happening."

"I didn't ask you to lay odds, just tell me what you'd say."

"I don't know." Mallory truthfully didn't know. She had a family, too, even if it was only one sister. Texas was a long way from Philadelphia. Mallory had fought to get accepted at this hospital. It afforded her everything she wanted in her late-starting career. She admitted she was comfortable here. She knew the lay of the land, the politics and personalities of the facility. She understood the rhythm of the city and its ebb and flow. She knew nothing about Texas, nothing about a family that gathered around so closely that it could be suffocating. But she'd never been afraid of challenges or adventures.

What bothered her most, she decided, was that Brad hadn't thought of her feelings, hadn't worried his decision would in any way affect her. She knew he was sensitive, but he reserved most of that sensitivity for his patients.

"There is a little good news to counter Brad's resignation." Dana was speaking again.

"What is that?" Mallory couldn't imagine anything eclipsing Brad's announcement.

"One of the coma patients, Margaret Keller, woke up about three-thirty this morning. Several of the staff say they thought the ghost had visited her just before she woke."

Tears came to Mallory's eyes and she smiled. At three-thirty this morning she'd been in Brad's arms. The world was being rocked for Mallory, but Margaret was returning to it. Maybe the balance had been off center and the two events evened it out.

"It's highly unusual for a resident to request a transfer without completing the rotation," Dr. Janis Campbell said. She was in charge of the residents and their assignments. She'd called Mallory to her office as a result of her request for reassignment.

"I understand that," Mallory said.

"Do you want to tell me why you are requesting this?"

Mallory kept the details sketchy, but told her that it was for personal reasons that involved Dr. Clayton.

While the administrator's expression didn't change, Mallory knew she had heard the rumors about the two of them. She reassigned Mallory to the coma wing.

"Dr. Carter from the coma wing has requested help. Would that be satisfactory with you?"

Mallory smiled. "I plan to go into neurology working with coma patients," she volunteered. "That would be perfect."

Mallory's heart was a little lighter when she left the office. She didn't have to see Brad every day until he left, and after he was gone, she wouldn't have to look across the floor and remember that he'd often stood there, glancing at her, caring for children who put their faith in him.

The drawback to the new assignment was the quiet nature of her duties. The work was demanding, but not in the same way. There wasn't the constant activity of seeing patients, talking to them, giving orders to nurses. Here, she had time to think, time to remember and dwell upon Brad's upcoming absence.

One night as she left the hospital and approached her car Brad stepped out of the shadows. "You're avoiding me."

Fear caused her stomach to drop before she realized he wasn't a drug-crazed assailant there to do her harm.

"Brad, you scared me."

"I'm sorry. I wanted to speak to you and you always seem to be busy or not around."

"It is a hospital. We're open twenty-four hours a day." She tried for lightness, but failed miserably.

Mallory pressed the button on her key ring and opened the door of her car.

"Can we go somewhere and talk?"

"Talk about what? Haven't you already said what you needed to say?"

"I want you to understand."

"Oh, Brad, I do understand." Mallory felt compassion for him. "I'm glad you found your mother. It was a fruitful search and you should be glad it ended this way. I lost both of my parents and I fully understand your need to be with yours. Do what you have to do."

She got into her car and started the engine. Brad kept the door open, preventing her from driving away.

"Mallory, I'm sorry."

"You have nothing to be sorry about. In your place I'd make the same decision. When are you leaving?" She didn't know why she asked. Closure maybe. A date after which she could be sure she didn't have to avoid him.

"Thanksgiving. I won't be returning after the holiday."

"That's appropriate," she whispered. "You have something extra special to be thankful for this year. And your family will be thrilled that you're back home. Good night, Brad."

She wrenched the door closed and drove off. Tears blurred her vision and she wiped them away.

The wind was fierce, as it was late in the year for ballooning, but Mallory went up anyway. She needed space, freedom, control over the things that were happening in her life. The wind batted at the balloon and she had to use all her energy to control it. Keith had been there to help her blow it up and then pack it up again. The day hadn't been that satisfying. Mallory thought of Brad being in the air with her. The last time she'd been out had been with him. Despite the need to work with the wind to keep the balloon on course, she still had time to remember that lovely day.

It seemed he'd invaded every part of her life. Mallory had even looked for the cabin he'd pointed out when they were ballooning together. She'd found it and wondered if he was there, but discarded the thought and concentrated on repacking the balloon.

She stayed and had lunch with Keith. Substituting sparkling cider for champagne, they laughed and enjoyed the early afternoon. Mallory waved as Keith pulled out of the parking lot. She followed, but her cell phone went off before she'd turned onto the main road.

"Hello," she said, seeing a number on the display panel that she didn't recognize.

"Mallory, it's Brad. I saw your balloon. I need your help."

She heard a groan as if someone was in pain. "Brad, are you hurt?"

"No," he said. "I'm at my cabin. Can you find it?"

"I think so."

"Good. Bring your medical bag."

Mallory instinctively knew something was wrong. She put the phone down and started for the cabin. She had only aerial directions to get to it, but there was only one road in and out that she had seen. She found it and turned left, heading back in the direction she had come. The river appeared on her left and she followed it until she came to a clearing. She immediately recognized Brad's car. A van sat next to it.

Grabbing her bag from the back seat of the truck, she rushed to the door. A woman she didn't know opened it. "Dr. Russell?" the stranger asked, her voice slightly breathless.

Mallory nodded.

"Come on in."

"Where's Brad?" Mallory inquired. She was sure he was hurt. Why else would he ask her to bring her medical bag.

"He's in here."

She followed the woman to a small room set up as a makeshift medical facility. It had little equipment. The examination table was an old kitchen table covered with a bedsheet, a piece of plastic and then a strip of polished white shelf paper. Brad stood near the wall, his hands raised as if he'd scrubbed for surgery. On the table was a little boy. A man stood over him, holding a bloody cloth against his leg.

Mallory's eyes shot from one to the other. "Him," Brad said succinctly.

She went to the table, immediately examining the boy.

"What happened?" she asked, quickly determining that his injuries were more than she could handle. He needed to get to a hospital.

"There was an accident," the woman said. "A fire on our boat. He tried to put it out and there was an explosion."

"We need a hospital." She glanced at Brad, and she saw that his hands had been burned. Second degree, she thought. He must be in excruciating pain.

"We've called for a medevac. It won't get here in time. He's bleeding too bad. You're going to have to help me stop it and keep him alive until they get here."

Indecision gripped Mallory, but she gazed into Brad's eyes. "I'll try," she said.

She glanced at the man and woman. "Are you the boys' parents? I'll need your consent to try to save his life."

"You have it," they said in unison.

"One other thing. I'm a resident doctor at Philadelphia General. I haven't finished my studies yet."

"But I'll be here to instruct her." Brad spoke up.

"Just save him," the woman begged with tears in her voice.

"All right. Is he allergic to any drugs?"

"Not that we know of," she answered.

As Mallory washed her hands and pulled on surgical gloves, she barked out orders. "You," she said to the mother, "take those white cloths and wrap them snugly around Brad's hands. Be careful, his burns are second degree and he's in terrible pain. Even if he doesn't look it."

The woman moved quickly to follow her instructions.

"What's the boy's name?"

"Chad. Chad Clarke."

Mallory pulled a needle and a vial from her bag. "What's that for?" Brad asked.

"Pain," she answered.

"You're going to need me alert."

She put them away again, knowing that was true. She turned to the father. "I'll take over here. I need you to get on the phone and make sure that medevac knows this is critical." She took a quick breath, then asked more softly, "Can you do that?" He nodded. "Do you know Chad's blood type?"

"Yes, O positive."

"Good. Tell the medevac team we'll need two units."

She shifted positions with him. After he left the room, Mallory removed the bloody cloth.

Brad came to her side after asking the mother to leave them and close the door. Reluctantly she did so. Then he whispered to Mallory what she should do. First she had to stop the bleeding. She had no blood to give the child to replace what he was losing.

Flying glass must have nicked an artery. She couldn't see for all the blood.

"Clamps are in the drawer."

Mallory looked down and found a drawer. Brad moved to open it.

"No," she said, worried about his hands.

"You're sterile," he reminded her, and pulled the drawer open. Mallory picked up surgical scissors and cut the cloths away. She started a saline IV from the emergency kit she carried with her. Brad had a general anesthetic, which she administered to keep the child from awakening. Then, following Brad's instructions, she started.

"You've done this before."

"The setting was different."

"Don't focus on the setting. Think about the map." He meant the area of the body she was working on. No other part existed unless it affected this part.

"How's his breathing?"

"Good. Go on."

Mallory worked carefully, finding the nick. The boy was lucky. The artery hadn't been severed, but was cut deeply. She clamped it and closed it. Brad talked to her every step of the way. He kept his voice even, unhurried and without tension. She still felt tension in everything she did. Her hands felt awkward and large working on the small artery. But Brad kept repeating that she was doing fine, that the child was in good hands and she would pull him through.

When he finally said they were done and she could close, she heard the rotors of a helicopter. Mallory ignored them and concentrated on her task. The child's color concerned her. He was paler than he should be. They had no monitors to give the boy's blood pressure readings, no anesthesiologist to keep track of the anesthetic. Mallory didn't like the conditions.

The medics arrived just as she finished.

She and Brad gave instructions to the flying doctors who would take the child to the closest hospital and continue treatment. One insisted on looking at Brad's hands and administered care to him. He refused to go to the hospital with them. The parents thanked them profusely, then got on board the helicopter.

Mallory sat down when all was finished. She needed to clean the room and dispose of the waste, but she was tired. Exhausted.

"You did fine, Mallory. If you hadn't been here that boy would have died."

Mallory got up and headed for the other room.

"Where are you going?"

"To clean up. We can't leave the place like that. You can't do it, and I have to get back to Philadelphia tonight."

"You could stay here."

Mallory's heart practically jumped out of her chest, urging her to accept the invitation. But her brain was in control and it told her to protect herself. If she was going to get through this heartache she had to cut the cord at the source.

"I can't," she said. She didn't elaborate. And she hoped he wouldn't ask.

"I could use your hands." He held up his, which were now completely covered in white gauze. "I can't even get undressed with these on." He'd been given a painkiller and Mallory could see it was affecting his speech and his mind. He was flirting with her openly, something he'd never done.

"I suppose I could drive you to the hospital. You really ought to see a doctor, anyway."

"See a doctor," he laughed. "I *am* a doctor."

"*You'd* better lie down," she advised. Mallory pushed him down on the sofa and left him there to sleep, while she cleaned the room. It took her nearly an hour to dispose of all the waste and disinfect everything. Cleaning gave her a new respect for the crews who came in after an operation and made a room ready for the next one.

Brad was sound asleep when she returned. The sedative had taken effect, otherwise he would be in excruciating pain. Mallory needed to get him to the hospital. When the pain medication wore off he would need additional care.

For a long moment she gazed at him. He looked like such a little boy in sleep. He didn't have the weight of the world on his shoulders, and his eyes weren't hooded or closed. She sat next to him, feeling the warmth of his hip next to hers. She touched his forehead and ran her hand down his cheek.

This was the man she loved. The one who knew her secrets and with whom she was willing to share more. But he was also leaving her in just a few weeks.

Like a cloud moving in over the mountains, tears filled her eyes, distorting her vision.

* * *

"Dr. Russell."

Mallory jumped at the sound of her name. She sat up with a start and rubbed her face. Disoriented, she looked around. Dr. Carter stood in front of the chair where she'd fallen asleep.

"What is it?"

"I'm afraid he's lapsed into a coma."

"Are you sure?" she asked, knowing Dr. Carter was the best there was.

"I'm sure."

Brad hadn't awakened when she'd tried to get him to her truck. He was heavy, but she'd managed to get him in the seat and buckled in. His skin had turned red and blotchy, symptoms Mallory recognized as an allergic reaction. He was reacting to the medication he'd been given.

With her heart in her throat she'd called 9-1-1 and rushed him to the hospital. The staff had taken over then, giving him whatever was needed. Mallory was pushed back, relegated to the secondary role of giving information on what had happened. What he had taken and how long ago.

"Do you think he'll…"

"Doctor, you know there's no way to tell in these cases. He's a strong man, healthy and in good physical condition. He's got those things going for him. How long he remains in this state would only be a guess." Dr. Carter was a compassionate man. His voice was caring and concerned.

"May I see him?"

He nodded.

Mallory got up. Brad's room was just down the hall from where she'd been waiting. She went in. The light over the bed was the only illumination. Because of his severe burns, Mallory couldn't take his hand the way she often did with coma victims. Nor did she know what to say to him.

"Brad, I'm so sorry," she finally murmured. "This is my fault. I didn't notice you were distressed. I thought you were just sleeping." Her voice cracked, and when she touched his arm, he was totally unresponsive. Mallory wasn't used to him being so still, so inert. Whenever she touched him, he always responded in some way.

"Brad, you have to wake up." Mallory took a seat next to the bed. She kept hold of Brad's arm, hugging it between her hands. "There's so much I need to tell you. I know you're leaving to go back to Texas, but I have to tell you I'm in love with you." She stopped, taking a breath and pushing back tears that threatened to fall from her eyes.

She went on with a less emotional topic, talking about the pediatrics ward. She told him he needed to wake up because the shelter needed him. The kids he pulled off the streets needed him and *she* needed him. She kept at it for hours, until a nurse came in and told her she had to get some sleep herself or she'd be no good for her own patients.

Mallory left and went home. The house felt more silent tonight than it had in previous nights without Brad being there. She looked at the phone and thought of calling the hospital to check on Brad's condition. But she'd only left there half an hour ago. If anything had changed she was sure someone would notify her.

There was one call she needed to make. She had to phone Brad's brother Owen and the rest of the Clayton family.

Rosa was the first to arrive, followed by Owen, Digger, Dean and Luanne. The entire family descended on the hospital. Mallory explained what had happened, and they took turns staying with him. All day and all night there was someone in Brad's room.

Mallory couldn't help resenting them for usurping her place. She wanted to sit with Brad, touch his arm and talk to him, but she couldn't.

Brad wasn't in the coma wing. His condition wasn't long-term, at least not yet. And his family was there. He didn't fit her profile of people who had no one—the patients she talked back to life. Brad had that kind of support. He had his family, people who loved him. Mallory tried to convince herself that everything that could be done for him was being done, but it wasn't working. She loved him, too, and wanted to be there, talking to him, bringing him back to her.

On the third night she ran into Rosa coming out of the room. Brad's sister looked tired and run-down, nearly bumping into the wall as the door closed behind her.

"Rosa, are you all right?"

She turned and recognized Mallory. "Hello," she said. "I was just going to get some coffee. Want to join me?"

"You don't need coffee. You need sleep," Mallory answered, but she walked with Brad's sister toward the cafeteria.

"I tried. I just can't seem to sleep." Rosa pushed her hair back. "It's so unfair, Mallory. He spends twenty years trying to find his birth mother and then this happens. Who knew he was allergic to a drug?"

"It's no one's fault," Mallory murmured comfortingly. "And he'll recover."

Rosa turned and gripped her arm. "Are you sure?"

"With you all here talking to him constantly and the support he's getting, I'm certain of it." Mallory prayed she was right. Not all her coma patients pulled through. Even some that were visited regularly by family and friends were still in comas, but Brad was different. Brad was hers.

"Could we sit down a moment?" Rosa said when they'd gone through the line and had cups of coffee in their hands.

"Sure." Mallory took a seat at a nearby table and sipped her coffee.

"Are you in love with him?"

Mallory managed to avoid choking. It was the last question she'd expected Rosa to ask. And she didn't know how to answer it. She was in love with Brad; of that she had no doubt. But she hadn't told Brad and she didn't know if he loved her. Should she tell his sister?

"I saw it in your eyes that day I came. When you two were in Texas it was obvious to all of us. Maybe Brad hasn't seen it yet. He's such a blockhead."

Mallory laughed. She hadn't laughed in days and the release felt good.

"So answer me," Rosa demanded.

"Where is this going?" Mallory hedged.

"If the doctors tell us they think he's going to be in this state for a long time, we're planning to move him to a hospital in Dallas."

A lightning bolt of pain shot through Mallory. Had she no control? She'd thought the worse that could happen would be to have him moved to the coma wing.

"He was leaving, anyway," Mallory said. She was amazed her voice sounded so calm. "He'd already resigned from the hospital and planned to return to Dallas at the end of the month. Whether I'm in love with him or not makes no difference."

"It's a defense, Mallory."

"What?"

"Brad feels everyone he ever loved left him. *He's* leaving so he won't be hurt."

Mallory thought a moment before answering. "Even if that is part of his reason for leaving, I can't change it."

"So you're just going to let him go without a fight?"

"Rosa, what do you want me to do?"

"Tell him how you feel."

"What difference could it make? If he had the same feelings for me, would he have resigned without even speaking to me about it?"

Rosa looked into her coffee cup.

"You know he would," Mallory continued. "He might be fighting his feelings, but if he is, I can't make him love me if he doesn't want to."

Rosa nodded and Mallory's heart sank even lower. Even so, she murmured, "Would you mind if I sit with him for a few minutes?"

Mallory left Rosa nursing her coffee. She didn't know how long she had. Any one of the family could show up to relieve Rosa at any time. His room was bright and filled with flowers, yet he lay as still as he had for the last few days.

She approached him slowly. Taking the chair where she'd sat the first night, she gently grasped his bandaged hand and held it to her cheek. She hadn't slept much in the last three days, either. She laughed, thinking Brad was sleeping for the both of them.

"Brad, I know you can hear my voice. You might not understand the words, but I'm going to say them anyway. This may be the last time I get to talk to you alone." Her voice cracked. She'd never been this attached to any of her coma patients. "I love you. I never thought I wanted to marry and have children, but I do. I want to marry you. I want us to have children together."

Tears gathered in her eyes and spilled down her cheeks. "I know you don't believe women have staying power where you're concerned. Rosa told me everyone you loved left you. I'm not like the others, Brad. I can't predict the future, but I promise you, I'll love you forever."

Mallory put her head down on the white sheet and

wept. "I need you, Brad. And you need me. Please wake up. Please come back."

She stayed like that, holding his hand, her tears wetting the sheet, until she heard the door open. Mallory lifted her head, using her fingertips to wipe away the tears. She stood and turned to Rosa.

"There's no change," she said, as if she were only his doctor reporting on his progress.

The two women passed each other, both knowing this was goodbye. It didn't matter if Brad woke up tomorrow or if he never woke up. He wouldn't stay with Mallory. And there was nothing she could do about it, except get used to the idea.

Chapter Twelve

Sheer exhaustion had Mallory asleep the moment she reached her bed. Days had passed since she'd talked to Brad, and his condition was no different. She hadn't been able to sleep or eat, and the nurses were beginning to comment on how tired she looked.

The ringing telephone woke her. It was dark and she was disoriented. Her head was heavy and her mind groggy. What time was it? she wondered. The digital clock showed it was after midnight.

"Dr. Russell," she said into the receiver.

"Brad woke up." Rosa's voice was unmistakable. She was greatly excited, shouting into the phone. Mallory's heart thudded, then hammered against her rib cage. Her breath came in short gasps, so fast that she thought she might hyperventilate. She concentrated on controlling it.

"Are you still there?" Rosa asked.

"Yes, I'm here." Mallory didn't know what to say. "Is he…is he all right? Has Dr. Carter seen him?"

"He left a few minutes ago. He said from what he can tell Brad should recover completely."

That's the way comas worked, Mallory thought. No one knew why they happened. There was speculation that they could be a healing process, an instinctual function that kicked in when the body needed to repair itself, shutting everything down until the process was complete. Only sometimes it never was and it claimed the victim. Thankfully, Brad wasn't one of them.

"I'm glad," Mallory told her. "Your family must be overjoyed."

"We are. Everyone's on their way over. Aren't you coming?"

Mallory tried to speak, but words didn't come out easily. "Brad and I…have said our goodbyes. Saying them again would be pointless."

"You know, Mallory, there comes a time when you have to fight for what you want."

Rosa hung up then. Mallory dropped the phone back in the cradle and slumped against the headboard.

"Brad is awake." She repeated it over and over, through the hands that covered her face, through the tears that ran down her cheeks. "He's awake."

Mallory opened the door and entered her kitchen. She dragged herself through her days, amazed that she could function as a doctor with the way her heart felt. Brad was gone. It was amazing how fast patients were sent home from the hospital. Three days after waking up he was released, and left for Texas with Owen almost immediately. Mallory hadn't seen him at all.

She put on water for tea. She lived these days on tea and coffee. She stared at the kettle, watching the spout as if she could predict when the steam would come out.

Her mind went back to Brad. She'd avoided his room at the hospital. Knowing he was going to recover was a relief. Seeing him again would only break her heart further.

She was glad there was no longer any chance of running into him during her working hours. Mallory wondered how long it would be before the pain in her heart went away.

"Mallory."

She jumped and turned around, a scream coming from her throat. Then she saw him.

"Brad, what are you doing here? You scared me to death." She put her hand to her chest where her heart was beating double-time. Brad held up her key.

"I found it in the open door."

Mallory had forgotten it. She opened her hand and he dropped the key in it.

"I can't live without you."

Did she hear him right? The water had begun to boil and the whistle of the teakettle muffled his voice. She glanced at the kettle and at the man, unsure which one to react to.

"What did you say?" Deciding on Brad, she faced him, ignoring the pot. He moved around her, took it from the burner and turned off the flame.

"I said I love you and I can't live without you."

Breath left Mallory's body and her knees weakened at the same time. She bent over.

Brad caught her and pulled her close.

"I didn't expect this reaction."

Mallory grabbed hold of him, but struggled to keep her mind clear and logical. "Brad, you're leaving. I have a commitment here."

"I know you do. I'm not leaving. I'm staying here."

"What? When? How?"

"I went back to Texas, and I missed you." He dropped a kiss on her lips. "You didn't even come and see me in the hospital."

"I did."

"But not when I was awake."

Mallory said nothing. She tried to pull herself out of his arms, but he tightened them.

"I got my job back at Philadelphia General."

Her heart nearly burst, then she remembered his mother. "What about your mom? You were going back to be close to her."

"She's only a three-hour plane ride away. And I've arranged with a local university to take me on as a teaching assistant. I'll be there two days every two weeks. I can see my mother then. The rest of the time I can spend with my wife."

"Wife? Brad, are you sure?" She could hardly get the words out.

"I'm sure." He kissed her forehead. Mallory struggled to keep hold of her senses.

"What about—" Her words were cut short by the pleasure that ran through her as his mouth settled on her neck. "What about people leaving you?"

"Rosa told me she talked to you about that."

"I can't guarantee you that this will last forever, that we won't grow apart."

"I can't promise you that, either," he said. "But I can promise that if you'll marry me, I'll try my best to make it forever." He looked deeply into her eyes. "What do you say?"

Mallory showed him. She kissed him, saying yes with each kiss she rained on his face.

"By the way," he said when she released his mouth for a moment. "That thing you said about us having children together. I want five."

"You said you didn't hear me!"

"I lied."

Mallory swung at him. He caught her arms and pushed them behind her, imprisoning her body against his. His mouth took hers and history began.

* * * * *

THE
ELLIOTTS
Mixing business with pleasure

The saga continues this February with

Taking Care
of Business

by

Brenda Jackson

They were as different as night and day.
But that wouldn't stop Tag Elliott from
making it his business to claim the only
woman he desired.

**Available this February from
Silhouette Desire.**

This January a new dynasty begins....

THE ELLIOTTS

Mixing business with pleasure

Billionaire's Proposition
by
Leanne Banks

Wealthy playboy Gannon Elliott will do anything to get Erika Layven working for his company again...including giving her the baby she so desperately craves!

Don't miss the exciting launch of a brand-new family dynasty... THE ELLIOTTS, available every month from Silhouette Desire starting January 2006!

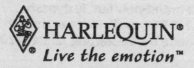

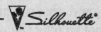
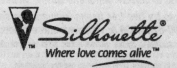